The Christmas Carousel
By Jill E. Van Horn

ISBN: 978-1-952661-47-1

Chapter One

Pin Cushion

A tiny droplet of water spattered her nose as she scrambled up the steps to *Patterns Boutique*. Looking down, she could see spots of water darkening the light cement like a leopard's coat. The thunder roared in the distance as she opened the front door.

"Happy Monday, Ruby!" Holly Edwards clutched her unopened frilly umbrella in her hand. "What a way to start a week."

Ruby walked out from the back of the store carrying several men's linen suits and hung them on the rack of new spring arrivals. "It's so good to see you entering my shop first thing every morning." She tossed her a smile and walked over to give her a hug before pulling back. "I see you've beaten the rain, your curls are still perfectly intact," she said, reaching out to touch one of her tight dark-brown coils.

"Barely." She wiped her forehead with the back of her hand and glanced down at her slightly damp red-and-white polka dot dress. "Looks like we're going to get our April showers after all." She propped her umbrella against the wall by the front door and walked over towards Ruby.

"Good. All of us gardeners are excited about it. *April showers bring May flowers*, you know. How was your weekend, Holly?"

Her arms felt weak just thinking about it. "Still unpacking boxes and trying to find a place for everything. I'm almost done with the alterations on Sara Jenkins's wedding dress. It's in the car for now—I didn't want to take a chance on it getting wet. But if the weather forecast is correct, the sun will be out by noon. Oh, and I was able to get my garden ready for planting. Thanks for letting me borrow your tiller."

Ruby waved her hand in the air. "That's what family's for. You can borrow it anytime. In fact, if you need any help planting, you've got the girls and Dan at your disposal. Just let me know if you need me to send them your way."

She gave little laugh. "I don't know if they'd appreciate you volunteering them for manual labor."

"Nonsense. They love it as much as I do." Ruby turned to look out the front window and frowned. Holly walked over and peered over her shoulder, listening as the wind outside picked up and water pelted the glass in a steady cadence.

She followed Ruby's line of sight and felt a chill run up her spine when her eyes beheld the small billboard across the street. "So sad, isn't it? It used to be such a cute place to visit."

The faded paint was peeling on the distressed wooden sign, but it was still legible. *Merrysville Amusement Park.* She looked beyond the entrance at the ancient fairgrounds. The ashen sky made the old deserted park appear impossibly gloomier than usual, so isolated and forgotten. Tall grass, weeds and vines had all but overtaken the lot where the walkways were now just paths of scattered leaves and litter.

Ruby turned around. "You read my mind, Holly. People used to come from all over the country to ride the

Christmas Carousel."

She smiled and tilted her head back, resting against a comfortable memory. "Yeah, I remember riding on it as a little girl. I never wanted it to end. The pink-and-white unicorn was my favorite. I remember holding onto the candy cane striped pole and waiting to rise all the way up to the tippy top so I could reach for the brass ring and win a free ride, but my short little arms wouldn't even come close no matter how far I stretched. I finally gave up though—Mom was worried that I'd fall off!"

Ruby clicked across the floor in her kitten heels toward the cash register. "I always wondered why they called it the Christmas Carousel. There's nothing Christmassy about it."

"I know." Her smile faded. "It's too bad that it was shut down."

A mysterious glimmer appeared behind Ruby's eyes with her smile. "But I've got some good news."

"Really? I guess my instincts were right. I was thinking as soon as I walked in this morning that you had a little more pep in your step."

Ruby's lips upturned into a wide grin. "Remember when I said I was trying to get approval to put in a community garden over there?"

She nodded.

"Well, I just found out at the town meeting last night that it was approved. And almost thirty people volunteered to help. We're starting to plant this weekend. So, I guess I'll need my tiller back."

"Absolutely. That's great, Ruby. I'd love to help in any way I can."

Ruby plopped down on her stool and bent over to pull open the bottom drawer of the cabinet and retrieved a new roll of receipt paper. "I'm counting on it, Holly. I knew you'd love it here. I'm so glad you decided to take my advice and move here to work with me."

"Me too. I know it's only an hour from Baltimore, but it

still feels like a million miles away." She walked over to the coffee maker in the corner. "Mom said I needed the change of scenery and I agreed. We both decided it was time for me to move out."

"And my favorite aunt was right. I'm proud of you for taking the initiative. Speaking of taking initiative, have you heard from Greg since you've been here?" Ruby began working to replace the empty roll of tape in the register, deftly pushing the paper through the tiny slot that she usually struggled with.

"Nope. And I doubt I will. I think he'll be really surprised when he finds out I moved here on my own." She scooped some nondairy creamer into her coffee mug and took a sip. "Wow. This is good coffee—strong. Did you get a new kind?"

Ruby laughed. "No, it's the same old Folgers—I just added a little more ground coffee and a little less water. It's highly concentrated high-octane energy in a cup."

"I wish I could make coffee."

"What? You mean you've never made coffee, Holly?" Ruby recoiled slightly and composed herself just as quickly. "You're kidding, right?"

"No. Mom always made the coffee. Gardening and mending socks were the only things she'd let me help with." She looked into Ruby's surprised eyes. She'd seen that look before. "Yep, Greg thought it was odd too. It was one of the many reasons he listed as to why I wasn't the right girl for him." She glanced down at the floor.

Ruby pushed her bangs from her eyes. "Don't worry, you can make it tomorrow morning. I'll show you how. And you'll find the right guy someday—someone who doesn't mind that you've never made coffee."

"Or cooked a meal." She couldn't help it, she might as well admit her lack of general household skills to Ruby, whose eyes grew larger by the second.

Ruby shook her head and smiled. "Unbelievable! Girl,

4

what am I going to do with you? Seriously though, speaking from experience, when it comes to love, it usually happens when you least expect it. Just look at me and Dan. We were friends since grade school. I never would have believed back then that I'd end up marrying him."

"Honestly, Ruby, finding another guy is the last thing on my mind right now. I'm still trying to get used to living on my own. I don't even know how to make eggs. Mom's been worried. She came up to visit over the weekend and brought me a homemade chicken tetrazzini casserole."

"That's okay. Baby steps, Holly, baby steps. We'll start with coffee, made the regular, boring way. How did you and Greg meet, anyway? I don't think you ever told me."

"Oh, we've been friends since childhood. Honestly, I don't really even remember when it turned romantic—if that's what you want to call it."

Ruby leaned forward and rested her chin in her hands on the counter. "Sounds like you need someone who will sweep you off of your feet."

The whole *white knight* thing. Now Ruby sounded like Mom. She really wasn't looking for someone to rescue her, just understand her and love her for who she was. Which was something she was still trying to figure out. "Like I said, Ruby, it's the last thing on my mind." Her thoughts shifted to business and she walked over to grab her clipboard to peruse her client list of alterations for the day. A few seconds later, when the front door chimed and swung wide open, she glanced up. Standing in the doorway was a tall figure with broad shoulders in a tan trench coat holding a damp paper shopping bag in one hand and a large dripping black umbrella in the other. His short brown bangs formed little spikes that were dripping water into his eyes. He put the bag down on the linoleum tiles covering the entry floor and turned around to lean his umbrella against the wall.

"Good morning, Ruby." The man squinted and ran his

fingers through his bangs and slicked them back. "It's a little windy out there. I had quite a struggle with my umbrella." He began unbuttoning his coat. "I brought one of my dad's spring Armani suits for you to alter. I was just going to throw it away, but he made me promise to wear it. He calls it his lucky suit. I figured the warm weather will be here soon, so—" he said, picking up the bag and turning around, and almost brushing noses with Holly.

"Hello. I'll take that." She reached for the handles of the bag and smiled, trying not to stare too long into his gorgeous hazel eyes. "I'm Holly."

He froze for a moment and stared at her as if he'd never seen a creature called a woman before. "Uh . . . I'm Hunter. Hunter Ashworth," he said. His voice sounded like he'd swallowed a handful of gravel, and he tried to clear his throat and gulp at the same time. He slowly released his grip on the bag.

"It's nice to meet you, Hunter." She pretended not to notice his catatonic state. When he'd first made eye contact with her, she could feel her cheeks start to warm, and they were growing hotter by the second.

"Hunter and I went to grade school together," Ruby said from her stool at the register. "This is my cousin, Holly. She'll be doing your alterations today."

Holly stood with her eyes fixed on Hunter. She hadn't heard a word her cousin said over the hammering of her own heart in her ears.

Hunter glanced at her and then looked at his watch. "Great. I guess I'll go put on the suit so we can get started. Time is money." He hung up his coat before rushing toward the dressing room, only to stop a few strides later to admire a suit on the rack of new spring arrivals that caught his eye. "Is this the new Armani?" He held it up to the light for closer scrutiny.

She wanted to speak, but her tongue was glued to the bottom of her mouth. She'd never been tongue-tied before, but then again, she'd never met a Hunter before.

"No, we're not getting any of those in until next month, I'm afraid," Ruby chirped in after looking at Holly.

He shrugged and placed it back on the rack before going into the dressing room.

Ruby snapped her fingers and whispered, "Holly, get a hold of yourself."

She blinked a few times and cleared her throat. "Sorry," she managed to squeak out before walking toward the mirrors.

A few minutes later, Hunter pulled back the curtain of the dressing room.

"Come on over." She was crouched next to a stool in the center of the alteration area. All she had to do was breathe in and breathe out. He was just a customer, no big deal.

Hunter shuffled over and stepped up on a stool positioned in front of four large floor-to-ceiling mirrors forming a partial octagon around him with a crystal chandelier hanging over his head. He looked down at Holly as he held up his light-blue pants with one hand. "They're a little big." He gave her a smile, his eyes meeting hers before traveling down to his feet. His pant cuffs draped a mile over the edge of the stool.

"Uh, it's an easy fix." She followed his gaze to the puddle of material around his ankles. "Your dad must be a big guy." She couldn't believe he'd considered just throwing away the perfectly nice, almost brand-new suit. And as much as she tried to push the thought from her mind, she couldn't help but notice the cute little indentations that formed in the middle of his cheeks when he smiled.

His phone rang and he pushed up the long sleeve of the linen jacket to grab it from his shirt pocket, while trying to keep his pants from falling down with his opposite elbow. "Speaking of my dad, excuse me Holly." He put the phone to his ear. "Hey, Dad."

Holly grabbed a safety pin from her sewing basket and held it up to show Hunter. She then walked behind him and lifted his suit jacket to cinch the waist of his pants before pinning it tightly.

Hunter let go of his pants and stood up straight, giving her a quick nod of approval as he listened to his father on the other end of the line. "Yes. I know. I can't believe it either. Yes. I was there last night when they made the decision. They better not get used to it. We'll let them have their little garden this year, but after that, it will be one of the new manufacturing locations of the Ashworth Furniture Company."

He ended the call and placed his phone back in his pocket. "Sorry Holly, I was just talking to my father about the park across the street."

She tried to put two and two together. "What about it?"

He straightened his shoulders and stuck out his chest. "You're looking at the newly appointed CEO of our family business, Ashworth Furniture Company. And my first decision as the new CEO is to build a factory right downtown. It'll mean lots of new jobs."

Ruby crossed her arms and marched toward them where Holly was busy pinning the cuff of one of his pant legs. "Did I hear you correctly, Hunter? I thought you voted in favor of our garden last night. Why didn't you say anything?"

"I'm sorry, Ruby. I should have mentioned it, but everyone seems so excited about the garden—although I have no idea why. Look on the bright side, at least you'll have this summer to have a garden, and I'm sure you can find another place next season. I mean, it is just a *garden*, after all."

"Just a *garden* that will be able to feed lots of families. Why can't you find another place for your factory? Maybe on the outskirts of town? Besides, that park across the street has a lot of sentimental value. You, of all people, should know that."

Hunter scoffed, ignoring Ruby's last comment. "Don't be so old-fashioned. I'm all about bringing in the new, not celebrating old worn-out traditions. You have to keep up with the times. One thing I've learned as I've gotten older is, we can never go back. Things are going to move forward with or without us. It's best to just realize that and get on board."

"Ouch!" He pulled back his foot and lost his balance, falling backward off of the stool. At the last second, he caught himself with his outstretched arm, just as his head came to within a half-inch of the wall mirror.

Ruby froze.

"Oh, my goodness! I'm so sorry, Hunter." She shot up from the floor. "Let me help." He looked at her in a daze and reached out his arm. She interlocked her hand with his and helped to pull him to his feet.

"No problem," he said, clearing his throat before grabbing his lapels and straightening his jacket on his broad shoulders. "Be careful where you stick those things." He jutted his chin toward her pin cushion.

She hung her head and muttered, "Sorry."

Ruby walked back toward her register and visibly wiped the hint of a smile from her face as she sat back down. "Good job, Holly," she whispered under her breath, "the lucky suit, not so lucky."

Hunter glanced at his watch again.

Holly sensed that he was in a rush, and he was being as subtle about it as a whack on the head. "You don't have to get up on the stool for the jacket. I'll just put a few pins in it and finish pinning your pants around your waist. Just stand up straight and put your arm out to the side." She grabbed some straight pins and deftly began to move her hands from one side of his waist to the other. When her cheek brushed against his chest, his woodsy aftershave overwhelmed her senses and made her sway. She leaned in toward him to keep her balance.

He put his hands on her shoulders and sucked in his abdomen. "Be careful."

"Sorry. Don't worry, I'm almost done." She pulled back and cleared her throat, avoiding eye contact, and then tugged on the side of his pant waist and secured it in place. When she was finished, she made herself look him in the eyes. "Does that feel okay?" Her hands shook as she tried to stick the extra little pin back into her pink tomato cushion while pushing thoughts from her head about his trim waistline. Why was she attracted to someone so totally out of touch with reality? She knew arrogant when she saw it.

"Yes," he said, nodding. "It's quite snug, but it will be fine."

"We have to make sure." She removed the pin from his pants and placed it between her lips for safe keeping.

He let out a sigh. "But really, it's fine."

"Just one more second." She took the pin from her mouth again and letting out a half inch of fabric before repinning his waist.

"Better?" She looked up at his face. Did he just roll his eyes at her?

"Much," he replied a little too quickly.

"Okay. But I want you to be sure. Move around a little."

"I'm sure. They're perfect. See?" He bent forward and backward at the waist with his hands on his hips.

"Great. Then we're done. You can relax now. Just take off the suit and leave it with us and I'll have it done in no time. You can pick it up next week."

He exhaled with visible relief. "Great."

She'd never seen someone walk so briskly to the dressing room. He strode out a couple of minutes later with his suit draped across his arm.

"Here you go." He handed the suit to her without as much as a look in her direction. "By the way, Ruby," he said, walking toward the register. "How's Dan doing?"

"Oh, he and the girls are doing well. You should call him sometime. He'd be happy to hear from his old high school buddy."

"Really? I don't think we have much in common anymore. I mean, he's a father now and tied down, I mean, has other priorities."

Ruby raised her eyebrows and looked Hunter over in his expensive suit and silk tie. "Maybe you're right. I mean after all, Dan's just a janitor at our daughters' school. Is that what you meant?"

"Ruby, no. Of course not. I'm sorry."

"Look Hunter, I know you thought he made the wrong choice by turning down the football scholarship just to stay here and marry me, but he didn't want to move to Baltimore for college." She shook her head. Anyway, that's water under the bridge. How's Mandy?"

Hunter cleared his throat. "Oh, we broke up last month. I'm seeing my masseuse Roxy now. She's great with her hands. I'll have to bring her by to check out your new spring dresses."

Holly stifled a giggle behind Hunter as she watched Ruby practically roll her eyes.

"So, Holly's wearing one of the new classics right now." Ruby's eyes drilled into hers and she could read her expression loud and clear: Behave! "It's from the *Reimagined Vintage* line. You know what they say, *fashion runs in a cycle*."

Hunter turned around to look at her and she scrambled to attention, mustered a huge grin, and curtsied, while gathering up her layered dress by its seams.

He gave her a cursory once-over. "Yes, it's nice, in a *cute granny* sort of way. I didn't notice it before."

Ouch. Was it just her or was there a sudden chill in the

room? She could almost hear herself deflating like a balloon, pierced by his arrow of apathy.

Ruby kept her composure and glanced out the front window. "It appears to be your lucky day. It stopped raining." She looked back at him. "Well, take care of yourself, Hunter. I'll call you when the suit's ready."

"Great. Sounds good. It was nice to meet you, Holly." He brushed by her before grabbing his coat and umbrella and rushing out the door.

Ruby let out a long sigh and looked at her. "You look absolutely stunning, Holly."

"I know you're just saying that, Ruby." She glanced down at her dress, the one she thought was so fun and frilly ten minutes ago, she now wanted to set on fire. On second thought, that would be such a waste. Maybe she'd donate it to charity. "Did you see how fast he ran out of here?"

"Are you kidding? Have you looked in a mirror lately? He's out of his mind."

Truth was, even being surrounded by mirrors all day, she tried her best to avoid them—always averting her eyes as she walked by, unless she had to make an adjustment to her contact lenses or tame a stray hair. She wasn't at all comfortable in her own skin, like her cousin Ruby was, who reminded her of Xena, the warrior princess—even taller with the kitten heels.

Ruby shook her head. "I don't know what happened to him. He used to be such a good guy. Now all he seems to care about is money and appearances. I'm surprised you didn't say anything about the garden, though. You know, let him know you're on board with me. Us *green thumbers* need to stick together."

"It didn't really seem like my place. I think I was just the hired help to him. Besides, he seemed okay. Maybe just a tad self-important." Holly walked toward the window to watch him slink into his new BMW convertible roadster. And gorgeous! Too bad his insides didn't match his outside.

"Just a *tad*? I can't believe he fell off of the stool. I've seen a few customers get pricked by one of my employees before, but they've never fallen off the stool. Accidents do happen, I guess." Ruby laughed to herself. "In a way, though, I think he did kind of deserve it."

She winked. "Who said it was an accident?"

Ruby stopped laughing and looked at her with a look of shock that slowly transformed into sheer admiration. "Maybe I underestimated you after all, girlfriend."

Chapter Two

Just Around the Corner

Her soaking wet golden retriever, Abbey, was already wagging her tail by the wrought iron fence of her front yard, barking, while she parked her car and stepped out.

"Hey, girl! What are you doing outside?"

Abbey jumped up on her as soon as she opened the front gate, sullying her new dress with muddy clumps of dirt just as her mom appeared on the small front porch to witness the smear campaign. She sucked in air through her teeth and crossed her arms.

"I'm sorry, Holly dear. She wanted to go out earlier and I guess I just forgot about closing the gate to the garden."

She bent over to hug Abbey as water dripped from the ends of her shaggy coat. "I guess it doesn't matter now, does it, Abbey?"

Abbey licked her face.

"Now that's unconditional love." Her mom crossed her arms. "I guess I'll be going to the dry cleaner's tomorrow morning."

Bathed in dirt, she stood to give her a light hug with her forearms, being sure to keep her distance. Her dress was now the color of dirt. Maybe she'd set it on fire after all. "It's okay, Mom, really." She scrunched her forehead. "Wait, didn't you say you were leaving this morning?"

"Well, I was, but then I thought about it. Your father's at home working on his sermon this week while they paint his office. It's probably better I stay here and help you so he can get his work done. I know you've still got some unpacking to do, and I was thinking maybe I could go get some groceries and make you some meals, and—"

"Hold on, Mom. How am I supposed to get used to living on my own if I'm not actually *living on my own?*"

"I know, honey. I guess I'm just not ready for my little girl to be a grown-up yet."

"I'm only an hour away."

Mom gave her a pleading look. "How about just one week? Then I'll leave and let you get on with your life. In the meantime, I'm sure you could use some help."

She crossed her arms. As much as she was trying to be independent, it did seem like a good idea. She was feeling a little homesick, after all. She'd lived at home while attending college. It truly was her first venture from the nest, and Mom knew it was necessary at some point, but that didn't mean she was thrilled about it. "Fine."

Mom clapped her hands together and headed for the front door. "Great. I made us a nice vegetable lasagna for dinner."

"Of course you did," Holly said under her breath as she followed her mom into the house. She turned to look at Abbey, shaking her index finger. "For now, you stay outside Abbey. I'll feed you after we eat." Abbey whimpered and lowered her belly onto the white wooden planks of the porch. She walked into the kitchen to find her mom wearing two potholders shaped like mittens that she'd never seen before and removing a stainless-steel tray of lasagna from the oven. "I'm going to go change. Maybe after dinner, we can start planting my garden—if you're up for it."

A smile crossed her face and lit up her eyes as she set the pan on the stovetop. "Of course. I'd love to, dear. In fact, I almost planted it for you today, but I figured you'd want to be involved."

"Thanks for waiting." She walked out of the kitchen, then paused and turned back. "Oh, by the way, Ruby and I are going to help plant a community garden on Saturday at the park across from her shop. I guess you can help with that."

Her mom beamed. "That sounds like fun."

A few minutes later, after she changed into a pair of cutoff overalls, she sat down at the table and did a double take. On her plate was a slice of lasagna that oozed over the edge of the plate. "Wow! It's huge."

"What, dear? I figured you'd be hungry—"

She heard her cell phone ring. "I better get that." She looked at her mom and then toward the knife in the pan. "Could you please cut that in half?" Her mom grimaced and nodded, sighing loudly as Holly rose from the table and grabbed her phone off the counter, glancing at the number. It seemed sort of familiar. "Hello?"

"Hi Holly. This is Greg."

She swallowed hard. Since she'd deleted his contact information, his name hadn't popped up on her screen. Now she wished she hadn't bothered to answer.

"I know I'm the last person you probably thought would be calling you."

You've got that right.

"Anyway, I'm sorry about the way we left things."

She knew there was a 'but' coming in there somewhere. She decided to wait it out. Make him sweat.

"But I was hoping you might be able to help me with one little thing."

So, he wants a favor, after everything he's said. Somehow it didn't surprise her. She had kind of expected it, but since she hadn't heard from him in almost a month, she figured he must have gotten someone else to help with the project she had been working on at his shop when he'd broken up with her. He must really be desperate.

"Are you there, Holly? Hello?"

"Oh, yes, I'm here." Look who's needy now, she almost said out loud.

"Well?"

She took a deep breath. "Okay. What's the *one little thing*, Greg?" She slammed her lips together with instant remorse. Why couldn't she just say no? Practice Holly, say those two little letters: N, O. No!

She could see her mom's ears perk up as she sat at the dining table. As long as she could remember, she'd listened in to her conversations, pretending that she wasn't, especially when it involved her love life.

Greg laughed. "I knew you'd help me. I'm actually right around the corner of your quaint little neighborhood. Is it okay if I just show you in person?"

Her mouth hinged open. Unbelievable. He really did think she had no backbone. Maybe he was right. "Well, I guess . . . since you're here."

Mom cleared her throat and whispered, "Is that Greg, sweetheart? Why don't you invite him for dinner?"

She put her hand over the phone. "Please, Mom." So, it was her mother who'd told him where she lived. She wondered what else they'd conspired over—she'd be discussing that with her later.

"Are you talking to me?" Greg asked.

"Oh. No. It's my mom. She's just visiting. She made dinner." Whoops, she wished she hadn't said that, but he probably knew that anyway. She glanced at her mom who was giving her beseeching eyes. Oh, where did her loyalties lie?

"That sounds nice," Greg replied.

She could hear it in his tone. He was probably thinking

how much of a child she was, having her mom come to visit and make her meals. As much as he'd always complained about her mom's control over her life, it didn't stop him from joining forces with her behind her back. Oh well. It didn't really matter now. Before she could clamp down on her tongue, the words spilled out. "If you haven't eaten yet, you're welcome to join us." There she goes again. Part of her wanted to kick herself for succumbing to her mom's silent pleading.

"Well, thanks, Holly. That's awfully nice of you—and unexpected. I'd love to."

After hanging up the phone, she turned to her mom. "I thought you didn't like Greg."

"Well. I've had some time to reconsider. I guess I have mixed emotions. He did say some not very nice things about you—and me! But I'm sure, deep down, he really still cares for you. And it would be nice for you to have someone in your life to support you, you know, be around to take care of you."

"You mean, like you're doing now?" She gave her a look that could scald water. "I thought we agreed it was time for me to be on my own. I'm perfectly capable of handling my own affairs. I don't need someone to help me with every single facet of my life."

"I understand, honey. But I guess I just feel bad, like maybe I'm part of the reason you've never really challenged yourself, Holly."

She gasped. "I can't believe you just said that. You never gave me the chance. I mean, look, even now, you're the one who doesn't want to leave."

"I'll leave now if you want." Her eyes welled up with tears and she reached for her napkin.

"I'm sorry, Mom. You know I love you. I guess I've just had a rough day. Of course I don't want you to leave. But promise me, after this week, you'll give me my space."

"Okay, dear. I promise." She sniffed away her tears and

crossed her finger over her heart. "I just don't know where this independent streak came from all of a sudden."

Abbey began to bark on the porch, and they turned their heads toward the front door. "That must be Greg." Holly scurried away, glad the conversation was over, but not so happy about answering the door.

"Howdy, howdy." He stood at the screen door with a wide smile on his face. "I see Abbey girl's been gardening."

"Yes. She loves it." She looked in his eyes through the screen. "You seem to be in a good mood. Maybe you could give Abbey a bath for me while I help you with your little favor?"

Greg nodded. "That sounds like a fair trade. But maybe you want to see what it is first," he replied, appraising her face and hair. "You look nice."

She ignored his compliment. "I think I already know what it is." She glanced out over his shoulder to the street. There it was in the back of his pickup truck, the apothecary cabinet she'd been working on for Mrs. Bradley. "Come on in. We can eat first."

"That sounds good to me. Hi Judith," Greg said as he followed Holly into the dining room. He looked around the room, glancing at the furniture and freshly painted walls the color of toffee. "Cute place." When she sat down, she noticed that her mom had moved her chair closer toward the front door, probably trying to listen in.

"Thanks. I just finished painting last week. I was thinking of painting a mural in here. The walls are sort of bare."

He nodded. "Good idea."

Her mom walked back to the table and placed a plate of lasagna on the placemat before him. "I fixed you a plate."

"I hope the lasagna tastes as good as it smells, and knowing you Judith, I'm sure it does," he said, cutting into the lasagna with his fork.

Mom smiled at the compliment. "Thank you. You always did know how to say the right thing, except for—"

She cut her mom's words short. "Uh, so, I guess Mrs. Bradley wants me to finish her cabinet for her?"

Greg nodded as he chewed, then took a sip of water and swallowed. "Yep. She wouldn't have it any other way. She came by the antique store the other day and I realized that I'd forgotten all about it. Let's just say she wasn't very happy to hear that you were gone."

"At least that makes one person."

"Oh, Holly. Everyone at the store misses you, and your talents. You have an artistic eye for things I'd never be able to see. Anyway, Mrs. Bradley wants you to paint flowers on the front of it. She doesn't care how long it takes. I tried to tell her you had a new job, but she was insistent. She just hopes to have it by Christmastime for her family to see when they come to visit." Greg pulled a piece of folded up paper from his pocket, unfolded it, and handed it to her across the table. "Here's a rough sketch of what she'd like."

Maybe he should have thought of all of this before he broke up with her. She reached for the paper. "I guess, if it's for Mrs. Bradley, I don't mind." She studied the picture of climbing vines and what appeared to be whimsical flowers similar to poinsettias before glancing at her mom who was chewing and nodding in agreement.

"That's very nice of you, dear," she said after she swallowed, "considering—"

She put down the sketch and pulled the napkin from her lap. "Well, I think I'm ready to go plant my garden now. Greg, I'll help you unload the cabinet and then you can give Abbey a bath before you go."

"Oh, I thought you were kidding about that," he said, looking up in surprise.

"Hardly. It's the least you can do."

"I'll meet you in the garden, dear." Mom gave her a wink as she rose from the table. "After I do the dishes and fold your laundry."

"Are you sure you don't want me to stick around and help you with the garden?" Greg had just finished giving Abbey her bath and she was resting on the screened-in back porch.

Holly hefted another bag of organic potting soil into the wheelbarrow. It groaned beneath the weight and she held her breath. She'd been milking every bit of work she could get from the hand-me-down gift from her father. Hopefully it wouldn't collapse now.

"No, it's okay. Just giving Abbey a bath was plenty. Mom and I have it from here." She glanced at the back porch where she saw her mom exit the back door, donned in her new pink garden gloves.

"Okay, I'm ready to work! Are you helping us Greg?" she asked, walking down the cobblestone path toward them. She'd changed into blue jeans and pink flowery rubber boots with a bandana tied around her head holding her short blonde curls away from her face. Even in such attire, she looked like she could be a model on the cover of *Southern Living* magazine.

Greg shrugged. "No. Holly said you guys don't need me, so I guess I'll be on my way."

Mom entered through the double gate and ignored her piercing, if-looks-could-kill-you'd-be-one-dead-momma glance behind Greg's back. "Nonsense. We can use all the help we can get."

Greg nodded. "Well, okay then. Let's get started. There's probably another hour of sunlight left."

Holly frowned as she watched him head for the back

of the porch where the palates of vegetable plants and packets of herb seeds were laid out, everything from cilantro to Greek oregano to purple basil. He was here to stay, at least for planting her garden. She sighed as he walked back to the garden carrying two large palates and placed them on the ground. "Maybe we can start with the tomatoes, and then, the bell peppers."

Mom grabbed a shovel. "Did you get any jalapenos this year, Holly? Remember how we had a bumper crop of jalapenos last season? I've still got over twenty jars of homemade salsa in my pantry."

"No, I figured I'd try something different this time, Mom. I got serranos and poblanos instead. I'd like to learn to make your guacamole with the serranos." She bent down and grabbed a six-pack of beefsteak tomato plants and began to pop them out of their plastic black case to loosen them, before replacing them and walking over to hand them to Greg. Next, she reached for the Romas.

"Good choice dear. Don't worry, I'll give you copies of all of your favorite recipes." Mom placed her foot onto the flat part of the shovel and jammed it into the rich dark soil.

Greg followed behind her mom, plopping plants into the holes and raking soil back over them. Holly watched as he picked up a fat squirming earthworm with two fingers and held it up in front of his face. "You've got some really good soil. I see a ton of these little wigglers."

She wrinkled her nose. "Ew! Please put him down." She didn't mind worms, but it reminded her of one time when she'd gone fishing as a girl with her dad. They bought some worms at the local gas station. When he opened the lid to show her, she'd almost passed out. Apparently, her dad had thought it was hilarious. What, Holly? They're just worms, he'd said. When they'd gotten home, he put what he referred to as the 'leftovers' in the refrigerator for their next adventure. She had nightmares for weeks.

Mom stopped in mid-shovel and glanced up. "You know, Greg, if you like gardening, maybe you should come up this weekend and help us plant the community garden across the street from my niece's shop downtown, *Patterns Boutique*, right Holly?"

Enough is enough. "Mother. Greg and I broke up, remember?" Her voice came out louder than she'd planned. She looked over and saw Greg sitting on his knees, hanging his head.

"Holly! I was just trying to be nice." Mom dropped the shovel and began to walk toward the house, throwing a hurtful glance at her over her shoulder. "It's obvious I'm not needed here."

The slam of the back door rang out and she felt a rush of blood fill the capillaries in her cheeks. "I'm sorry, Greg. I guess this is just a little too awkward for me." She crouched down next to him and wiped her forehead with her forearm. "My mom can be a little overbearing sometimes—not to mention, a little overdramatic."

"She means well, Holly. I know what I've said about her in the past. But she only acts that way because she loves you." He stood up, using the shovel as a prop. "Here, let me help you up. We've got more planting to do."

She sighed and took his hand, feeling just a teeny bit guilty for her little outburst. "I know. And you know what? Maybe she's right. We need all the help we can get for the community garden, so if you're free—"

He leaned on his shovel and winked. "I just might be."

Chapter Three

Digging up the Past

Holly woke Saturday morning to the unpleasant shrill of her mom hollering her name from the kitchen.

"Holly! Holly! Please get up. I can't find Abbey."

"What do you mean?" Her heart raced as she stumbled from her bed with one eye still plastered shut with sleep and pulled open the top drawer of her dresser to grab a pair of socks. She pulled on a sock while she hopped into the kitchen, trying to navigate the room without colliding with the refrigerator. After wiping her eyes with her fists, she looked at her mom's face, ridden with concern.

"She was sitting with me on the back porch, and then Dan stopped by to pick up the tiller, and I guess I forgot about her. When I came inside to get another cup of coffee, I realized she was gone. I was just about to go outside—"

"I'll go find her. I'm sure she's in the backyard somewhere." She dashed onto the back porch in a pink T-shirt and purple plaid pajama bottoms to slip into her garden boots before her mom could finish her sentence. The brilliant rays of sunshine made her squint when she stepped off the porch. "Abbey! Abbey!" She marched around the yard while holding her hand above her eyes hoping the neighbors weren't up yet.

Mom called out from the porch. "You don't suppose she could've gotten into the garden, do you, dear?"

She shrugged and looked toward the fenced-in garden. "I doubt it, the gate's closed—but I guess anything's possible." She walked over toward the garden on tiptoes, holding her breath. As soon as she got close enough, relief washed over her, and she let out a long exhale. She could glimpse the ends of little tufts of red hair over the white picket fence.

"I found her, Mom."

"Oh, thank goodness. I was—"

As she drew closer to the garden, she gasped. "Uh, oh! Abbey!"

"What? Is she okay?" Mom sounded panicked.

She quickly surveyed the garden, hardly able to comprehend what she was seeing. Next to Abbey there was a large, fresh crater in the dirt. And next to that, two of her uprooted beefsteak tomato plants, hardly salvageable. It looked like their roots had already wilted, dehydrated by the strong morning rays of sunshine.

"Oh no, Abbey!" She did a double take, stricken by Abbey's expression. In all the years that she'd had Abbey, she'd not seen it before. Through her panting, the silly dog was *smiling* at her, as if proud of her work. Well, on the bright side, at least she wasn't muddy.

"She's okay. But the garden isn't. Abbey! Come!" she yelled, patting her hands on her thighs.

Abbey stopped panting and began to bark. She put her paws down into the crater and began to sling soil with her two front paws, digging deeper into the ground.

She flung open the gate and stalked into the garden. "No, Abbey. Bad girl!" Abbey began to whimper as Holly rushed to her side and grabbed her collar. "You're not allowed in the garden, Abbey. When did you learn to jump fences? Now I have to replant the tomatoes." She looked down at Abbey's sweet little furry face as she walked her toward the garden's entrance. "Don't give me that look, girl. It's not going to work this time."

Abbey blinked and looked away. "You stay here," she commanded before walking back to pick up the skeleton-like plants and place them back in their respective holes. She quickly scraped dirt over them with the edge of her boot. "This will have to do for now."

After making sure the gate was secure, she began to walk back toward the house. Where was Abbey? She looked back over her shoulder and saw her sitting by the gate. "Come on, girl, let's go!"

Abbey wouldn't budge.

"Abbey, I said, let's go."

Slowly Abbey stood and began to follow her back to the porch. "What is it with you, today? Maybe just trying to get used to the new place, huh girl?"

Abbey began to bark and wag her tail.

On the porch, she kicked off her boots and sighed, before crouching down to pet her. "I know how you feel. I'm trying to make it feel like home for the both of us."

Mom appeared at the screen door. "Thank God she's okay." Seven years ago, her mom had gone to the pound and found Abbey. Holly was just about to graduate, and her mom had managed to find the scrawniest puppy anyone had ever seen for a graduation present. Even in high school, Holly had compassion for little animals. Her mom had told her as soon as she saw the puppy's huge brown eyes looking up at her from the concrete floor of the shelter, she'd fallen in love and knew that Holly would adore her. And her mom was right. Abbey won her heart and became her best friend almost immediately.

"Apparently, she has new talents of which we weren't aware: jumping fences and uprooting plants. They'll be okay though, I think. I'm going to go water the garden, and Abbey's going to stay inside. Right, Abbey?" She watched as Abbey walked over and curled up on her plaid dog bed on the porch and lower her snout to the floor between her two front paws before closing her eyes. "I know, girl, digging up dirt is hard work. I'm sure you're tired."

A furrow formed between her mom's eyebrows and she shook her head. "That is so strange. She's never bothered our garden at home." She looked at her watch. "Well, we have about an hour before we have to leave. Did you hear from Greg? Is he going to come help us with the garden today?"

"I'm not sure. I texted him the address, but he still hasn't given me an answer. He said he'd show up if he could."

"Okay. Well, since I'm leaving after we get back, I think I'll make us some sandwiches for lunch, and I'll make you another lasagna that you can eat during the week. And I already made you my special macaroni tuna salad. It's in the refrigerator."

"Thanks Mom. At least I won't go hungry anytime soon," she said as she headed back to the garden.

"We're all here," Holly said over the *mwah mwah* sounds of her mom giving the girls and Ruby kisses.

Her mom bent over to hug Danny, the eight-year-old, who was dressed in a pink floral skirt and a *Frozen* T-shirt. "My, my, my, and look how you all have grown!"

The six-year-old twins, Taylor and Carol, who were dressed in matching green-and-white seersucker rompers, were busy fighting over a plastic toy shovel. Dan stepped in and took it away right as Carol was about to bop Taylor over the head. "Girls, we need to share. Do you know how to share?"

"Yes, Daddy," they replied, nodding their little heads.

"Good. Now let's say hi to your mom's Auntie Judy and cousin Holly."

"Yes, Daddy. Hi Auntie Judy. Hi Holly."

Holly laughed. "Hi girls. Could you be more adorable?"

"I can't believe how they've grown either, Aunt Judy—and I get to see them every day." Ruby put her arm around Danny. "They grow out of their clothes so fast, especially this one here."

Danny put her hands on her hips. "That means I get all of the new outfits, and my sisters get my hand-me-downs."

Holly smiled to herself and remembered when Ruby was pregnant with Danny. According to the obstetrician and two ultrasounds, Danny was supposed to be a boy, so, along with an all-blue nursery and Humpty-Dumpty themed wallpaper, Ruby planned to name her after her father. But she had to change plans after Danny pleasantly surprised both them and the obstetrician during the delivery. Later on, when Ruby announced she was pregnant with twins, they decided to choose names that would fit either a boy or a girl, just in case.

"So, where would you like us to start, Ruby?" Holly looked around the park. She counted at least fifteen volunteers by the gardening area, and many more walking around the park, picking up trash on the ground, pulling weeds, and hand-pruning nearby overgrown bushes. It was obvious to her that the people of this town of less than two thousand residents were passionate about their community's well-being.

"Well, I was thinking. Dan is going to start tilling a second plot right here. Mr. Hardgrave just finished tilling the first plot over there." She pointed toward an older gentleman wearing a straw hat and a pair of denim overalls on the south side of the park opposite the shop. "And do you see that van over there?"

Holly turned around and saw a large white van that had *Merrysville Shrub and Nursery* inscribed in italics on its side in glittery green paint. She and her mom answered in unison.

"Yes."

"Good. Mr. and Mrs. Smitty are donating the flowers and vegetable plants this year. They brought a van full of stuff for us to plant."

"We're on it."

As they made their way toward the van, she felt a tap on her shoulder and whipped around. "Greg!"

"Hey guys."

She smiled. "I'm glad you made it."

His eyes widened. "You actually said that like you meant it."

She didn't miss a beat. "And surprisingly, I think I did."

"Oh, you two. Stop flirting or people might think you're a couple."

"We're not flirting, Mom. If we were flirting, I'd do this." She proceeded to take his orange-and-white baseball cap from his head and pull it down snuggly over her ponytail onto her own.

Greg patted the top of her head. "That looks good on you, Holly. You can keep it."

"Oh, how sweet." She cupped her chin in her hands and batted her lashes.

It was then, out of the corner of her eye, that she noticed a small group of businessmen and women walking toward them, like they were on a tour. She locked eyes with Hunter Ashworth, dressed in a tan suit, who was walking with another very tall, older gentleman on one side, and a dark-haired brunette in a tight-fitting, anything-but-business, red-and-white floral sundress and three-inch white heels on the other. Suddenly she felt self-conscious and insignificant—even more so than usual—in her faded denim shorts and vintage *Pink Panther* T-shirt, wearing her ex-boyfriend's baseball cap. From the grin on Hunter's face, it appeared that he'd been watching them for some time.

"Hey there. It's Holly, right?" Hunter asked as they approached.

She felt her cheeks flush and wished she could just poof into thin air. "Uh . . . yes, and this is my mother, Judith, and my . . . friend, Greg."

"It's nice to meet you both. I see you're sticking with your vintage look," he added, eyeing her faded pink T-shirt. The brunette briskly nudged him in the side with her elbow. "Oh, this is Roxy. Roxy, this is the lady who helped me with my suit alterations at Ruby's shop."

"It's a pleasure," Roxy said, extending her hand. "I'm excited to visit the little shop," she said, squeezing Holly's fingers with her newly manicured hand. "It sounds darling."

"Thanks," Holly said, trying to give her a sincere smile.

"Watch out!" Danny screamed from a distance as one of the twins ran up and collided with Roxy. It looked like Taylor had taken the shovel from Carol and she was chasing her, trying to get it back. Unfortunately, neither one of them was paying attention to the statuesque roadblock standing in their way.

Roxy screamed as she got knocked off balance, her foot twisting sideways and popping right out of her shoe on impact. "Ow! Where are your parents, little girl?" She bent over to put her shoe back on that was now smudged with dirt. "You shouldn't be allowed to run around unattended like this. Look at my new shoes!"

Taylor immediately burst into tears and Holly walked over to give her a hug.

Just as her mom opened her mouth to speak, Ruby ran up to them. "Sorry," she said, looking at Roxy. "Oh, hi, Hunter."

"Hi, Ruby." Hunter leaned over and quickly whispered something into Roxy's ear that made her face soften.

Ruby turned her attention to Taylor and crouched down beside her. "Are you okay, honey?"

"She's okay. She's a big girl. Right Taylor?" Holly asked.

Taylor nodded, sniffling back the tears and wiping her nose with the back of her hand.

"Daddy said to *share* the shovel, remember? I don't want you getting hurt."

"Okay, Mommy," she said in between her little gasps as they walked off hand-in-hand toward the second garden plot that Dan was tilling.

Holly stood back up and widened her eyes. The longer she stood there, watching Roxy try to wipe the little smear of dirt off her shoe, obviously more important than the delicate spirit of a child, the more irritated she became. She was about to reach her boiling point when Hunter jumped in. "And this is my father, Raymond."

"Please call me Ray," he said in a booming voice, his lips parting to reveal bleached white teeth as he extended his large hand toward her.

She exhaled, letting the steam dissipate that was coming out of her ears. What good would it do to say anything now? She smiled at Ray and shook his hand. He looked younger than his years, and he obviously worked out. She wondered if his tanned skin was natural.

Ray shook all of their hands and glanced into the distance. "As much as we'd love to stay and chat, it looks like you folks are busy. And we've got a tour to take of one of our company's new locations. So, if you're ready, Son, I think we should get out of their hair."

"Alright, Dad."

"But next time I'm in town visiting, maybe I'll be helping out here with the garden," he said to Holly as they walked off.

"You don't mean that, Dad, do you?" she heard Hunter say in the distance. "I can't imagine wanting to come back *here*, of all places, after you retire and move to Hawaii."

Holly frowned. He had to know she could hear him. Why did he have to be so derogatory?

Greg whistled under his breath after he was sure they were out of earshot. "A power couple. Talk about high-maintenance," he said, shaking his head.

She flattened her lips. "Which one?"

Her mom and Greg let out small laughs.

"It's hard to say. Take your pick," Greg replied. "I guess those two deserve each other."

She watched from a distance as Hunter's entourage walked through the skeleton of the long-ago pristine Christmas Village and stop near the dilapidated carousel partially hidden by sheets of plywood covered in sprays of graffiti. She could see two men in hard hats standing there, awaiting their arrival. "Hunter said they'd be putting their new facility here before next spring."

"That's a shame." Mom sighed as she scanned the grounds. "This place brings back fond memories." After a minute, she turned back to face them. "Well, I guess there's nothing we can do about it. Let's go meet the Smittys. At least the town can have a nice garden this year."

"You're right, Judith. We just need to focus on the positive," Greg said as they walked over to offer their assistance in planting.

"Hello there, folks. I'm Ed Smitty, and this is my wife, Beth. So glad you could join us today." Ed was a stocky older gentleman wearing a camouflage floppy hat and thick leather work gloves, standing next to the back of his opened van.

Greg extended his hand. "Nice to meet you both. Where would you like us to start?"

"Well, we've got lots of volunteers already planting the vegetables, so maybe you three could go help Beth with the flowers? We've got pansies, marigolds to keep the pests away, and snapdragons. And then there're the bulbs: tulips, daffodils—if I had to list all of them, we'd be here until nightfall," he said, letting out a chuckle as he hooked his thumbs into his suspenders. "Basically, we have anything you can think of."

"Wow, I can hardly wait." Holly took the initiative to help Beth who had just finished lathering a thick layer of sunscreen on every square inch of her unprotected pale skin. She was a tall, thin woman with blonde hair that was neatly pinned into a bun, and she was wearing a pretty white long-sleeve shirt with a matching lacey visor.

"Great. You can help me with the palates." Beth smiled and replaced her white-rimmed sunglasses with lenses that obscured at least the upper third of her face before climbing into the back of the van and reached out her hand to pull her up. "You know, it's a shame that they're going to turn this park into another factory," she said as she picked up a palate of pansies.

"Yes. I agree. We were just talking about that," Mom replied, as she took a palate from Beth and loaded it onto a wheeled cart.

Beth continued. "And believe me, I'm not the only one who feels that way. See those men over there?" She pointed toward Hunter's well-dressed group of businesspeople who were now standing in front of the old boarded-up fun house. "That's Raymond and Hunter Ashworth. They're the ones responsible. It's the son, Hunter, who made the decision. Ever since it was reported in the paper, he hasn't been very popular with the townspeople."

Mom raised her eyebrows. "Yes. I just met them. I do understand what you're saying, but I guess, looking at it from his position, it would be good for creating jobs."

Beth nodded. "That's what Hunter keeps saying, but there are many other places he could build his factory, and he knows it."

"Well, maybe the townspeople can convince him once he sees how nice the new garden turns out," Mom said.

"It's doubtful." Beth glanced toward her plants and then across the way at Hunter. "He seems set in his ways."

A couple of hours later, they stepped back to admire their work. It was looking like a new park, at least from the street.

Greg put up his hand to give high fives all around. "Looks like a success, you guys. We raised the property value by at least a grand so far."

Holly slapped his palm. "Yes, but it looks priceless. Come on, let's go find Ruby and Dan."

As they headed back, she spotted them taking a break under the shade of a large mimosa tree, enjoying their escape from the penetrating rays of midday sunshine. The girls were sipping Capri Suns and sharing tuna salad sandwiches at a small, weather-beaten picnic table, while Ruby and Dan were sitting cross-legged on a checkered blanket, drinking iced tea and eating slices of orange cheese and Ritz crackers. Ruby looked at Greg and then threw her a puzzled glance.

"Ruby, Dan, this is my friend Greg."

"It's a pleasure," Ruby said nonchalantly, giving a slight head nod.

She was grateful, and even slightly impressed, that Ruby was able to hide her surprise so well. After all, she'd told Ruby straight from her own lips that she'd probably never hear from nor see Greg again after everything he'd said when he'd broken things off with her.

"That looks wonderful," Mom said, eyeing their

lunches.

Ruby laughed. "Yes, it's great. The girls decided they like tuna salad now, so Dan and I get to eat like we're in first grade again," she said, holding up a cracker. "There's celery with peanut butter and raisins on top if anyone wants any."

"Sounds delicious, but we brought our own. I'll go get our cooler and we can join you guys." Holly turned to head for her car.

Greg yelled out, "Wait, I'll go with you if you don't mind."

She nodded.

A few minutes later they returned with a large white cooler filled with food and drinks.

"What a perfect day. Not too hot, and not too cool," Mom said, sitting down next to the girls at the picnic table. "And don't worry, Greg. I made an extra sandwich. Help yourself."

"Thanks, Judith, don't mind if I do. I'm starving. Gardening is hard work." He reached into the cooler and grabbed a sandwich, turkey on marbled rye. He then grabbed a second sandwich, unwrapped it, and handed it to Holly. "You like ham, right?"

"Sure. Thanks." She took the sandwich and began to nibble on it.

"So, Ruby, Beth Smitty made it sound like there isn't any chance of Hunter Ashworth changing his mind about building his factory here at the park," Mom said.

"Yep, I agree. He's changed a lot since high school. I remember how he used to talk about how much he loved this park as a little boy and how his great-grandfather helped Hunter's great-great-grandfather build that carousel over there. He was so proud of it. And Dan and he used to be really good friends, but he won't even give him the time of day now."

Holly leaned in. "That's too bad. Have you tried to talk

to him, Dan?"

"No. He didn't even acknowledge me today when he walked by."

"Does anyone know Roxy. Could someone talk to her?" Mom asked.

Dan shook his head. "I don't think that would make a difference. He's usually dating a new woman every other month."

"And besides," Ruby added, "as you could see from earlier today, I don't really think she cares too much for children, and certainly not amusement parks. They're in their own little world."

Holly swallowed and wiped her hands on her napkin. "I don't get it. His father seems like such a nice guy too. I wish he'd intervene."

They finished eating in silence. A few minutes later, a group of several volunteers walked by talking to each other loud enough for all of them sitting at the table to hear.

"Too bad the Ashworths couldn't just take their company and move away. The factory will be such an *eyesore* compared to this."

"Yeah, but what about the jobs?" another voice asked.

"Hunter Ashworth doesn't care about creating jobs, he just cares about himself."

"I wonder what happened to Hunter?" another woman asked, her voice trailing off. The question hung in the air.

Dan's face twisted into a scowl as he looked up at the rest of them. "Money and success happened to Hunter," he whispered.

They'd just gotten back from the park and said goodbye

to Greg before coming inside. Mom walked into the living room and stared at a stack of boxes in the corner that she'd filled with clothing that Holly had outgrown, or more specifically, styles that had outgrown her. "Are you sure you don't want me to stay to help you with anything else, dear? I could help you organize your books or take some of your stuff to the thrift store."

"No Mom, you've done so much already. I can take it later and drop it off." She glanced at her phone. "Besides, I think the store closed at five today."

Mom frowned.

"I know what you're thinking, Mom. I know you think I'm a pack rat. Even though I could *probably* turn some of them into my own original fashions, and some of those clothes will *probably* be back in style someday, I promise to get rid of everything."

Mom sighed. "Honey, I don't think you want to wait twenty or thirty years for that to happen."

"Funny, Mom."

"I know I taught you not to be wasteful, but honestly, dear, that was before your father and I could afford to buy new clothes."

"Well, you know as well as I how much fun it is to make old things new again."

She walked over and gave her a hug. "Yes dear. I appreciate the process as much as you, and that's one of the things that make you and I alike."

It'd been a running joke in their family. Congregants from her father's church used to say that the pastor's job was to redeem souls while his wife and daughter redeemed anything and everything else they could get their hands on, from distressed furniture and old clothing to stray puppies and kittens.

"So, you're keeping the hat, I see." She looked at Greg's baseball cap still perched on her head.

She shrugged and turned to open the curtain just in time

to see Greg drive off. "Yes, I guess so."

"Do you think you two will get back together?"

"I have no idea, Mom. I guess we'll just have to see what happens. For now, though, I'm perfectly happy living here in Pennsylvania."

Mom looked at the clock. "Well, I guess I better get going. It sounds like you've got things under control. Besides, your father is starting to get a little gripey about not having his homemade meals. I still have time to get back and make his dinner. He's got to get up early to preach in the morning."

"I'm sure he misses you for more than your meals, Mom. You guys hardly ever spend time apart like this."

"I guess you're right, Holly. I'm looking forward to getting back home now that I know you're doing so well. But are you sure you don't want me to do anything else before I go?"

She flattened her lips and crossed her arms, giving her a stern look. "I've got it covered."

"Fine. Well, I'll see you soon, dear." Mom kissed her on both cheeks and looked her in the eyes. "Maybe next weekend?"

She led her mom toward the front door and opened it. "We'll see."

"Okay, honey, I'll see you soon."

Holly tilted her head down and coaxed her reluctant mom out onto the front porch by poking her in the back with her fingertips. "Bye, Mom."

She watched as her mom made one step toward her car and turned around to wave. "Say goodbye to Abbey for me."

"Okay, I will." She leaned over the railing of the porch, waving and blowing kisses. After watching her mom finally drive off, she walked back inside, closed the door, and leaned back to rest her body against it. *Whew!* Finally, she could breathe again. She took in a breath, audible in the stillness of the house.

But something wasn't right; it seemed too quiet.

Where is Abbey? It was the first time she'd even thought about her dog since they'd gotten home. A sense of unease pulsed through her and made her shutter. "Abbey!"

No answer.

Let's see. I let her out when we got back. Did I let her back in? she asked herself, biting her lower lip.

"Abbey," she yelled again as she stumbled for the back door. *Not again!*

She ran outside, frantically looking for Abbey. Her eyes were drawn to the garden. It had been almost a week since she'd ventured beyond the forbidden gate. She'd assumed that Abbey had forgotten about it. As much as she cringed at the thought of her digging up her plants again, she hoped that she would be there, waiting behind the fence.

As she got closer, her panic dissipated when her eyes zeroed in on Abbey's sleek golden coat barely visible through the pickets. She let out a sigh and spoke in a soothing voice as she opened the garden gate. "Abbey, you've got to stop sneaking in here."

Abbey was lying next to a newly dug crater in the same spot as the last, panting. The tomato plants lay on their side, uprooted again. She sat up and looked at her with wide eyes and gave a loud bark. *Rruff.*

"What is it, girl?" As she got closer, she could see that the hole was much deeper now, and there was something way at the bottom that looked like the tattered edge of a piece of burlap poking through the dirt. There were several torn pieces of burlap scattered around Abbey and the hole, and it appeared that she'd tried to yank whatever it was from the ground but had only succeeded in tearing bits of burlap off in the process.

She stood with her hands on her hips and sighed. "Well, I wasn't planning on doing anymore gardening today, but maybe I should go get my shovel."

Abbey's ears were at full attention. She let out another, more intense, *RRUFF.*

"Okay, Abbey. You talked me into it. I'll be right back." She headed for her garden shed. A minute later she was standing next to Abbey with a shovel, pulling on her gloves. "I don't know how the tiller didn't pull this up," she said to Abbey who raised her eyebrows and tilted her head as she stuck the shovel into the crater next to the burlap and stepped on it with her foot.

Abbey proceeded to jump up and down on her front paws in a rocking fashion and then take off, running a lap around the garden and barking.

"Calm down, girl. We might be here a while."

Abbey walked over and reared back on her haunches, sitting down on the ground a few feet from the hole, panting.

The layer of dirt below the topsoil was unyielding. She stepped onto the other side of the shovel and jumped, grunting, trying to bring down as much force as she could to get the shovel to plunge into the hard soil. The shovel sank about halfway. "Little by little," she said, jumping off the shovel and prying back on the handle like a crowbar to loosen the dirt.

After proceeding to dig in the same fashion in a circle around the burlap, she was able to loosen enough soil to stick the shovel underneath what appeared to be a sack. She heard the sound of scraping metal as she pushed down on the handle, slowly easing the bag caked with brown clay out of the ground and setting it next to the hole. There was definitely something in the bag; it looked like the outline of an oblong box. She shuttered as she pushed images from her mind that suddenly appeared of real-life detective crime scenes she'd seen on television.

Abbey barked again, wagging her tail as she walked over to examine the contents with her dirt-covered snout.

"What is it?" She watched as Abbey tried to open the

bag with her nose and stick her head into it. "Let me help you, Abbey."

At least she was wearing gardening gloves, no telling what she was about to touch. She got down on her knees next to her dog, clenching her teeth as she grabbed one corner of the bag and held it up, shaking it gently to dispel its contents. Out of one eye, she watched a rusty metal box, roughly the size of a box of tissues, tumble out of the bag and come to rest next to her knee.

She sat in the dirt on her knees and sighed with relief. It looked harmless, sort of. *Not creepy at all.* She picked it up and slowly pried open the corroded lid with her fingers, squinting as she peered at it. Underneath was a tuft of threadbare faded blue velvet that had seen better days, but considering where she'd found it, was in remarkable condition. She let out her breath and tilted her head from side to side to stretch her neck muscles as she set the lid down on the ground and then carefully brought the box to her lap.

On top of the fabric, she noticed tiny decomposing fragments of what looked to be pieces of a stick. She picked up one of the fragments for closer inspection as Abbey tried to bury her snout in the box, making a snorting sound as she tried to uncover the object underneath. Something was certainly attracting her olfactory bulb that was beyond human discernment.

"Well, girl, shall we see what's inside?"

Abbey sat down next to her and stared at the box, wagging her tail, swishing it back and forth, stirring up a little dust cloud. A string of drool dripped from the corner of her mouth when she threw the wood fragments on the ground.

"I'll take that as a yes." She took a deep breath and crinkled her nose before finally pulling back on the edge of the blue velvet cloth.

Chapter Four

Planting
1998

"What's a time capsule, Grandpa Joe?" the little boy asked, as he tripped over his two-sizes-too-big old work boots, skipping to keep up with him as he headed for the picnic area at the end of the yard by his wife's favorite English lavender rose bush. He watched as his grandson stopped to pick up a stick for his grandpa's Border collie, Ralphie, and thrown it halfway across the yard. Ralphie barked as he ran to retrieve it and galloped back with the stick in his mouth before proceeding to rub it against the boy's calloused palm.

"Maybe later, Ralphie. We've got something we've gotta do," he said, waving his hand in the air, as he carried a large shovel on his opposite shoulder. Ralphie pranced along beside him, continuing to poke his hand with the little stick until he gave in. "Alright. Just one more time," the little boy said, lobbing the stick into the air.

When his grandson arrived at the bush, now dragging the shovel behind him as he walked, Joe pulled the metal box out from under his arm and crouched down next to it. "Come here, Son. Have a seat."

Joe watched him sit down on the garden bench next to the rose bush and wipe his forehead with his shirt sleeve. It was an especially muggy day in Merrysville, even for August, and the simple act of walking outside became an arduous act, like walking through a murky lake up to your neck. And as much as their grandson had complained this morning, his wife had still made him wear a long-sleeve brown shirt and dark-green jeans since he was going to be outside digging in the dirt around the sharp thorns of her prized roses. He couldn't help but feel a bit sorry for him.

"A time capsule is something that will help me communicate with someone in the future."

His grandson looked confused. "Communicate what? To who?"

He shrugged. "I'm not sure. I guess to anyone who's willing to search for it." *Maybe even my older self.* "It's something that will hopefully cause people to wonder about the past, to explore their present, and maybe even to dream about their future."

His grandson's face looked strained and he averted his eyes down to his fingers grasping the handle of the shovel. "Why are you burying it?"

"Well, Son, I'm not really burying it at all—I'm *planting* it."

Now his grandson looked really confused, so he explained. "You bury dead things. You *plant* things that you want to grow and produce. And in this case, let's just say, I'm hoping to grow dreams."

"I . . . uh, guess that makes sense. Are you going to tell me what's in the box, Grandpa?" he asked, taking a seat next to him in the dirt.

"It's something my father—your great-grandfather—gave to me when I was about your age. It has special meaning for me, not just for my past, but also for my future, and yours. He made it with his own two hands. Who knows, maybe someday you'll come across it again," he said as Ralphie set down the stick next to his grandson and began to lick the salty sweat from his face.

"Stop it, Ralphie." His grandson giggled as he wiped a streak of saliva from his cheek.

"Can I put something in the box, Grandpa?" he asked, picking Ralphie's stick off of the ground and breaking it in half.

He smiled. "Sure, Son," he said, taking the stick from his grandson's hand. "I think that's a great idea."

Chapter Five

Digging up the Past

Holly hadn't seen anything like it before. It appeared to be a smooth wooden egg made out of very pretty dark wood, possibly black walnut. It had a thick coat of lacquer covering layers of decoupaged lavender roses on its front, and when she looked closely, she could tell it was made from two separate pieces that had been glued together.

She brought the egg toward her ear and shook it. Not a sound. By its weight it seemed like solid wood, but it was hard to tell.

"What do you think, girl?" She took another look into the box and saw a piece of yellowed paper on the bottom. She reached her hand in and pulled it out. It was rolled up like a little scroll. She gasped when she realized she was able make out the cursive writing.

To whoever discovers this treasure, may your dreams come true, just as mine are at this very moment. - J.A.

Her head reared back. *Wow! A time capsule?* "This is certainly unexpected, isn't it, Abbey?" She read the words on the tiny scroll through a second and third time. She turned the egg around in her gloved hands, examining its seam and looking for any other clues. "I wonder who buried this? Maybe it's from hundreds of years ago!" She could continue to guess forever, but right now, it didn't look like she'd be getting any answers. She felt special nonetheless, like she was a part of history.

She tucked the egg gently back into the box and walked inside, carrying it under her arm with Abbey next to her, matching her stride.

After kicking off her shoes and setting her newly unearthed prize on the kitchen table, she turned to look at Abbey who sat on the ceramic-tile floor next to her, panting. "Where do you think I should put it?"

Rruff!

She laughed to herself. "The mantle, you say? Okay, the mantle it is." She walked over toward the fireplace, posing the egg on the mantle in a position to display the delicate decoupage artwork on its front. She tucked the tiny scroll back into the box and placed it next to the egg to keep it from rolling. "There. I think it looks perfect."

Abbey walked over to the fireplace and lay down next to it. For some reason, it seemed she didn't want to leave its sight. It was as if some kind of invisible force, imperceptible to mere humans, had designated her the guard dog.

She bent down and picked up the dog bed. "Well, I guess I'll move your dog bed over here for now, then," she said, plopping the bed down on the carpet next to the fireplace.

Abbey stepped onto her bed and proceeded to curl into a ball before looking up at her. She felt a pang in her heart. It was undisputable this time—as sure as the sun rises in the east, her precious dog was smiling at her.

Chapter Six

Dropped
Seven Months Later

"So, cuz, I've been meaning to ask you, how's Greg?" Ruby asked, holding the door open for their last customer, Mrs. Carlisle, the wife of the local orthodontist, while she lugged two very large aqua-blue shopping bags through the narrow doorframe. She'd spent the morning and a lot of money at *Patterns Boutique's* special early bird Black Friday sale and they'd both been more than happy to assist her.

Holly plopped down on the bone-colored leather chair by the dressing room and kicked off her high heels before grabbing her foot and crossing it over her leg to massage the arch with her thumbs. A glow of sheer ecstasy lit up her face as she leaned her head back. "Ah! I've been wanting to do that all morning. Greg. Yes, I guess he's doing well. I talked to him last week. He seemed very busy."

Ruby walked over and sat in the chair opposite her, giving her a quizzical look. "When's the last time you saw him? I thought you guys were dating again."

"Yeah, at first, I kind of did too. But I've actually only seen him a few times since we planted the garden across the street. He says he's been busy ever since he lost a second employee, after I left, and he had to start working on the weekends. And now, with the holidays upon us, he says the shop's been crazier than ever. But he does call faithfully to check on my progress with the apothecary cabinet—and to see how I'm doing, I guess."

"And?"

"It's almost done." She closed her eyes and let her foot drop to the floor. "I've had more time since I finished canning all of my vegetables. My shelves are stocked until next spring."

"Good," Ruby replied. "But what I meant was, what about you? How's your progress?"

She didn't speak.

"Holly?"

Her eyes popped open. "Sorry, I was just thinking."

Ruby looked at her with half of her mouth turned down. "Would you mind if I asked you something?"

She shifted her thighs in the chair and sat up. "No, go right ahead."

Ruby hesitated for a second. "It's actually more of a statement. It kind of sounds like Greg might have ulterior motives. Maybe he was just cozying up to you to get you to paint the cabinet."

She took a deep breath. "Believe me, Ruby, I've thought the same thing. It's okay, though. I'm not going to put myself in a position to get hurt again. But I think he really does miss me, especially since I told him I need my space."

"You did? Good for you, girl," Ruby said, leaning forward to give her a high five.

"Honestly, I'm not sure what's going to happen. It's strange, the less interested I seem in him, the more interested he seems in me."

"Sounds like he likes the thrill of the chase. So, what have you been doing with yourself, besides working? I guess I should have known something was up. You've seemed a little quiet lately. And I need to apologize. I've been so busy with running this boutique and taking care of the girls that I haven't even taken the time to catch up with you."

"It's okay, Ruby. I've been fine. I've been doing a little bit of exploring on my own, taking Abbey hiking and stuff like that. I'm proving to myself that I'm not the scared little sheltered momma's-girl that he broke up with."

Ruby laughed and clapped her hands together. "And it's driving him crazy, for sure."

"I haven't even let Mom come visit for a whole month."

"Aw, poor Aunt Judy. I bet she's beside herself, missing her little girl."

"I thought the same thing at first, but now I'm not so sure. She's started her own online wreath-making company and just sent me a picture of her new puppy, Oscar. I'll have to show him to you. He's adorable."

"Wow," Ruby said, reeling back her head. "I must say, I'm impressed with your new level of independence—both of you!"

"Thanks, Ruby. But I think I'm still trying to figure things out. I keep thinking about what my mom said when I first moved here."

"What did she say?"

"Well, she said I didn't challenge myself."

Ruby nodded, as if trying to find the right words. "I think you're trying to, a little bit. I mean, at least now you can make coffee."

"Yeah, but it's nowhere near as good as yours."

Ruby tilted her head. "True. But you'll figure it out. Anyway, you moved here. That's something, right? And just look at your mom, starting her own company, now, in this season of her life. See, you've got your whole life ahead of you. The sky's the limit."

"Thanks, Ruby. I think I needed to hear that, scratch that, I *know* I needed to hear that."

"Let Aunt Judy know she can call me anytime for business advice—hey, I know—maybe I can sell some of her wreaths here in the store."

"That's a good idea, Ruby. It sounds like a win-win. I'll ask her about that next time I talk to her."

Ruby jumped up from her seat. "Whoops, I almost forgot. I have to lock the door for our lunch break. And I don't know about you, but I need a nap," she said, rushing toward the door. Just as Ruby was flipping the *Open* sign over to *Closed*, the front door chimed.

"Yeah, I'll probably be in my pajamas by six tonight." Holly turned her head and looked out over the top of her chair, blinking twice, as if seeing a mirage. It was Hunter Ashworth, and he didn't seem very chipper.

"Hi Ruby," he said. And by the lackluster quality of his voice, she knew she'd guessed right.

"Hunter! I was just about to close for lunch. We've got new hours for the holidays," she said as Hunter stepped inside with a petite blonde woman following behind him wearing some sort of exotic fur with spots and stripes.

Holly could feel a sudden rush of cold air whistle through the small shop. Even from a distance, she could tell that Ruby's pronouncement hadn't bothered Hunter one bit. He actually seemed relieved when he looked at his companion.

"I'm sorry Kat. I guess we'll have to come back."

"Maybe you could make one teeny-weeny exception, just this once?" Kat pleaded, staring at Ruby with her heavily mascaraed lashes and a puffed-out bottom lip. "I'm planning to spend a lot of mon-ey," she sang out while looking at Hunter. "His money, I should say, right baby?" Kat tugged on his arm, causing him to turn a pretty shade of rosy red in the cheeks that matched her nails.

"Well, I suppose—just this once. It's the biggest

shopping day of the year, right?" Ruby asked facetiously.

"Aren't they all, Miss Ruby?" Kat replied, patting her on the hand. "We've been in almost every store in this town. Some of them twice. My baby loves to spoil me."

Holly couldn't believe her ears. Miss Ruby? Now that took the cake. How old was his latest fling anyway? She didn't look much younger than her, but she was sure acting childish. She hardly wanted to, but she stood and walked toward them. Evidently, it had been a short and rocky road with Roxy. She was dying to ask how good old Roxy was doing, with her magical hands, and put him on the spot. "Hi Mr. Ashworth," she settled on. She turned toward Kat. "I'm Holly Edwards. I'll be your personal assistant today, if that's okay with you."

Ruby gave her a sly smile; it seemed she was impressed with her assertiveness. "If you've got this, Holly, I'm going to go grab us some lunch at *The Market Deli* down the street."

Holly nodded.

As Ruby grabbed her purse and headed for the door, Kat grabbed her arm. "Sure Holly, you lead the way."

After what seemed like hours, Kat finally entered the dressing room, which she'd helped her stock with over twenty dresses, a few suits, and several boxes of shoes. Holly sat down in the waiting area across from Hunter who was sitting in a leather chair, resting with his feet on the matching leather ottoman.

Holly called out, "Okay, Kat, we're ready when you are. Why don't you start with that cute little pink tweed suit with the gold buttons?"

"That's a great idea, Holly," she replied from behind the curtain. "Since you're so good at this, why don't you see if you can pick out a suit for Hunter too?"

"Sounds good, Kat." She looked at Hunter and raised her eyebrows. He sat with his head resting against his propped-up arm and rubbed his eyes. She was surprised to see him wearing casual clothes—dark Levi's and a tan sweater. He didn't even blink at Kat's suggestion.

He looked up at her and frowned. He definitely didn't seem like he wanted to get out of his chair. Perhaps she could start by trying to make conversation. "So, you're not working today, Hunter?"

His eyebrows shot up. "What? Says who? This is the hardest work I've done all year."

She almost burst out in laughter. "She does seem a little peppy."

"For getting me up to shop at three this morning, she's *a lot* peppy."

Holly stood and walked over toward the men's suits. "So, where have you been lately? I haven't seen you since the park."

He glanced at her from over his shoulder. "Well, I've been traveling a lot, trying to get acquainted with all of the ins and outs of the business and meeting all of our employees across the United States. And obviously, trying to keep a low profile. I'm sure you know why."

Holly nodded as she walked back over to him with a navy-blue wool Armani suit on a hanger. "Yes, I've seen the papers. What do you think?" She held up the suit for him to see in the light.

Hunter glanced up; his eyes red and lids droopy. "It's fine. Do you want me to try it on? This time, no stool."

She smiled. "No, no need for that. I wrote down your measurements and have them in a little file by the desk up front. I can just tailor it for you, and even deliver it to your home if you'd like, at no extra charge."

"Really?" He sat forward, looking as if she was offering a huge favor.

"We do it for all of our customers." *The good ones and the arrogant ones.* She hoped he'd realize he wasn't in any way getting special treatment.

He sank back into his seat. "Oh."

She couldn't hold it in any longer; she had to ask. "So, you're still going through with the factory? Even with the entire town giving you the cold shoulder?"

Just then, Kat burst through the curtains of the dressing room. "I love it. What do you think, Hunter?" She smiled widely as she modeled the suit, turning from one side to the other and then twirling in a circle. "It's perfect for the office."

"It's nice, Kat. You should get it," he replied, glancing up, looking like he was still trying to think of an answer to her question.

"Really? Okay!" She bounced on the balls of her feet. "Maybe I should try on the pink heels with it."

"Yes. They'll look great, I'm sure, Kat," she said as bubbly Kat sprang back into her curtained cubby hole.

She looked at Hunter, her question still lingering in the air.

He sighed. "Yes, we're still going through with it. The first of March is the day we break ground for the new factory."

Not bothering to hide her disappointment, she puffed her cheeks and blew out the air like a deflated birthday balloon. "That's too bad."

"Let's talk about something else. So, how have *you* been?" He looked at her, truly looked at her for the first time that morning. "You seem different today."

She could feel her heart skip a beat. "Really? How?"

Hunter flattened his lips and searched her face. "I'm not sure. Maybe just more confident?"

"Hmm." She couldn't deny it, she felt proud.

"And you look nice in your dress . . . even though I thought you looked better in shorts and a baseball cap. I bet your boyfriend thinks so too."

She couldn't hide her shock. "Really?" As much as she loved hearing the words, it was completely inappropriate. What was he thinking? He was with his girlfriend, and he was flirting with her. But she could see why the women were so drawn to him, even if he was a—

"Really," he replied as he looked at her through piercing eyes.

"Thanks," she said, hearing her own voice coming out in a whisper. She looked down at her hands and shifted in her seat.

"Okay, I'm back," Ruby said, throwing open the door. "I got you an egg salad sandwich, Holly." She set down a large brown sack by the register. "Come and get it."

Thank God. Holly cleared her throat and practically jumped out of her chair. "Great. I love egg salad." She'd never been so excited to see someone in her life. Talk about awkward. "I'll be right back, Hunter."

An hour later, after modeling everything in her dressing room, Kat decided on purchasing, or having Hunter purchase, only one suit, eight dresses, and three pairs of shoes, including the pink ones. Ruby gladly rang it up along with Hunter's new suit.

Holly stood next to Ruby at the register. "I should have that suit done by next week, Hunter. I've got your address on file. I'll call you when I'm ready to deliver it."

"Thanks, Holly," he replied, his shoulders lagging, glancing at Kat who was admiring herself in the mirror, "for everything."

By the end of the day, her prediction had proven to be right on target. It was almost six and she was just stepping into her red-and-green polka dot pajama bottoms, exhausted by the day's events.

She was thankful that Ruby had decided to close the

shop a couple of hours early—after the flow of customers had trickled down to an occasional drip. When she'd left work and walked to her car that afternoon, the street had been deserted. It seemed everyone in Merrysville had risen at the crack of dawn and decided, after a long day of shopping, to turn in early.

She wrapped a towel around her wet hair and walked into the kitchen to fill her copper tea kettle with water. There was nothing better than a nice cup of peppermint tea on a cold night after a long, hot bath. She looked at Abbey, sound asleep. Since the day she'd found the wooden egg in the garden, Abbey's dog bed had stayed by the mantle. But now that she was implementing the gas fireplace to stay warm, she'd had to scooch it back a foot, against Abbey's whining protests.

The low sputtering sound of the tea kettle rose to a high-pitched whistle, causing Abbey to lift her head.

"It's okay, girl. It's just the hot water."

Abbey lowered her head and continued to watch she as she dropped her tea bag into her mug and opened the cabinet door to retrieve the jar of wildflower honey.

She was feeling a bit hungry and a little lonely. She'd driven to her parents' house for Thanksgiving dinner yesterday and her mom had stocked her up with leftovers. And she'd only spent a few hours with Greg, whom she invited over for dessert later in the afternoon; and most of that was in front of the television set, watching football. She sighed as her eyes perused the masking tape labels of the Tupperware containers: turkey breast, corn bread stuffing, herbed stuffing, mashed potatoes, gravy, green beans, sweet potato casserole, and cranberry-orange relish. So much food! And no one to share it with—except Abbey.

After deciding on a turkey sandwich, and a side of sweet potatoes with miniature marshmallows, she set down a small plate of turkey and potatoes for Abbey, who gobbled it down in no time flat. She walked into the living room and set her mug onto the coffee table before lowering onto the couch. Food was the one thing that always got Abbey off of her dog bed. She glanced at her hand-me-down artificial Christmas tree from her parents, disassembled and in a box by the corner next to the fireplace. Next to it was an extra-large box filled with Christmas decorations, lights, and ornaments that she'd dragged from her spare bedroom closet out into the living room a few days ago. As part of the Edwards' family tradition, they'd always put up their tree the day after Thanksgiving, but today, she was feeling a total lack of motivation to even stay upright, let alone decorate her Christmas tree.

But it was tradition. As much as she wanted to sit and rest, she couldn't help but feel drawn to the tree and the oversized cardboard box. How could she possibly break the family's tradition on the very first Christmas she'd be celebrating in her new home? Besides, maybe the festive ritual would help her feel less lonely. Carrying her mug of lukewarm tea, she stood and walked over toward the boxes. She set her mug down carefully on the mantle and began to unpack the tree.

After wrestling with the base of the tree, she was able to connect the three levels and plug in the lights. "There. That didn't take long at all. Now for the decorations." She reached into the box for the silver garland. After wrapping it around the tree, she bent over and picked up a box of ornaments containing little gold, glittery stars.

Her phone vibrated on the coffee table as she opened the lid and she quickly set the box on the edge of the mantle before answering it.

"Hi, honey."

"Hi Mom, how are you?"

"I'm fine. How about you sweetheart?"

"A little stuffed, thanks to you."

Mom laughed. "So, have you decorated your tree yet?"

"That's what I'm doing right now as a matter of fact."

"Good. I'm glad to hear it. You'll have to send me a picture when you're through."

"Will do. How's Oscar doing?"

"He's okay. I think he's been a little sad since Abbey left. They seem to like each other pretty well, don't they?"

"Yep. They were instant friends from the day they met," she replied, fondly recalling how her mom had brought the little white Pomeranian with her to visit a few months earlier. Abbey had immediately walked over and began to sniff her back, and then proceed to lick the side of her head.

"Well, honey, I just wanted to check in with you. I hope you're not feeling too lonely. Is Greg planning to visit you again soon?"

She braced herself. It was time to tell her the truth. "I'm not sure Mom. We're both pretty busy right now. And, honestly, I don't want to feel like I'm settling."

Mom was quiet for a moment. "Well . . . I suppose if things are meant to be, it'll all work out. And if it's not Greg, I'm sure eventually the right man will come along and sweep you off of your feet. And he'll be even better than anything you could have ever dreamed of."

Mr. White Knight again. "Yes, that's what I've been told, by all of the *married* people I know."

"See, dear. It will happen. We're all living proof."

She was unconvinced. "Okay, Mom. I'm sure you're right. Well, I better get back to my decorating."

After ending the call, she walked back over to the mantle. "Where was I? Oh, yeah, the stars!"

She turned to reach for the box of stars, and accidentally pushed it into the metal box, causing the wooden egg next to it to start to roll toward the edge of the mantle. She could feel her heart drop to her knees as she stretched out her hand. Abbey tilted her head and barked as the egg plunked into her palm.

"Whew, that was close." She replaced the egg next to the box and went back to her tree. After balancing on a chair to put the star on top, she plugged the lights into the wall and stood back to admire her work. "Looks beautiful, doesn't it, Abbey?"

Abbey barked.

"Thanks, girl. I can always count on you."

Her thoughts turned to her conversation with her mom—and to Greg. Was she settling? Or was she in love with him? She wasn't sure. But if she didn't know by now, she was pretty sure the answer was 'No.' She looked at the clock, sleep clouding her eyes, and yawned, wondering how she'd managed to stay up so late.

Walking back over toward the mantle, she replayed her conversation with her mother:

Someday the right man will come along and sweep you off of your feet.

"Does a man like that even exist? If so, I sure wish I could find one," she said out loud, tripping over the corner of Abbey's dog bed as she grabbed for the handle of her mug.

It all happened in slow motion, as if she was standing outside of herself, watching with eyes as big as Christmas ornaments as the mug brushed a little too hard against the box, sending the egg rolling right off the opposite end of the mantle. "Nooo!"

She reached for it a little too late. Her heart did a flip-flop as she watched the egg drop onto the porcelain tiles of the hearth and break in half.

Abbey leapt out of her dog bed as it came crashing down and ran to hide behind her.

"It's okay, girl," she said, not sure exactly who she was trying to soothe, Abbey or herself. "Go lie down."

Abbey whimpered and lowered her tail as she walked back to her bed.

Reluctantly, she looked at the egg and fell to her knees.

It had split into two pieces on the floor, the top piece resting askew on the bottom. "It's not that bad. Maybe I can fix it."

When she reached for the top of the egg, she let out a tiny gasp. "What's this?" She set aside the top piece and stared at what was underneath. More blue velvet cloth, in pristine condition. She didn't hesitate. She picked up the bottom half of the egg and set it in her lap, her heart doing another somersault, as she pulled back the delicate material.

Inside was a miniature wooden carousel ornament. She brought her hand to her face, and gasped. It was beautiful—the craftsmanship, so intricate. She slowly reached down and picked the carousel up, holding it by a golden loop of string, and slowly turned it around with her fingers. *Could it be?* She blinked, trying to comprehend what she was seeing—a tiny unicorn with rainbow wings on a little pink-and-white striped pole. *Wow.* This wasn't just any old carousel, this was the Merrysville Christmas Carousel! Turning the little ornament over in her hand, she looked at its smooth base. In small block lettering printed on the bottom was: The Christmas Carousel 1930.

She didn't know how long she'd been sitting there in silence, with Abbey looking on from her bed, examining the ornament, but when her foot began to zing with pins and needles, she realized it was time to get up. "Well, Abbey, I think I'll hang this on the tree. At least I'll have a reminder of the carousel, even if the real one's going to be destroyed." She shook out her leg and limped on the good one over to the tree to hang the ornament with Abbey following behind her. "And let me guess. Now, you want your dog bed over here." She put her hands on her hips as her guard dog stretched out on the floor next to the Christmas tree.

Chapter Seven

Circling in for a Challenge
Dream a Little Dream

Intrigued, Holly walked the path, brightly lit by strands of glowing white stars strung on wooden red-and-white striped candy canes, toward the carousel, drawn by the sound of Gavioli organ music echoing in the air. Each step sent a tingle from her little toe all the way to the nerve endings on the nape of her neck. She turned to look at the fun house where distorted mirrors evenly spaced across its front substituted for windows. To her surprise, she caught a small army of her own reflection, eight feet tall and as thin as sheets of paper marching by.

The sugary scent of cotton candy drifted in the chilly night air, along with the familiar aroma of buttery popcorn and roasted peanuts. She tucked her head lower into her coat, shivering, before remembering the Ferris wheel. She looked to her left. There it was in the distance, in all its brilliant and colorful glory, bright as the sun making its revolutions. She smiled as she remembered how scared she'd been as a little girl, squeezing her eyes shut as her cart stalled at the top and began rocking back and forth, thanks to Ruby. Now though, the ride was empty. She looked again toward the popcorn and cotton candy stands, both treats in surplus; but otherwise the stands were deserted. She realized she was all alone. No reverberations of laughter in the distance or screams of elated terror as children raced through the sky in their rickety wooden roller coaster carts, just the never-ending sound of festive organ music swirling in the air, growing louder with each of her footfalls.

Her memories had been holding back on her—the deserted park seemed more alive than ever. How did I forget how magical it all had been? she wondered, not bothering to question where she was going, or why. She was headed toward the carousel, inexplicably drawn by the music. Finally, she stepped into the clearing, the sight of it taking her breath away.

"Step right up folks, step right up. Take a ride on the magical Christmas Carousel. Who knows, maybe you'll even be lucky enough to grab the brass ring!" a carousel barker shouted as he stood in his red-and-white striped vest and black top hat in front of the wonderfully magnificent golden entrance gate. "It'll be the ride of your life, Holly."

I'm not alone after all. She quickened her pace, forgetting about the chill—or had the night air started to warm? Wait, how had he known her name?

She was a few feet away now, taking one last stride to stand directly in front of him.

"Good evening, Holly. My name is Joe. Thanks for coming. Ralphie and I have been waiting for you," he said as a black-and-white Border collie ran out from behind a row of cherry laurel bushes and came to sit next to his feet. Joe was a white-haired gentleman with an expansive girth, with red suspenders holding up his black dress pants. *Roly-poly* came to her mind as she looked through his wire-rimmed spectacles perched halfway down his nose into his clear blue, kind eyes.

She narrowed her eyes. Had she met him before? "How

do you know my name?" Her voice came out as shaky as she felt. She looked down and saw that, under her coat, she was wearing her flannel pajamas and slippers. "Oh, wait, never mind. I get it. This is a dream."

There was a certain sparkle in his eye when he shrugged his shoulders. "If you say so, Holly," he replied, raising and lowering his brows. "Would you like to take a ride?"

She looked around and smiled, electrified. It was amazing, how vivid everything seemed. "Sure, why not? It's only a dream. I might as well have a good time."

Joe proceeded to pull back on the latch of the gate and leaned forward in a bow before putting out his arm to direct her. "After you, Holly," he said, holding the gate wide open.

"Thank you, Joe." She passed through, her widened eyes immediately beginning to search for the unicorn with rainbow wings. She ran around the side of the carousel, in a flight of fancy, past the majestic black horse in shining armor, past the crouching tiger with a saddle of flowers. On the other side she spotted it, just for her, the flying white unicorn. She put her foot in the leather strap and grabbed the pink-and-white pole, swinging her leg over the unicorn's wings. When she looked down next to her, Joe was sitting in a cushioned Bertazzon gold sleigh with a canopy, while Ralphie sat by his side, panting.

"What . . . how did you beat me? Oh, I almost forgot—"

"This is a dream?" he guessed, narrowing his eyes as he finished her sentence.

She nodded. "Exactly."

Joe sat back and put up his feet while loosening his bow tie. "Ah, it's nice to get a break." He leaned his arm back on the edge of the sleigh and snapped his fingers, causing the carousel to begin to turn. "Isn't the music delightful?"

She unbuttoned her coat now that a balmy breeze had

blown into this small corner of her fantasy world. "Yes, it's *all* delightful." As they revolved, she glanced around the park. In the distance she could see the vacant Tilt-A-Whirl spinning and the empty bumper cars bumping. "Where is everyone?"

"You tell me, Holly. This is *your* dream, correct?"

She put up a finger. "You got me there." She removed her bulky coat and positioned it in her lap.

"I'll take that for you," Joe said, reaching for her coat and placing it across from him on the empty cushioned seat.

She grabbed the pole by instinct as the carousel sped up, little by little. "Thank you, Joe, so . . . are you going to tell me why?"

"Why what, my dear?"

"Why you've been waiting for me."

"Oh, yes, I did say that, didn't I, Ralphie?" He looked at Ralphie, who raised his nose in the air and began to sniff as they reached a comfortable speed. "Well, I'm not sure how I know, exactly. I just got a sense that you'd show up—and probably have a few questions before we get started."

She pursed her lips. "Hmm. Yes, I was going to ask about the carousel—but 'get started' with what?"

Joe tipped his head back and laughed, patting his stomach lightly with his hands. "You'll soon see. But your instincts were correct. First, let me tell you about the carousel, and perhaps it will answer some of your other questions."

She acquiesced with a slight tilt of her head, and the music instantly lowered in volume.

He looked at her out of the corner of his eye, as if searching for her approval before continuing. "My father helped his father build this when he was a teenager."

"Let me guess, in 1930?"

"You're absolutely correct, my dear," he bellowed with

the enthusiasm of a game show host. "You're catching on quick."

"I saw it on the bottom of my Christmas Carousel ornament."

A glint formed behind his eyes. "Ah, yes, the ornament. That carousel ornament was given to me by my father before he passed away. I forgot all about it until recently."

"So, was it you who buried it?"

"*Planted* it, my dear. I like to say I *planted* it. You're thinking just like my grandson," he muttered under his breath just loud enough for her to hear.

"Well, why did you *plant* it, then?"

"Well, right around the time I planted it, I think it's been about twenty or so years now, my life was about to change. My dreams were just starting to come true. I was full of hope for the future and I wanted something to commemorate it with."

"I'm not sure that I understand."

Joe took a deep breath and sat back. "I come from a long line of craftsmen. As you can see, this carousel, as well as the ornament replica, were all made by hand, custom-designed by my grandfather and father. Right around the time I planted this, I was about to carry the torch for them—I didn't realize how it would change me, though," he finished, his voice tapering to an almost inaudible volume.

"What do you mean?"

"Until very recently, I had stopped caring about the carousel. It brought back too many memories for me. You see, I met my wife on this carousel. But after my business became successful, beyond my wildest dreams, I sort of forgot about the little things that make the world go 'round—no pun intended."

She gave him a little smile. "Go on."

"I stopped spending time at home or with my wife and son. I got entirely wrapped up in work and stopped caring about anyone but myself. And when Wilma passed away five years ago, I felt that I owed it to her, but at that time, I was too depressed to do anything about it. You want to talk about regrets? I could preach a sermon on it."

She was beginning to feel compassion for him. "Wilma was your wife?"

He looked down, silent. After a minute he raised his head and nodded. "I became a recluse after that. I didn't really care about anything. There I was, CEO of one of the biggest furniture manufacturing companies in history and I was miserable. I used to say to myself I was the poorest rich person in the world."

"I'm sorry, Joe."

He perked up in his seat. "Anyway, my dear, now that we've gotten that out of the way, let's move on."

Ralphie looked at Joe and barked.

She laughed. "I think Ralphie's on board. Okay. Let's talk about this 'work' we've got to do."

Joe cleared his throat. "I'm afraid my grandson is about to follow in my footsteps. He's all about the bottom dollar. He's got his mind on his money and money on his mind. Thankfully I was able to have a heart-to-heart with my son and was able to get him to see the light, but my grandson's a whole 'nother story. He's just like me, or like I *was*— spitting image. He doesn't seem to realize that along with his authority comes more responsibility toward humanity. Like this park, for instance, the town deserves better—and it's his job to steward it. And that's where you and I come in, dear. I'd like to rebuild it, especially this carousel."

"I agree wholeheartedly. But what can I do? I'm no carpenter."

"I think, with some hard work, you could figure out a way to bring it back to life. And perhaps help my grandson in the process."

"Your grandson? How? Why me?"

He looked toward the heavens. "Things happen for a

reason, I believe, Holly."

She shrugged. What did she have to lose? "Sure, I'll play along—seeing that this is just a dream. I'm sure I can make it happen with the snap of my fingers—just like you made this carousel turn. And I think most of the townspeople would be elated to have their park back to its former glory. I hear people talking about it every day."

He clapped his hands together. "Great! I thought you'd be up for the challenge."

The word hit her like a fist in the gut. *A Challenge. Just what I need, a challenge, according to Mom.* "Sure Joe, I can do it. Why not?" She looked around at the other animals on the carousel, the bronzed horses, the cheetah, the crown-wearing zebra in front of her. "But I do have a question. Why is this called the Christmas Carousel?"

Joe inhaled and reached into his vest pocket, retrieving a silver pocket watch. "Well, dear, it turns out that it was supposed to be an actual Christmas Carousel with Santa and his reindeers in tow, but since it began operating in the spring, we put those in storage—and just never got around to putting them on for Christmas. You see those empty spots on the outer edge over there?" he asked, pointing to an area in front of her. "That's where Santa was going to go. And behind you, there's a few spots for the reindeer." He leaned forward and looked over his shoulder. "If memory serves me right—they're in that storage shed over there." He pointed past the row of winterberry shrubs bordering the fence, toward the pavilioned picnic area. Standing beyond that, in between two dimly lit streetlights, was a two-story grayish-brown shed with a corrugated metal roof.

"Wow, I'm glad I asked. I'd always wondered about that—and why there were some vacant spots. Now it makes sense—as much sense as it can for a dream like this, anyway."

Joe flattened his lips, a pensive look perched on his

face. "Perhaps I could offer a suggestion, Holly. When you do refurbish this old carousel, maybe *you* could add them." He smiled so wide she could see his gums. "It is getting to be that magical time of year, isn't it?"

"Well, I can redo it all right now." She put her fingers together, about to snap, when she remembered something. "Oh, by the way, who's your grandson?"

"That, my dear, should be obvious by now," he replied and winked as the caroused sped up, spinning faster and faster as the music began to crescendo.

She snapped her fingers. *Nothing.* "Wait! What's going on, Joe?" she yelled over her shoulder, wrinkling her forehead.

"It's time to reach for the brass ring, Holly," he yelled, appearing next to the carousel with Ralphie by his side, standing and clapping his hands together in rhythm to the music. "I think you'll be able to do it this time."

She bit her lower lip and sat straight up, nodding to the beat as the carousel spun. She needed to time it perfectly. Yes, she was up for this challenge too. As she approached the mechanical arm holding the shiny brass ring, she inhaled sharply.

"Are you going to grab for it, Holly?"

Concentrate, Holly. She held her arm bent in front of her, raising it a little higher as the carousel whirled. Almost there. "Just . . . one . . . more . . . second," she said, standing up in her saddle straps, leaning to the side, grunting, as she straightened her arm and stretched her fingers as far as they could stretch.

Chapter Eight

The World of *Make You Believe*

For the last few days, since waking up from her dream, Holly had been unable, and a little unwilling, to think of much of anything else but. She'd gone to bed every night with anticipation, hoping she'd be able to revisit the Merrysville Amusement Park and the Christmas Carousel in her dreams, only to wake each morning more profoundly disappointed than the previous. By week's end, she figured she'd just journal it, every single detail, before it became a foggy memory.

And as she drove to work this morning, she thought about Abbey. Holly had noticed that Abbey seemed to be acting differently since her dream. She'd gone back to acting the way she used to—sleeping on the bed at night, curled into a ball by Holly's feet, instead of by the Christmas tree. Perhaps it was just a coincidence. Perhaps not.

"Only twenty-three more shopping days until Christmas," Ruby sang as she entered the front door bright and early, at the end of the busiest shopping month *Patterns Boutique* had ever seen. Thankfully, she'd still had time to finish altering Hunter Ashworth's suit.

"I know. It's been a little crazy, hasn't it?"

"A little?" Ruby said, putting her hand on her hip. "From the Queen of Understatement herself."

Holly smiled, causing her lips to crack. She walked over to her purse to dig for some ChapStick.

"I hear it's going to snow tonight," Ruby said.

"It's about time. It's not Christmas without snow. I just hope Greg will be able to come up to get the cabinet," she said, after spreading the Piña Colada-scented waxy balm on her lips.

Ruby straightened up from behind the register. "You mean, it's *done*?"

She smiled. "Yes, it's done!"

"That's great, Holly. I'm sure it's beautiful."

"I'll take a few pictures before he picks it up to show you. And, guess what else is done?"

"What?"

"Mr. Ashworth's suit."

"Maybe you should take it to him today, before the snow."

"Yes, that's exactly what I was thinking." She paused, reflecting on the mental struggle she'd been having all week. She wanted to mention the ornament and her dream to Ruby but wasn't sure exactly *how*. How could she express the sheer exhilaration she'd felt as she strived to reach for the brass ring as something so commonplace as words? Besides, it was her own little piece of the extraordinary, and she wasn't sure if she was quite ready to share it. But at the same time, she figured there was some underlying meaning to all of it, and maybe Ruby could provide some insight into the history of the little carousel ornament or provide some kind of rudimentary dream interpretation. Did she dare reveal the raggedy shards of her subconscious?

"Is there something wrong, Holly? You seem to be lost in thought."

"Huh?" she said, quickly turning her head toward Ruby.

"If you want, I can deliver the suit," Ruby offered, "in case you don't feel comfortable."

"Oh, no, it's not that. I was just thinking." She looked at the clock. They still had twenty minutes before the store was to open.

"About what?"

"Remember last spring when I showed you that wooden egg that Abbey found buried in my garden?"

"Yeah, I remember," Ruby said and gave her a wink. "Did it hatch?"

She maintained a straight face. "Sort of."

Ruby's eyes got large. "Really?" she asked, her voice now an octave lower.

"I dropped it and it broke in half."

"Aw, it was so pretty too."

"It's okay. If it hadn't broken, I would've never found what was inside."

Ruby brought her hand to the side of her face, her unblinking eyes fixed on Holly. "I almost don't want to ask. But I can't resist. What was inside?"

"A Christmas ornament."

"Really? That's odd—and interesting."

"And not just any ornament. It's a tiny Merrysville Christmas Carousel ornament."

Ruby crossed her arms. "Now that's very interesting. Did you bring it with you? I've never seen one of those. I didn't even know the Ashworths ever even made Christmas ornaments."

"The Ashworths? What makes you think it was made by them?"

Ruby couldn't hide her surprise. "Well, because they built the carousel . . . and, of course, the park."

She was completely thrown off. "Wow! I totally should have known that!" It was almost like part of her had known, though. "Maybe I just kind of forgot. I probably heard it from someone."

"Maybe so . . . and do you remember the time we were at the park and we actually ran into Hunter and his grandfather?"

Her eyes narrowed. "Hmm . . . no, I don't think I do," she replied, slowly scraping her teeth back and forth on her bottom lip, trying to will forth the memory.

"It's okay, Holly, you were only eight or nine at the time. We bumped into him a couple of times you could say. I remember waiting in line to ride the Ferris wheel and we saw Hunter walk up with his father. It looked like Hunter had been crying."

"Why?"

Ruby shrugged. "I don't know, and obviously, I never asked him. He seemed really embarrassed." Ruby began to sort through a rack of women's clothing and pulled out several of the women's dresses.

"Well, how do you think the time capsule ended up in my yard?"

Ruby looked up. "You know, I'm pretty sure Hunter's grandfather used to live in your neighborhood, now that I think about it. Maybe he used to live in your house. It would be easy to find out—just ask Hunter when you go deliver the suit."

Holly walked over to take a seat on the arm of the leather chair by the dressing room. "Wait, so let me get this straight. You're saying that the Ashworth's have always owned the park? They actually built the park?"

"Yep. And the carousel."

"So, why in the world did they let it go to pot? Especially the carousel, if it was so important to the family."

"They never came right out and said why, but I suspect it was because of some family issues. After Hunter's grandma died, I noticed a change in him, and now that I think about it, that's about the time the park closed down."

A surge of adrenaline shot through her chest and her pulse quickened. "Do you know what his grandma's name was?" She grabbed the arm of the chair and held her breath, not sure if she wanted to know. Her dream was becoming a little too close to reality. *Please don't say it. Please don't say Wilma.*

Ruby glanced up to the right, thinking. "Nope, I can't remember."

She let out her air in a rush. Her thoughts were swirling. Should she mention the dream? And if the ornament belonged to the Ashworth family, should she give it back? From the words on the scroll, it didn't seem like he wanted it back.

"Are you okay, Holly? You look a little spooked." Ruby walked back toward the register, throwing her a tentative glance.

"Oh, no, I'm fine." She let out a nervous giggle. "I was just thinking. It's amazing how our minds can imagine such unbelievable stuff, especially in our dreams."

"I suppose you're right. I've had a few crazy dreams. Have *you* had any lately?" she asked, crossing her arms.

She fully recognized that she'd opened the door wide open to that question and marched right through it. "Yes, as a matter of fact, I have."

"We still have a few more minutes before the shop opens. Feel like sharing?"

"Sure. I, um, dreamed I was at the amusement park across the street and it was better than I could have ever imagined. And it was so vivid, Ruby!"

"Sounds nice."

"Yeah, it was very nostalgic. And there was this charming gentleman, Joe, the carousel operator, who asked me to rebuild the carousel."

"Isn't it interesting how our subconscious makes itself known, even if it has to do it in our dreams? Finding that time capsule really had an impact on you. Obviously, you love the park as much as the rest of us."

She heaved a sigh. She figured that's what Ruby would say, and she was probably right. "It sure is." She'd said enough for now. She was still trying to wrap her head around the whole thing. She'd never experienced a dream like that before. It was just so incredibly *real.*

Holly made sure to shoot him a text before showing up at his house. He'd texted her back moments later, instructing her to just drop it off; so she was quite surprised to hear someone finagling with the latch on the other side of the front door, and even more so when Hunter pulled it open a few seconds later with a look of expectancy carved into the contours of his face.

"Well, hello Mr. Ashworth," she said, trying to hold back a smile. "I brought your suit." She stood on his polished concrete porch, his suit in plastic draped over her arm.

"Holly, please call me Hunter. No need for formality."

His soft tone of voice made her heart skip a beat. She'd just finished promising herself in the car on the way over that, after dropping off the suit, she would forget all about Hunter Ashworth (and his roasting hot smile) and the silly Christmas ornament, but now that he was standing in front of her, she found herself with another decision to make.

She held up the suit, holding her breath, hoping he'd just take it and send her on her way.

"Come on in, please," he said, backing away to reveal the mosaic tiled entryway and art deco chandelier hanging overhead. "You can just hang the suit on the coatrack."

Oh brother! She looked up, slowly letting out air to

calm the jitters that had sprung up out of nowhere. "Wow, it's gorgeous," she said breathily, as she walked across the threshold to hang up the suit. "And very modern."

"Thanks, Holly. That's my style. A little different than yours, I'd say."

She looked into his eyes, and her lips gave way to the smile she'd been trying to quash. "It fits you."

"Oh, I've got to check on something. Follow me," he said, turning on his heels as he headed down the hall.

Well, so much for leaving right away. She took another breath. "So, glad to see you survived Black Friday. Any plans to return to the shop before Christmas?" She was trying desperately to make small talk as she followed him into his gourmet kitchen. She didn't notice until now that the house seemed strangely dim. Feeling slightly uneasy, she glanced into the living room, noticing that all of the curtains were drawn. But when she made her way to the spacious kitchen, it was nice and bright.

Hunter grimaced. "I sure hope not—no offense," he said, standing next to the built-in double ovens. He turned on the oven light and peered in.

She allowed herself to relax a bit and laughed at his candor. "I could say I feel sorry for you, but I don't."

"Not even a little bit?" he asked, bringing his thumb and index finger a millimeter apart in the air.

She shook her head. "Nope. You made the decision, after all."

"Hey, would you like something to drink? I've got tea, soda, water, coffee, you name it."

"No thanks, I should probably be getting back to the shop."

Hunter looked at the clock. "It's lunchtime. Do you mean to tell me that Ruby makes you work through lunch?"

He had her there. "No, but I do need to eat."

Something seemed a little off with Hunter. He didn't seem quite as arrogant today. He seemed *cordial*. But it was awfully quiet in this big, cheerless house. Had she interrupted something? He didn't act like it. But it didn't seem like the right time to bring up the ornament, either.

"Well, you're in luck. I've got a pizza in the oven. It just so happens that I've been working at home the past few days and I'm in need of some company. What do you say?"

"Reheated takeout?"

He laughed. "I didn't realize you had such low expectations of me. No, actually, I made it myself. It'll be ready in a minute."

She reared her head back. "Really? You can cook?"

"Sure—well, I bought the dough, but I made the sauce. I think it's pretty good too. Guess you'll have to see for yourself."

This was not at all what she was expecting from Hunter Ashworth. "Okay. I guess I could try a slice."

"Great." He opened the oven door and pulled out the pizza before grabbing a pizza cutter from the top drawer. After serving her a slice of sausage, green pepper and mushroom; and himself two, he offered to take her on a tour of his manor.

"And now, the last room, my home office, also known as the library," he said, after touring the rest of the downstairs.

"I must say, this is impressive, Hunter. Thanks for the tour. And the pizza was pretty good too."

Hunter looked at the clock, suddenly appearing to be in a rush. "Thanks Holly. Well, I guess I should be getting back to work. Thanks for bringing my suit by. Let me walk you out." And that was it. In the blink of an eye, the nice leisurely, easy-going Hunter disappeared and was replaced with the all-business version. *Shazam!*

"Yes, time is money, I hear."

As she turned to exit the room, a black-and-white photo caught her eye. It was a picture of Hunter and an older gentleman. And even though he was younger in the picture, she recognized those clear blue eyes. It was the man from her dream. She gasped, her breath catching in her lungs as she stopped to stare.

"That's me and Grandpa Joe. I'm surprised you even noticed it. Most women that come to visit don't even pay attention."

Most women that visit? Awkward comment. She'd let it slide. She was too busy grabbing onto her earlobes to make sure she'd heard him correctly. "Did you say Grandpa Joe?" She attempted to maintain a calm demeanor. On the inside, however, she was hopping up and down like the Easter Bunny—the Easter Bunny who'd seen a ghost.

"Yes," he replied, a serious edge to his voice. He looked down.

Her instincts were telling her something wasn't right. She felt like she should know what it was—the same feeling she'd had earlier at the shop about the Ashworths' owning the park. She looked at him, dressed in all black. "Are you okay, Hunter?"

"Yes. I'm sorry. I'm fine. My grandpa passed away last week. Right after we left the shop, I got the call. It was in the paper, I figured you already knew."

She put her hand to her throat, not even sure how to comprehend what was happening. "I'm so sorry, Hunter."

Now it all made sense.

"He'd been sick for a while. I'd been meaning to visit him for the past few months, but I'd been so busy, I hadn't gotten the chance. I didn't even see him on Thanksgiving. I was traveling a lot with Kat."

"Is there anything I can do?" she asked, unsure of what else she could say to this man in front of her who seemed ridden with guilt. As much as she wished she could say something to make it better, her instincts said to keep silent. This wasn't the time to bring up the ornament or the dream. He'd probably think she was making it all up anyway, in some strange way to make him feel better.

"Nothing I can think of." He looked her in the eye. "Like I said, Holly, I appreciate you stopping by."

As she stepped back onto the front porch, she remembered the question she'd meant to ask: Did your grandfather ever live in the Garden Terrace neighborhood? She hesitated for only an instant before continuing to walk to her car. No, she didn't need to ask it now. She was quite sure she already knew the answer.

She couldn't wait for work to end so she could go home and reexamine the carousel. She felt like a bouncy ball without any walls to bounce off. After returning to the shop, she mentioned to Ruby that Joe Ashworth had recently passed away, only to find out that she was already aware.

"Yes, there was an article about him in the paper last week," she said, digging through the recycling bin in the small break room they usually shared at lunchtime.

"Where have I been?" She plopped down in one of the plastic folding chairs, upset with herself for living in such a big bubble.

"Ah-ha! Here it is," Ruby said. "I thought you knew or I would've said something. She handed her the article. How's Hunter doing?"

She shrugged. "He seems okay." *The Queen of Understatement strikes again.* Honestly, he did seem sweet. Humility suits him very well—better than any Armani suit ever could. When she'd gotten into her car to leave Hunter's house, she felt like every muscle was fighting against a magnetic force of attraction trying to draw her back, but that was something she planned on keeping to herself. "He's sad of course—said he didn't really get to say goodbye." Looking down at the article in her hand, she had to force herself to stay calm. There it was in black and white—a recent photograph of Joseph Ashworth. He was the man in her dream, there was no doubt about it.

"That's too bad. I think they were pretty close."

She nodded, speechless. And although she'd spent the rest of the afternoon assisting a shopper with matching her suit with the perfect blouse and shoes, her mind had drifted back to the carousel, and to the man with the clear blue eyes, Hunter's grandfather.

When she finally pulled up to her home, emotionally and mentally drained from the day's events, Abbey was waiting by the door to greet her. "Hey girl," she said, crouching on the floor to give her a hug. "You're exactly who I need to see right now. It looks like you and I need to take a closer look at that ornament you've been guarding."

Abbey barked and wagged her tail as she followed her toward the Christmas tree. At this point, she wasn't even sure what she was looking for, other than more confirmation to add to the already overwhelmingly large pile of evidence that it really was Hunter's grandfather who she'd seen in her dream. Still, something drew her to the tree. She carefully tugged at the golden string, carefully lifting it over the plastic dark-green pine needles to remove the ornament from the branch and walked into the kitchen. She put the ornament down on the table and slapped her hands together, causing Abbey's ears to raise to attention. "Let's get out the magnifying glass." She opened the bottom drawer of one of the kitchen cabinets designated 'Junk Drawer No. 1' and rummaged through it until her hand came upon the two-dollar magnifying glass with plastic black handle that she figured she'd probably never need.

Well, I need it now. She walked back over to the switch

on the wall and pushed the dimmer up as far as it would go to give the utmost illumination to her little white-tiled kitchen table and the ornament. "Let's see what we have here," she said, taking a seat before raising the magnifying glass to her eye.

Turns out, she was right the first time; she didn't really need the magnifying glass after all. Scratched in tiny letters on the side of the base of the ornament, plain as the nose on her face, were the initials, J.A. She put down the ornament and sat back in her chair. So, she had a dream about someone she'd never even met who recently passed on from this world. What did it all mean? She hadn't a clue. "Well Abbey, some things just can't be explained," she said as Abbey tilted her head, trying to comprehend. "Like Ruby said, our subconscious makes itself known even in our dreams."

And that was that. Eventually she'd have to put this behind her. But as she stood up, she couldn't squelch the question that came to her mind:

Was it, Holly? Was it really just a dream?

Chapter Nine

Hunter's Prize
Revisiting a Dream

It was a lovely summer day. She was wearing a nice white halter dress that blew gently in the breeze, splashing her legs with swathes of linen as she walked toward him, carrying a pink-and-blue cloud of cotton candy floating on a paper funnel.

As she got closer, she conjured her best look of displeasure. "We have to stop meeting like this, Joe."

His wing tipped shoes scuttled over the flagstone to meet her. "It's not going to work, Holly. You can frown all you want, but deep down, I know you love it. It's in your DNA," he replied, slightly out of breath.

She tore off a piece of pink spun sugar and popped it into her mouth as he opened his pocket watch. "I suppose you're right. So, what's the rush?"

"I don't mean to hurry. But time is ticking."

"And time is money, right Joe?"

He smiled. "It's way more than that, Holly. Way more." He paused for a second. "So, do you still think this is a dream?" he asked, putting out his arm to escort her to the carousel.

She flattened her lips that were now dyed a pale shade of purple. So many questions popped into her mind. "How is any of this possible? Why didn't you just tell me the truth?"

"Would you have believed me?" he asked tilting his face toward hers.

"Um, I guess not," she replied, hopping up onto her favorite four-legged creature, the flying unicorn. "But then again, I don't really know. I'm still not sure what the truth is."

"That's fair, Holly. Why don't you let me explain, at least, try to?" He took his seat on the sleigh and snapping his fingers. Instantly, the carousel began to turn.

"Wait, where's Ralphie?"

"Oh, he's around here somewhere. You know how dogs are."

"Indeed, I do. My dog's the reason I'm here, you could say."

"Maybe," Joe replied, nodding. "Or maybe she was the vehicle that got you here, and another vehicle would have shown up if it hadn't been her."

Before she could shape her lips to form a question, Joe interrupted. "Like you said, some things just can't be explained."

Holly could feel her mouth go dry. He'd somehow heard her conversation with Abbey. "Well, could you please tell me then, what *can* be explained?"

"I think it's better that I just show you," Joe said, and snapped his fingers again.

Just like that Joe and Holly stood by the Whack-a-

Mole, watching a group of young girls cheering on their chubby redheaded friend. She'd just beaten a grown-up in her favorite game, winning one of the second-tier prizes, a stuffed tiger, and stood on her tiptoes to hand the game operator, a freckle-faced teenage boy wearing a vintage U2 *Joshua Tree* T-shirt under his Merrysville Amusement Park apron, another dollar bill.

"It's my last one," she said in a voice only he could hear.

"You can do it, Sally," her friends began to yell encouragingly as she eyed a yellow overall-wearing, four-foot-tall pink gorilla with a ring of daisies on its head hanging a few feet away.

Just as she was taking her stance, grabbing the handle of her whacking stick with both hands, a little boy, who looked to be about nine years old, walked over toward the game booth and pointed at the bottom row of prizes. "Look Dad, Whack-a-Mole! I bet I can win that green leopard over there. Can I play, Dad? Please?" he asked, looking from Sally to the frenzied young man in his twenties digging in his pockets for more change. "There're only two other players. I have good odds."

His dad laughed. "That's a good point, Hunter." It was all in fun. Hunter had no idea that his father could now afford to buy him any stuffed animal he wanted, and for probably less than what he'd have to dish out for him to play to win a ten-cent toy.

"Looks like we might have another player here, girls," the game operator announced into his megaphone as he looked at Hunter. "And he just might be a *worthy* contender," he added, throwing a smirk toward the red-faced twenty-something.

Hunter's dad reached into the back pocket of his Levi's and whipped out his billfold before slapping a five into the game operator's hand. "Here, just use this up," he said to the operator. "He loves this game."

The operator winked. "Anyone else? Any other takers for Whack-a-Mole?" His megaphone reverberated loud enough for people over twenty yards away to turn their heads. "How about you, young lady?" he asked a pretty blonde teen who was walking hand-in-hand with her gangly boyfriend. She smiled and shook her head, before averting her eyes toward the ground.

"I guess that's one way to meet the ladies," Hunter's dad said, laughing to himself. "Gotta give you credit for that."

"Yes, sir. I have no shame," he replied, puffing out his chest. "She's in my history class." He glanced down at the three people posed with their padded implements of destruction tethered to the game with short pieces of rope. "Okay, looks like we're ready to roll. Just watch the countdown clock, contestants. And a three, and a two, and a one, and a GO!" he yelled over the sound of the echoing buzzer.

Hunter bit his tongue as he concentrated, and began pounding his padded stick, bopping the heads of the insidious smiling moles.

"You can do it, Hunter," his father yelled as he watched him scan each hole, on the hunt for the next head to pop up.

"Go, Sally," the girls sang out in unison. "Sally, Sally, Sally," they chanted.

A siren began to wail. "Time's up!" the operator yelled.

Hunter looked up at the top of his game board. His siren was flashing. "Yes!" he exclaimed, jumping up and down.

The twenty-something walked off, head down, muttering something to himself.

"Thanks for playing, sir. Better luck next time," the operator called after him. "Looks like we have a winner folks." He turned toward Hunter. "What's your name, young man?"

"Hunter, sir."

"Well, what would you like, Hunter? The sky's the

limit." Hunter's face lit up. "Just kidding, I've just always wanted to say that. Anyway, you get your choice of anything on the bottom row."

"That green leopard over there!" Hunter yelled, unfazed, pointing to the stuffed animal on the end of the row.

As the operator reached to grab his prize, Hunter looked at Sally. The little girl looked like she was about to cry.

"It's okay, Sally," one of the girls said, giving her a hug as she turned to walk away. "Maybe we can come back some other time."

Sally hung her head, sniffling. "No, my mom said this was it. Said we can't afford it."

"Hey, little girl!" Hunter yelled.

Sally turned her head as Hunter walked over to her. "Me?" she asked.

"Yah. You can take my games. I've got four left. I've already got what I wanted."

"Really?" A guarded smile emerged on her face.

"Sure," he said, looking toward his dad with a raised eyebrow. "That's okay, right Dad?"

His dad nodded. It looked like Hunter had rendered him speechless.

"Thank you!" she said, hopping back toward her station at the game.

"No problem." He walked back to meet his dad with his green leopard tucked snuggly under his arm.

The game operator gave Ray a thumbs up.

"Ready to go ride the Ferris wheel, Dad?"

His dad put out his hand. The spark in his eyes said it all: There wasn't anything Hunter couldn't ask for after that.

Holly turned to Joe. "That was so sweet! It makes me want to cry."

"Oh, it's not over yet. And believe me, I wish it was.

Have a look," he said, pointing back toward Hunter and Ray.

Hunter skipped backwards with his new stuffed leopard, donned Frisco, toward the Ferris wheel. "Hey, Dad, maybe we can go to the arcade after we ride." He was out of breath, watching as someone bent over to slide a quarter into the slot of the Skee-Ball machine.

"Watch out, Son," Ray yelled one second too late as Hunter collided with something in his path. *Umph!*

Hunter turned to see what he'd bumped into. The 'what' turned out to be a 'who,' a young girl about his age, wearing thick-lensed glasses with tortoiseshell rims, who'd been holding her Hello Kitty wallet in one hand and a taller girl's hand in the other, at least, until he'd come galloping along.

"Ow," she yelled, rubbing her shoulder as she sat on the ground.

"I'm so sorry," Hunter said, extending his hand to help her up. "Are you okay?"

"Yeah, I think so," she replied, frowning as she glanced at her elbow.

"Let's each take one hand," the other girl offered, extending her arm.

After the girl was off the ground, she dusted off her backside with a flat palm and straightened her glasses that had almost flown from her face on impact. "Thanks," she said, looking at him for the first time. Her eyes traveled to the leopard. "Cute."

"Thanks," he replied. "So are you," he said, winking. "I like your glasses—they make you look smart."

She giggled. "I meant the stuffed animal."

"Oh," Hunter replied, his eyes averting toward the ground.

"Are you sure you're okay, dear?" Ray asked the girl. He'd been standing there, holding his breath until she was off the ground and moving all of her limbs.

"Yes, sir," she replied.

His dad turned to him. "Son, you've got to pay attention to where you're going."

"Sorry, Dad," Hunter said, biting his lower lip and shuffling his feet.

"Oh no, it's our fault. Holly wasn't paying attention," the taller girl interjected, yanking on the girl's hand. "Come on, Holly, let's go ride the Ferris wheel."

"Okay, Ruby," she replied and turned to walk away.

Hunter noticed something out of the corner of his eye on the ground. "Wait, you forgot this!" he yelled, bending over to pick up her wallet.

Holly rushed back. "Thank you, I must have dropped it," she said, as he placed it into her hand. "Bye!"

Just as she skipped away, his grandparents, Wilma and Joe, were approaching his father. "Hey, Ray," Joe said. "I was hoping we could find you here."

"Dad? What brings you out here to the park?" Ray put out his arms and hugged them.

"Your mom. She insisted I needed a break. And, of course, I had a couple of business concerns I wanted to talk to you about."

"Joe! This is supposed to be a social time. You promised!" Wilma said.

"Grandpa!" Hunter exclaimed, running up and giving Joe a hug with one arm, and holding Frisco with the other.

Joe glanced at the stuffed animal in his arms. "Hi Hunter. It's good to see you."

"Look what I won, Grandma!" he said, holding up Frisco.

"It's cute, dear," Wilma replied. "Let me take a look," she added, taking it from his hand.

"Why'd you go waste your money on that Ray? You know those things are cheaper than dirt," he said in a low voice. "And they look like it too."

Even though Joe spoke quietly, Hunter overheard. After his grandma gave Frisco back to him, he walked over to a nearby bench and sat, hunched over, with Frisco in his lap, resting his chin in his hands, as he waited for his father and grandfather to finish their conversation.

"Hunter, are you ready to go ride the Ferris wheel?" Ray yelled a few minutes later, looking at him over at the bench. "Come on, Son," he said, motioning with his arm.

Hunter held Frisco up in front of him and wiped the tears that had welled up in his eyes as he sat the toy down on the bench next to him, propping him upright. "You can stay here, Frisco. Maybe someone will find you and take you home," he said, before running to meet his dad, empty-handed.

"Where's your prize, Son?"

"I changed my mind. It's not as nice as I thought it was. Besides, I probably can't ride the Ferris wheel with it anyway," he said, reaching for his father's hand.

Holly abruptly found herself back on the saddle of the unicorn, her arms hugging the striped pole. She glanced at the sleigh. Joe was sitting there, legs propped on the opposite seat, with Ralphie by his side. She was still shaken by what she'd just seen. "You've got to promise to warn me next time. The trip was a little bumpy, you know."

"For you and me both." He gave her a sad smile, causing little wrinkles to form at the corner of his eyes. "That never gets any easier to watch. Let me explain. You see, only a couple of years after I planted your carousel ornament with my grandson, my company was soaring. I stopped spending a lot of time with Hunter, but when I did,

I was usually so stressed with work that I was only there in body, not spirit. And I wasn't exactly *in good spirits* most of the time, you might say. I became gruff."

"When I showed up at the park that day, I was upset about a business deal and took it out on little Hunter. Wilma was the one who'd dragged me to the park in the first place, saying I needed to have some fun, take a break." Joe hung his head. "Hunter just wanted to show me the toy he'd won all by himself, she'd said afterward, get my approval. He longed for my approval she always said. I think I broke his spirit that day. Wilma was mad at me for a long time after that. Told me to apologize, but I never did."

Wow! She remembered it all now—wasn't sure how she'd even managed to forget. All those years ago, she'd met Hunter Ashworth, when he was a caring and sweet young boy.

Joe held a box of tissues toward Holly.

"This isn't just about restoring the carousel, is it?" she asked quietly, pulling one from the box to wipe her eyes.

"Like I said before, I want Hunter to learn from my mistakes and change before it's too late. He's just wasting time and wasting his precious gifts and talents on things that don't end up amounting to a hill of beans. His soul is searching for something more, and I'm hoping that you'll help him realize that."

"You really think he'll listen to me?"

"Why not? He seems to like you Holly. I can tell."

Holly reared her head back. There was absolutely no way that was true.

"You're surprised? Go, talk to him Holly. Get him to think about his priorities. Start with the park. I know his father will agree. Ray is different than I was. He always seemed to appreciate the little things in life. Now he's made the decision to focus on what's most important. I know, behind the scenes, Ray's doing what he can to persuade Hunter to make the right decisions for the town, but in the end, the choice is his."

It was a tall order, she knew, but right now, she didn't want to think about it. There were more urgent matters to tend to. Holly tilted her head down at Joe and raised her eyebrows, staring into his eyes.

"What?" he asked.

"Are you going to do it?"

"Oh yes, I almost forgot. It's what you've been waiting for all night, isn't it?" He snapped his fingers.

The carousel began to spin wildly, increasing its speed even more than the last time, as the mechanical arm dispensed the shiny brass ring. The jaunty organ music seemed to play louder and grow faster right along with it.

"Reach for it, Holly, reach for it!"

She held her face into the breeze, feeling exuberant as her heart rate and every other molecule of her being was entrained to the beat of the music. "I have a good feeling about this, Joe!" she yelled over her shoulder before turning back to concentrate on her timing.

On the count of three. One . . . two . . .

She lay in bed, looking at her clenched fist, half-expecting to see the brass ring. She could've sworn her fingertips had brushed the smooth, cool metal if only for a second.

This is crazy. For all her contemplations about life and her miniscule role in the world, she never would have imagined this scenario. She felt like she was stepping into, and out of, a completely unknown dimension, her foot tentatively stepping over an invisible line, followed by her body plunging headfirst, into a land where time was undefined, and a new reality was created merely by believing it was possible. She had half a mind to start calling out to Joe, to see if he'd show up in her bedroom, crossing the same boundaries she'd only been able to cross in her sleep.

The sound of Abbey's bark brought her back. She sat up and looked at the clock, and then at Abbey who was sitting on the bed by her feet, staring at her. "Looks like we slept in today, girl. Guess I was pretty busy last night. Maybe next time, you can come with me."

Abbey stood and stretched her body before jumping off the bed, wagging her tail as she made a beeline for the kitchen.

Holly threw off the covers. "Okay girl, I can take a hint. Maybe we can talk about it over breakfast."

Chapter Ten

I'm Not Convinced

I'm impressed! One thing was sure, Holly realized, pulling back the curtain and staring out the window: When it snowed in Merrysville, it really snowed! She'd been a little surprised when Greg texted that he wouldn't be able to make it to pick up the apothecary cabinet as planned due to the weather, until she looked out the window and saw what he meant. After her pupils adjusted to the blinding reflection, she realized it must have snowed over fifteen inches, like a fleet of trucks had backed up and dumped mounds of the delicate white powder, creating a blanket of shimmering white over the entire neighborhood. She had to look twice to make sure it was really her car she was seeing parked in front of her house, its nondescript shape blending in with the tall row of icy white bushes lining the sidewalk.

NO PROBLEM, YOU CAN COME NEXT WEEK, she'd texted back a few minutes later.

Her phone buzzed with his response: a thumbs up sign. So personal, Greg. Way to make an effort.

She texted back an image of a snowflake, just for fun.

Her phone vibrated again. It was a text from Ruby:

HEY HOLLY, LOOKS LIKE WE GOT A LITTLE SNOW. LOL. DID YOU SEE THE ARTICLE ABOUT HUNTER AND THE PARK IN THE PAPER?

NO, I'M NOT SURE IF I GOT THE PAPER. IT'S BURIED UNDER AN AVALANCHE IF I DID.

YOU SHOULD CHECK IT OUT ONLINE—ON THE MERRYSVILLE BANNER WEBSITE.

OKAY, Holly typed, and added the snowflake again, just for fun.

She sat down on the couch and searched for the article on the local newspaper's website. There it was, on the front page in all capitals. "THE MERRYSVILLE GRINCH OFFERS EARLY PRESENT." And below it, a picture of Hunter Ashworth. She wasn't sure where they'd gotten the picture, but it was literally the creepiest 'smile' she'd ever seen.

She only needed to read the first paragraph to see what the problem was. She looked again at the photograph. Under it was a quote. "I pride myself on providing work for our community—an antiquated community that must work to keep up with the times and hopefully become a beacon of progress for generations to come."

Holly put her head back and moaned before continuing. After quickly scanning the rest of the article she threw her phone on the couch cushion next to her. He was going to start construction early, as soon as January, by the sound of things. She'd been holding onto the tiniest shred of hope that in the end he'd change his mind, but now, it looked like his mind was set. And he obviously didn't care about the town or his worsening reputation among its people.

But as much as she hated the idea of the factory being built across the street, and his ridiculous and insulting quote, she couldn't help but feel a teensy bit sorry for the Merrysville Grinch. Her mind turned quickly toward her last meeting with Joe. Deep down inside, Hunter had to care, at least a little, about the park, didn't he? How could she get him to realize it?

She spent the weekend thinking of a way to stop, or at

least delay Hunter long enough to be able to get through to him. Some traditions needed to be upheld, especially ones with so much history behind them, like the park. So, by Monday, after she'd shoveled her sidewalk and the snowplows had cleared the roads, she drove to work with the framework of a plan, still under construction in the alcoves of her mind, hoping that Ruby could help fill in some of the details.

"Good morning, Holly!" Danny yelled, her long spiral curls bouncing behind her as she ran to the front door of the shop and threw herself with wide open arms into her outstretched arms.

"Danny, honey, what a surprise!"

Ruby laughed from behind the register. "School's out for Christmas break, and just in the nick of time I'd say. Not like the school buses could get down some of the backroads around here. But I hear sunny skies are in order for the rest of the week. Hopefully it will melt most of the snow."

"No way, Mommy. We want to go sledding," Danny replied, stepping back and stomping her little foot.

"We'll see." Ruby glanced at Holly. "As you can see, they're brimming with energy."

"So, Danny," Holly said, bending over to face her, eye to eye, "will you be helping us out today?"

Danny shook her head. "No, Daddy's coming back to get us in a little bit. He's at the school cleaning," she replied as one of the twins walked out from the break room, carrying a picture that she'd been coloring.

"Holly's here!" Carol yelled, running toward her. "Here Holly, this is for you," she said just as Taylor popped her head out from around the corner to wave.

"Hi Holly!" Taylor yelled.

"Thank you, Carol!" she replied, taking it from her outstretched arm. "Oh, wow, this looks like Santa's sleigh."

"Yep. It's Santa and his reindeer," she said, nodding

emphatically. "See, there's Rudolph." She pointed to a red circle on the snout of the four-legged stick figure leading the pack.

"Dan's taking advantage of the kids being out of school. They're polishing all of the floors to get them ready for the new year." Ruby turned toward her daughters. "Girls, why don't you head back to the break room and draw something else for Holly? I'm sure she'd love it."

"Okay, Mommy," Carol replied, scurrying back to the break room.

"Mommy, can I try on a dress?" Danny asked, her little hands folded together into a prayer under her chin.

Ruby gave her a stern look and put her hands on her hips. "Do you promise to be very careful?"

"Yes, Mommy. I promise," she replied, nodding with wide eyes.

"Okay. Just one, okay?"

Danny jumped up and down. "Thank you, Mommy!" she yelled before running off to find her perfect dress.

"For being named after Dan, she sure is my girliest girl. She reminds me of you a little bit, Holly," Ruby said as she watched her daughter flip through the racks of women's clothing, pausing every few seconds to contemplate a dress. "So, how are you Holly? Did you have a good weekend?"

Holly walked over to the stool by the register. "As a matter of fact, I did," she said, plunking herself down on a stool. "It was quite fun shoveling the front walkway, and even more exciting shoveling a path for Abbey in the backyard to be able to do her *business*, if you know what I mean."

"I'm jealous. All I did was make cookies, and I have zero left to show for it," Ruby said, making an 'O' shape in the air with her fingers. "The girls and Dan ate them all before they even had the chance to cool."

Holly laughed, snapping her fingers. "Darn, I would've loved to try one. But, in all seriousness, I was kind of glad to be homebound. It gave me some time to work on something."

"Oh really? I thought you were done with the apothecary cabinet. It looked absolutely gorgeous from the pictures you sent."

"Yes. I'm done with that. I was working on something a little more abstract—an idea for rebuilding the park." She reached into her purse and pulled out a small bundle of tissue paper.

"Wait. What do you mean?" Ruby froze, her eyes becoming thin like coin slots. "The park across the street?"

She nodded. "I was thinking of a way to have a Christmas Village for the children, and maybe get the carousel up and running again."

"Holly? Didn't you read the article? Hunter Ashworth is going to be breaking ground for his new factory next month. I hate to say it Holly, but I think it's too late."

"It's never too late, Ruby."

"Is this about that dream you had?"

The question took her by surprise. She wasn't quite ready to try to explain her 'dream' to her cousin. "Well, you can't say it's a bad idea. Just think, we could have one last farewell to celebrate the park. We obviously don't have time to get the whole park up and running, but we could rent some rides and just work on fixing up the carousel— and this time, making it the way it was meant to be. The children would absolutely love it."

"What do you mean, *the way it was meant to be*?"

"Well, remember when we were wondering why it was called the Christmas Carousel?"

"Yes?" Ruby said cautiously.

"Well . . . I did a little research and found out that it was supposed to have a Santa and reindeers on it, but they were never added."

"Interesting. How exactly did you find that out, Holly?"

"I have my ways," she replied in a mysterious tone.

"Have you asked Hunter about all of this?" Ruby asked, putting her wrist to her hip as she leaned forward over the register to look her straight in the eyes.

"I was actually thinking about paying him a visit over lunch."

"Well, Holly—*if* you can perform the miraculous task of getting the Merrysville Grinch to agree, I'll help you in any way I can."

"Great! And I can start the conversation with this," she said, unwrapping her little bundle and pulling out the Christmas Carousel ornament before dangling it in front of Ruby on its little golden string.

"Wow, that's gorgeous. May I?"

Holly smiled as Ruby reached for it. "Yes, it is, isn't it? It's exactly like the real one." She watched as Ruby twirled it around on her finger. "Maybe, once Hunter sees this, and how amazing the park will look once the Christmas Carousel's up and running, he'll change his mind and we can save the park!" Holly stood up from the stool to greet a customer who'd just walked in. "Excuse me," she said quietly. "Looks like we've got our first customer of the day."

"Baby steps, Holly, baby steps," Ruby called out behind her.

Holly hadn't practiced exactly what she was going to say when she got there. She didn't want to come off sounding rehearsed. But at the same time, she didn't want it to seem like a spur-of-the-moment, just-off-the-top-of-my-head idea either. She desperately wanted to be taken seriously. This was her chance to do something bigger than herself. It was a *challenge*, as her mother would say. And, of course, she didn't want to disappoint Joe.

Before she'd gotten in her car, she texted Hunter to see if he was at his office. Seeing how he'd been acting the week before, she figured the chances were about fifty-fifty. He texted her back fairly quickly that he was indeed at work and had a few minutes to talk about the "important thing" she'd texted him about. Since it was lunchtime, there were only a few cars in the parking lot when she arrived at the Ashworth Furniture Company's management offices. She parked her little white Honda next to the BMW parked in the spot reserved for the CEO. Hunter's name was typed on the placard in bright blue letters under the word RESERVED.

"Oh, hi Holly. What brings you to this part of town?" Kat asked, looking up from the front desk where she was typing on her computer keyboard when she entered the small lobby. "Need some new furniture? The store is down the street. These are just the offices."

She identified the new suit Kat was wearing immediately as the pink one from the shop. "Hi Kat, I didn't realize you worked here. I almost didn't recognize you with your hair up," she said, trying to hide her shock. Hunter was dating his secretary, why did this not surprise her? "It makes you look—professional."

"Thanks, Holly."

"I'm actually here to see Hun—Mr. Ashworth," she replied, correcting herself quickly.

"Can I tell him what it's about?" Kat asked, glancing at her cumbrous snow boots, before her eyes traveled up to her gray puffy coat and matching gray pom-pom ski hat.

She watched as Kat's demeanor changed, sitting up a little straighter, her shoulders stiffening and the muscles of her face tightening. She was becoming—*territorial*. "Um, just had some quick questions about the park across the street and wanted to make sure his suit worked out okay."

She was surprised with how easily her words rolled off her tongue on the fly.

"He's pretty busy right now," Kat said staring her straight in the eyes, all traces of cordiality *poofing* into thin air. "But I'll buzz him for you." She cleared her throat and pushed down on the intercom button. "Honey?" she asked, her voice transforming into fluffy whipped butter.

"Yes," came the gruff response over a string of static.

She put her lips within an inch of the speaker. "Holly— from the boutique—is here to see you."

"Send her in."

Kat looked at her with eyebrows raised. "I guess you can go in. Just through the doors and to your right, but you might want to remove those first," she said, pointing her chin toward Holly's feet.

"Oops, sorry," she said, looking down to see the small puddle of gray slush that had slid from her boots onto the floor. She walked to the towel that someone had placed on the floor and pulled off her boots. It hadn't even crossed her mind to bring other shoes.

Kat shrugged. "No big deal. The maintenance man will get to it eventually."

"Thanks, Kat." As she walked past her desk, she could see a copy of the *Merrysville Banner* turned to the article about Hunter. She quickly averted her eyes and continued through the doors and to the right, popping her head into the first doorway. There he was, standing behind his desk wearing his new suit, holding a stack of books in his hands.

He looked at her with a sincere smile as he set the small pile down into a cardboard box resting on his desk. "Hi, Holly. I was intrigued by your text. What's this very 'important thing' you need to discuss?"

She scanned him and then the room, noticing several large cardboard boxes scattered on the floor around his office, and one that was already packed, on the floor next to a stark shelf that she assumed used to house his books.

"Um, it looks like your suit fits nicely. It's a good color for you."

"Is that why you came by? To see if my suit fits?" he snorted, continuing to load the box with papers and other items on top of the desk.

She let out a huff of air. "No. I, um . . . are you going somewhere, Hunter?"

"Soon. To headquarters, in Baltimore. My father and Kat both think I should relocate to headquarters for the new year. Kat loves the idea of living in a big city—it only makes sense. Especially after, well, the glowing article in the paper over the weekend."

It dawned on her. "Oh, yes, that. Is that why everything seems a little off around here?"

"That's part of it. I guess I'm still grieving, along with a lot of the employees. My grandfather will be greatly missed by many."

"I understand completely, Hunter."

"Well, would you like to have a seat?" He gave her a look that made her feel just shy of two feet tall and pulled out his chair. "I haven't got much time. I've got an *important* business meeting to attend."

"Sure," she said nervously. *Now there's the arrogant Hunter I know and love. And he doesn't even realize it.*

He slid the box over on his desk, allowing him to see her in his line of sight. "So, what's up?" he asked, glancing at the clock on the wall behind her as he clasped his hands together on the desk, directly on top of the "Merrysville Grinch" article.

She shifted on her leather cushion and took a breath as his sparkling eyes stared intently into hers. *Why did he have to look so good?* She searched for the right words to begin. "Well, I've been thinking of how to say this, but . . . I think it's better if I just let you see it." She reached into her purse to pull out the Christmas Carousel ornament, holding it up by its little string.

99

He leaned forward as a strange look spread over his face; a spark of familiarity overridden by the shock of incomprehension. "Where'd you get that?" he finally said after sitting back in his chair.

"Do you want to see it?"

"Nah, I know what it is. But how did you get it?"

"I found it in my backyard. Well, actually my dog Abbey dug it up in the garden under one of my tomato plants and—"

"You must live at Grandpa's old house," he said in a whisper. "Do you live in *Garden Terrace*?"

Holly nodded.

"I forgot all about it. The magical Christmas Carousel. Huh, after all these years, I finally get to see what Grandpa put in the time capsule."

"You didn't know about it?"

"Well, I was there when he buried the time capsule, but I didn't know what was in it."

"*Planted.*"

"What did you say?" he asked, his head reeling back slightly, his eyebrows furrowing.

"When he *planted* it, you mean."

"Yah, *planted* it," he said, shooting her a quizzical look. He gazed at the carousel for another few seconds, seemingly letting the surprise discovery settle in. "Was there anything else in the box?"

"Just a few pieces of wood, like little sticks."

"Ralphie," he whispered.

"Ralphie?"

"Grandpa's dog. He'd been making me play fetch. I asked Grandpa if he could put his stick in the time capsule, so he did."

"Aw, that was sweet." No wonder Abbey couldn't tear herself away, she could smell the other dog's scent even after all of this time.

He leaned forward. "So, is that what you wanted? To

show me the carousel?"

"Well, I guess that was part of it. But I'd really like to talk to you about a proposal I have for the park."

He rolled his eyes. "Holly, I'm so tired of hearing about the park."

"I know, Hunter. But I was thinking. Maybe I can help you."

"*You*, help *me*?" he asked, crossing his arms. "This should be good." He sat back in his chair with a skeptical sneer on his face. "What makes you think I need any help?"

"The article," she replied, unable to back down. She'd come this far, after all. "I have an idea that will help you maybe win back the trust and respect of the townspeople."

"Like I said Holly, I'm leaving this town."

"Yes, but Ashworth Furniture Company will still be here. Isn't that reason enough?" She could hear her own voice becoming more commanding with each syllable. "At least hear me out." At this point, her heart was pounding in her ears, and she felt like she could pass out from lack of blood flow to her brain, but she was determined to continue.

Hunter threw up his arms. "Okay, okay. I'll hear you out. The floor is yours."

She leaned forward in her seat. "Great! Well, I was thinking that we could have one final celebration at the park, a farewell, I guess you could say, for Christmas. Since it would take too long to get all of the rides up and running, we could rent some rides for the children. Except for the carousel. We could find the rest of the parts of the carousel and restore it for Christmas. We could call it *Christmas at Merrysville*. Simple enough, right?"

Hunter studied her face, looking at her as if a second head had sprouted from her neck. "You're serious, aren't you?"

"Of course." Her smile began to fade when she realized her idea wasn't as well-received as she'd hoped. She glanced at the "Merrysville Grinch" headline on his desk. "And it would certainly help your image."

After what felt like a full minute of staring down at his desk, he let out a big sigh and shook his head. "That's the problem with people like you, Holly."

"What do you mean, *people like me?*"

"People full of pipe dreams with no real knowledge of what it takes to execute a plan. There's a big difference between the fantasy world you're living in and the business world in which I operate."

Her jaw dropped to her knees. She wasn't sure how to respond. "I think you meant that as an insult, but I'd rather be living in my world any day, than your world of business plans and progress that treads on people's lives."

Hunter stood from his chair. "You know, I'm sorry Holly. I should apologize. I think you caught me at my most vulnerable last week at my house. I think I must have given you the impression that I wanted to be friends. But our relationship is only business. I don't have time for friends. I probably should have never agreed to see you."

She screwed her face into an unreadable mask, hiding her emotions most deliberately from this man in front of her who was intentionally pushing her away. And being a jerk. "You know, Hunter, I just have to keep reminding myself, it's the people that lash out with angry, hurtful words that need the most help. Somewhere inside, under all of your pain, is a sweet little boy with a tender heart that loves to hug stuffed animals and share Whack-a-Mole games with less fortunate little girls." She rose from her chair, locking eyes with him as he froze in place with his mouth hanging open. "And compliment gawky little girls with glasses," she said under her breath.

The intercom buzzed, echoing loudly in the silence of his office. "Hunter honey. Your next appointment has arrived."

Hunter pushed the button on the intercom. "It'll just be

a minute," he said, still staring at her.

She shrugged. "I give up," she said in a low voice. "Here," she said holding out the carousel to Hunter.

"I don't want it."

"Just take it, Mr. Ashworth, it's yours after all." She set it on his desk before turning to race out the door.

He stayed standing as he watched her leave before picking up the carousel ornament. After examining the carved creatures suspended on their little striped poles and the Bertazzon sleigh for a minute, turning it gently in the palm of his hand, he sniffed and fell back into his chair. What had Holly meant by *finding the rest of the parts of the carousel*? How did she seem to know things?

"Oh well, it doesn't matter now," he said abruptly, before tossing the wooden carousel into the trash can next to his desk.

Some things just weren't worth the trouble.

"*What* doesn't matter now, Son?" his father asked, walking into his office as he unbuttoned his coat.

"So, you're my next appointment, Dad?" Hunter asked, slightly amused. "It's nothing. I was just talking to myself."

"Who was that lady I saw in the lobby? She rushed out without a word, and she didn't look very happy. Do I know her? She seemed familiar."

"That would have been Miss Holly *Do-Gooder*."

Dad scratched his head. "Do-Gooder?"

"Well, you know, she was one of the people involved with the community garden last summer."

"Oh, yes, that's right!" He pointed his large index

finger and thumb at him. "I remember now. She seemed very nice. So, I'm almost afraid to ask. What did you say to make that sweet young lady so unhappy?"

"What do you mean, Dad?"

"Please, Son," Ray replied, looking up at him from under a wrinkled forehead. "Don't give me that innocent look. As we all know from the recent article in the paper, we've got some issues to address with the townspeople. You're not exactly a teddy bear when it comes to public relations."

"Yes, the Merrysville Grinch told Holly there really isn't a Santa Claus after all."

"This isn't funny, Son," Ray replied, pulling up a seat. "I see some serious damage control in our future."

"Do you see me laughing?" he asked, pointing to his strained and flattened lips. He sat back and put his hands behind his head. "Anyway, she's not as sweet as you might think. In fact, she reminded me a little of a bulldog. So pushy."

Ray threw his head back and laughed magnanimously. "Pushy, huh? I'm envisioning black pots and kettles as we speak. So, what was she being *pushy* about?"

He sat up in his chair. "The park. She wants us, or more specifically, wants to help *me* with my reputation by opening the park for Christmas—restore the carousel, bring in rented rides, and who knows what else."

"Well, she may have a point there, Son. We always do some sort of yearly humanitarian project for the community. It wouldn't hurt for you, as the new CEO, to announce something like that. Maybe save a little face—"

"But I've got a factory to build."

"Don't underestimate the importance of good public relations, Hunter. Wouldn't you rather wake up to a headline that says something like, *CEO Creates Christmas Cheer*?"

He looked at his desk, and the article. "What do you

think Grandpa would do?"

His dad thought for a moment and replied in a soft tone, "I know for a while there he was over his head in business, but you must have noticed how he'd changed in the past few years, after Mom died. He's the one who talked me into retiring early."

"Yeah, the last time I talked to him he asked me if I was happy. I thought it was a strange question. I don't get it, Dad. Isn't the company everything to this family?"

Dad leaned back, causing his little chair to creak with the shift in weight. "It wouldn't be anything without the people's support. Your grandfather was a very wise man. What did you tell him? Are you happy, Son?"

He bit down on his lower lip, unwilling to let him probe. "You have a point, Dad. I can't deny that. You know, Holly mentioned something about finding the rest of the parts of the carousel. Do you know what she might've been talking about?"

"Hmm. Now that you mention it, I think there were other animals that they had in storage somewhere that were supposed to be added for Christmas, but I don't remember now. I never saw them."

"How would she have known about them?" he asked, giving his dad a puzzled look.

"I have no idea, Son. Maybe she has family from back in the day who'd heard about it. Hard to say. Anyway, Hunter, I think that young lady might just have a good idea on her hands. It could definitely solve this publicity nightmare. Just think, your mom and I will be in Hawaii after Christmas and you'll be in Baltimore. Wouldn't it be nice to leave on a positive note, with a special celebration? It would be the Ashworth family's gift to the town of Merrysville."

"I'll think about it, Dad."

Dad stood to leave. "Great! Just let me know how I can be of service."

After he left, Hunter sat back in his chair. He couldn't quite put his finger on it, but something was up. He leaned forward to look into his trash can.

And somehow, the simple wooden Christmas ornament, now laying on a heap of discarded crumpled papers, had set it all in motion.

Chapter Eleven

Teamwork Makes the *DREAM* Work

"So, how'd it go?" Ruby asked in a voice that reverberated off the walls, accentuated by the stillness of the empty shop, as soon as Holly opened the front door. "By the look on your face, I'm not even sure I need to ask." Ruby watched her slowly remove her coat and bend down to remove her boots. "I swear, Danny would've stayed here all afternoon trying on every single dress and pair of shoes on the sales floor if I would've let her."

A frown glued to her face, she walked over to where Ruby was sitting by the cash register.

Ruby raised her eyebrows, waiting for her to open her mouth.

"You know how people say *it could've been worse?*" she asked, crossing her arms as she sat down on the stool.

"Yes?" Ruby replied, continuing to stare at her glum face.

"Well, this was not one of those cases." Her shoulders caved inward as she slouched forward. "It literally couldn't've been worse. He's so arrogant. I don't think he has a sentimental bone in his body."

"Yikes. I'm sorry, Holly."

"I just don't get it. What does he have to lose?"

"Well, just thinking of it from his perspective, as a business owner, I'd say he could lose *money*. Restoring the carousel and renting rides would probably cost quite a bit. But at the same time, he'd be making money from admissions, so I don't know. It could all balance out."

"Well, it would be great for his reputation—and the company's. I think it would go a long way in making people want to buy Ashworth furniture."

Ruby tilted her head from side to side. "After everything's said and done, it could end up making him a little profit, both financially and socially speaking. Maybe you should just give him time to think about it."

She shook her head. "Time is something we don't have much of. I don't know. He's planning on moving to Baltimore. Maybe he's just giving up on this town."

"He's moving? Wow. I'm kind of surprised. He's lived here his whole life—and so has the rest of the family."

"He wants to be near their headquarters. I think it has to do with Kat too. He said she likes the city." She put her hand on her hip and leaned forward. "Did you know she was his secretary?"

"No. How convenient. I'll have to make sure we get in some more cute suits for her to wear to work. Let me write that down," Ruby said, grabbing for her note pad.

"Oh, Ruby. Always thinking of how to grow your business. I guess I can't blame you."

Ruby looked at her watch. "Speaking of the business, I think the snow's keeping everyone away. Let's say we close up shop early today?"

"Sounds good to me."

"While I do our daily bookkeeping, would you mind doing a little cleaning on the sales floor before we go, Holly?"

"Sure. Too bad you haven't come up with a way to ward off bad weather." She headed for the cleaning supply closet.

"You know, speaking of that, I have an idea."

She raised her eyebrows. "Why does that not surprise me?"

"I've been tossing around the idea of making an online virtual boutique. Customers could just enter their sizes and try clothes on virtually. It would open up the market to customers from all over, and it wouldn't matter if we had a blizzard," Ruby said, tapping her pen on the counter.

"See, I knew it. You think of everything." She grabbed the glass cleaner from the shelf and walked over toward the dressing area, stopping to stare at the bottom of the mirrors. "The mirrors are a little more smudged than usual." Fingerprints about two feet from the bottom were covering the glass in a random pattern, along with full palm prints patterned into the shape of hearts along the bottom.

Ruby looked up. "Yes. Credit goes to my lovely girls for that."

"They must've had fun." She imagined what it was they'd been talking about while making their marks on the glass. The wonders of being a kid again. Funny, she'd just had a taste of that on the carousel. She crouched down onto her knees to clean the mirror, avoiding her reflection. Nevertheless, she caught a glimpse of herself with her long hair spilling down freely on the sides of her face, over the front of her white lacey blouse.

Her hand continued in a circular motion as images flooded her mind. Plain as day she could visualize herself as a young girl of about Danny's age playing dress up in her room while her mom, dressed in a frilly apron, prepared dinner:

"Why don't you go and play, sweetheart? I don't want you to get burned. You know how this stuff splatters."

"Okay, Mommy," Holly replied. As she turned, she could hear the sizzle of oil as her mom grabbed the tongs and began to place large pieces of flour-and-herb-coated chicken parts one by one into the skillet on the stovetop. Ten minutes later, as the aroma of fried chicken filled the air, she stood in front of her mom's dressing mirror, bright red matte lipstick blurring the natural lip line, as she puckered her mouth and blew herself a kiss. She wore a home-sewn ruffled red dress with large rhinestone buttons sewn up the front. She imagined they were diamonds, and she, the wife of the president. The sleeves draped widely over her shoulders, with cuffs hanging well past her small fingers, and the hem of the silky material, edged with ribbon, grazed the floor. Her tiny toes curled awkwardly as they slid forward into the narrow tips of her mom's sizeable black patent leather high heels. She pushed back her sleeve, revealing red fingernails, and brought her hand to her neckline to feel cool smooth round pearls in her fingers. With her other hand, she pulled up on the hem of her dress, wondering if her feet would ever grow large enough to fill her mommy's shoes.

"That certainly looks scintillatingly spotless, Holly," Ruby said from behind her.

She looked up and saw Ruby watching her, hands on hips, a look of curiosity encamped on her face. "Oh, sorry. I think I was daydreaming."

"That's okay, Holly. I was just asking if you wanted to go home. Or if you want, you can stay here and clean the rest of the night."

"Um, let me think. It's a toughy, but I think I'll choose *go home*."

Ruby reached out her arm. "Sounds good. Let me help you up."

It was midweek. Holly looked out her window, glad that she could finally see her sidewalk. Ice that looked a little like dirty chunks of Styrofoam mixed in with the gravel lining the edges of the road was the only piece of evidence remaining from the snowfall; ephemeral as it was under the daily battering of the sun's strong rays. *If only Hunter's heart would thaw like that.* Just as she turned to pour herself a second cup of Folgers that she'd proudly brewed herself, her phone rang.

"Hey Holly. I hope I caught you in time. Where are you?" Ruby said, her voice sounding fraught.

"I'm still at home."

"Oh good! Sorry I'm calling on such short notice, but Danny woke up today with the sniffles, and since Dan's going to be working at the school, I'm going to stay home with the girls. Hopefully the twins haven't caught it. So far, they sound fine."

"I hope so too, Ruby!" Holly could hear Danny in the background pleading with her mother to go sledding, even if there was hardly any snow left to sled on.

No Danny, you need to stay inside to make sure you're well, sweetheart, she heard Ruby mutter. *Next snowstorm, honey, I promise.*

"So, I guess the shop will stay closed today, which is too bad, seeing that the snow has finally cleared," Ruby said into the receiver.

"I can open up the shop for you, Ruby. That's what I'm here for, isn't it? I've been working with you long enough." She was feeling a little surprised with herself. But she was feeling good, stepping up to the plate to handle something on her own and helping out her cousin in the process.

There was silence on the other end. "Are you sure, Holly?"

"Sure, I'm sure. I have my key. And I can make coffee too—I know the drill. If I have any problems, I can just call you."

"I guess you're right. I just don't want you to feel any pressure."

"Please. It's nothing, Ruby. I'm glad to do it."

"Oh, thank you, Holly! You're a lifesaver. And remember, call me if you need anything, anything at all."

"Don't worry, Ruby. It's all under control."

She'd been going nonstop ever since opening up the shop. By midmorning, Holly had to admit things had been moving along swimmingly, even if she had to say so herself. Ruby would be pleased when she found out a handful of regular customers had stopped by, as well as a new one.

"Hello, welcome to *Patterns Boutique,*" she said, rushing toward the front door to greet the smiling fresh face. "Let me help you with your coat." Holly held onto the beautiful cream suede coat while the woman slid out her arms and then turned to face her.

"Thank you, dear. Margaret said nice women worked here, and she was right." The woman glanced at her sweater dress and brown leather boots. "But she forgot to say fashionable as well." "I'm Karen Young," she said, extending her hand, "a friend of Janice Carlisle. Please, call me Karen."

"I'm Holly. Yes, Mrs. Carlisle is wonderful. We do so appreciate her patronage and enjoy her company."

"And she thoroughly enjoys yours as well. Anyway, Holly, Janice was wearing a gorgeous tiffany-blue wool dress when I saw her at church last week and she said she got it here. So, I was hoping you might have others, perhaps in another color? I wouldn't want to get the exact dress—I like being original."

She smiled and nodded. "I know the exact one. And yes, as a matter of fact, we have another spectacular dress made by the same designer that I think you'll love—one that will certainly highlight the green and gold flecks in your eyes." She turned on her toes. "Follow me."

"Great!" Karen replied, bouncing on her bent knees, and putting out her arm like a cheerleader waving a pompom. Holly swayed to her left to avoid getting bopped in the nose. "Oh dear, I'm so sorry. I get a little excited when it comes to new clothing."

"I understand completely," she said, tossing her head back and laughing as she led her to the back of the store. After supplying her with two sizes of the dress and stocking the try-on room with several other similar dresses and three outfits Karen just couldn't resist, she walked to the front of the store, at Karen's urging. *I might be here a while. I'm sure you have better things to do than wait for me to try on all of this clothing,* she'd told her.

She dropped down into her chair behind the register, unable to suppress a growing smile. She was feeling proud of herself—of her confidence to run the shop by herself. It couldn't've been going any better. She picked up her cell phone. Just as she was about to call Ruby to fill her in, she realized she'd missed a call. She scrunched her forehead and looked at the number, unable to recognize it. It didn't look like whoever it was left a message. *Oh well, maybe they'll call back.*

The sound of the front door chime caused her to raise her head. Standing in the doorway was Hunter Ashworth, the absolute last person she thought would have the audacity to grace the steps of *Patterns Boutique* with his awe-inspiring presence.

Her jaw fell slack as she stuttered, "Hello," giving her mind time to race through the gamut of words she could possibly choose to say after the way their last meeting had ended.

"Hi Holly," he said, looking around the shop as he took a step toward her. "I tried to call, but you didn't answer, and I happened to be driving by and saw your car, so I decided to stop in," he said, glancing down at the floor and then looking up to meet her eyes. "You probably didn't expect to see me anytime soon, did you?"

That was true. He'd read her mind like an open book. She couldn't speak, so she did the next best thing, she crossed her arms and glared at him intently.

"I know, you're upset with me. I get that," he said, taking another step in her direction. "I just want you to know that I've had some time to think about what you said, and, I, um—"

"Yes?" she asked, tilting her head toward him and continuing to look sternly into his eyes. She wasn't about to let him off the hook without making it very clear that she was not going be a pushover. He sure was irresistible, though, when he was eating humble pie.

"I'm sorry for responding without thinking it through. And, I'm sorry for what I said about you. I didn't mean it as an insult. I really do appreciate your opinion."

Her heart skipped a beat. "Well, I accept your apology, Hunter. I hope we can continue our *business* relationship, even if you won't be living here."

Hunter sighed. "I deserve that. If I had time for friends, you'd be at the top of my list."

It was sort of endearing, she'd give him that, and it was probably the best she was going to get from Hunter today. Baby steps, as Ruby would say. "So, is that all you wanted?" She couldn't help but note how the tables had turned, and by the look that crossed his face she figured he was thinking the same thing.

"Well, no. Actually, I've come to tell you that I'm willing to hear you out. I was speaking with my father, and we both feel that opening the park one last time would be nice for the community—if it's possible."

Maybe there's hope for him, after all. "Really?" She looked toward the dressing room. Karen was still inside trying on clothes. "Excuse me, Hunter, I'll be right back." She stood and glided to the back of the store, feeling light on her feet. "Karen, are you doing okay in there? Is there anything else you need right now?"

Karen poked her head out from the curtain. "I'm fine Holly, you just keep talking to that handsome man out there," she replied in a quiet voice and winked. "Don't worry about me," she added before shutting the curtain.

Her mouth dropped open in surprise and she giggled to herself as she made her way back to the register and sat. "Would you like to have a seat, Hunter?" she asked, pointing to the stool. She cleared her throat and waited for him to get comfortable. "So, what are you actually saying?"

"Well, I'm willing to listen to your proposal—to see if we even have time for a Christmas Village. And of course, cost is always a factor."

"I guess it would depend on how many people we could get to pitch in. I'm sure that having volunteers would help significantly."

"Yes, and you seem to have a connection with the community, based on what I've seen with the gardens. And obviously, Ruby, too." His eyes surveyed the room. "By the way, where is Ruby?"

"She's home tending to her daughter Danny. Sounds like she has a little cold."

"Oh. That's too bad. I was hoping we could talk to her about having a community meeting to discuss our options and make some plans. We'll have to move quick, though,"

Hunter said.

"Say no more. I'll text her and see if we can't get a meeting together by tomorrow night at the community center. She's got a Facebook page, and she has a newsletter she sends out by email. I'll see if she can make an announcement. I'm sure lots of people will show up."

"Great. Let's see if we can make it for seven tomorrow night, then. I'll let my dad know as well."

She smiled. "Thank you, Hunter. I think you'll see you're making the right decision."

"I guess time will tell," he said, glancing at his watch. "Well, I better get going."

"See you tomorrow night," she said as he stood and headed for the exit, her eyes tracing his moves. As he reached the door, he stopped in his tracks and turned to glance back over his shoulder, looking as if he had something else to say.

She raised her eyebrows.

"Um, bye, Holly," he said before turning to leave.

Whatever it was, she guessed he changed his mind. Watching him go, she wondered if he'd felt the electricity in the atmosphere that she had. She was sure he must have noticed; maybe he was just good at covering it up. Besides, he was dating someone else, and so was she, well, sort of. Not that dating Hunter was part of the challenge anyway.

By late afternoon, she decided to call Ruby with an update on the sales and to discuss the upcoming meeting that had yet to be scheduled. Ruby was more than willing to jump on board to help with bringing the townspeople together for a meeting on Thursday evening. And thankfully, Danny had seemed to have all but conquered her illness with an abundance of freshly squeezed orange juice, chicken noodle soup, and plenty of rest.

"No problem Holly, I'll send out the email tonight, and by tomorrow night we should have quite a group.

Everyone, I mean every single person I know, loves that park, so I won't be surprised if it's standing room only. I just have one question, though."

She knew what was coming. "Yes?"

"How'd you do it?"

She thought of Joe. "Christmastime truly is the season for miracles—that's all I can say." But as much as she was thrilled with her progress and wanted to revel in it, she was slowly descending to earth from her short stint on cloud nine. "But, there's still a lot of work ahead."

"I agree. And I think nothing *but* a miracle can explain Hunter's change of heart. Thank you for doing such a wonderful job today. Sounds like the sales were off the charts. I'll come in early tomorrow to clean up and get ready for the day. Why don't you just go ahead and wrap up for the day? I'm sure you're tired."

"On the contrary, Ruby, I have a newfound energy. But I'll lock up. It's about that time.

The Merrysville Community Center was a few blocks from the center of downtown, on the opposite side of the old park. It had been built only twenty years prior to provide a place for children to go after school to play sports, as well as provide a wide variety of exercise classes for adults and seniors, workshops, and meeting rooms for other community groups in town—anything from the local SBA to the Merrysville Runner's Club. Holly stood in the doorway of the large gymnasium, leaning on the doorframe in her comfy jeans and favorite checkered flannel. By seven o'clock, she'd counted over forty people, most of them parents of young children, as they entered the room, with several more stragglers entering the double doors at the end of the hall.

She looked again. As they got closer, she could identify the stragglers as Hunter and Kat, followed by Ray Ashworth.

"I'm glad you all could make it. Looks like everyone's here that's going to come. So, we should probably get started or we might be here all night."

"Great," Hunter replied, looking at Kat, who was wearing her leather high-heeled boots and a silky dress under a short black wool coat. "It's okay. This shouldn't take long."

"Good, because I made dinner reservations at Nell's for eight-thirty," she replied sulkily, as she removed her gloves and loosened her scarf. "And it wasn't easy with the holidays. They were almost booked solid."

Holly turned and walked into the gymnasium, wondering how it was possible that she'd already had enough of Kat for one evening and it was just getting started. After everyone had taken their seats on the first couple of rows of bleachers, she introduced herself to the group.

"Good evening everyone. Thank you so much for coming. I'm Holly Edwards, cousin of Ruby," she said, pointing to Ruby who was seated in the first row next to Dan and the girls. "She and I will be the go-to people for this project. As you are aware from the email, Hunter Ashworth and his father, Ray, are interested in sponsoring a Christmas Village at the old park." She pointed to the two men sitting on the row next to Ruby and Dan. "Our hope is that we can have the park up and running for Christmas Eve and Christmas Day as well as the following weekend, all the way 'til New Year's.

Some people began to clap while others murmured.

She put her hands up in the air and the room fell quiet. "I appreciate the enthusiasm! And I know, we only have fourteen days to get this done. But I want to talk about the possibilities here, not reasons why it can't happen."

"I think most of us here are on your side, Holly," someone yelled.

People began to clap.

"Thank you." After the cheers died down, she continued. "I'd like to first give you all an overview of my ideas and then I'll take some questions. As I mentioned to Hunter the other day, I'd like to see if we can open the village with some rented rides for the children and also get the carousel up and running. In order to do that, we're going to need volunteers in the following areas: marketing, promotions, ticket sales, food preparation, of course, renting rides, and restoration of the carousel. After we have all of that figured out, we'll need people to volunteer their time to run the rides and the food stands."

"I know someone who has a food truck," someone yelled out, "and a cotton candy machine."

"Great. I'd like to go through the list one by one and get your ideas. I've also created sign-up sheets, so please, before you leave tonight, make sure you do sign up for what you're interested in and leave your phone number and email in case we don't have it yet."

A hand went up in the second row. It was the owner of the local bakery, Mrs. Piatt. "I think your categories sound fine, Holly. But maybe we can also do a fund raiser, like a holiday bazaar. We have so many talented artisans. I can donate some baked goods and I know a lot of us here can donate some of our crafts and specialty foods so some of the proceeds can go toward paying for this."

"I can donate some of my wreaths," a female yelled.

"I have dried lavender and goat's milk soap," a young man in the front row called out.

"I think that's a great idea, Mrs. Piatt, would you like to take charge of that?" Holly asked. She glanced at Hunter and Kat, who'd leaned in and whispered something in his ear and then proceeded to laugh.

"Absolutely," Mrs. Piatt replied, smiling.

"This sounds great, and I don't mean to rain on your parade, but what if it snows?" an older gentleman, whom Holly didn't recognize, asked.

Out of the corner of her eye she saw Kat nodding. She was obviously not on board with the decision to have a Christmas Village.

Hunter Ashworth stood, causing Kat to pull on his sleeve, trying to get him to sit back down. Holly was thankful that he stood his ground. "I'll answer that, Don," he said, rising and walking to the front to stand next to Holly. She noticed that Kat had crossed her arms and seemed to be squirming in her seat. "We're fully prepared for snow. We have access to snowblowers, tractors, outdoor heaters, you name it. I think Ms. Edwards here has put a lot of thought into this. For me and my father here, we're willing to give this a try."

Everyone began to clap, and she waited for the applause to die down. "Okay everyone. I think we got a little bit off track. Let's go through the list."

"You got it," someone yelled.

After she finished discussing the first few items, she arrived at the restoration of the carousel. She'd been waiting for this moment, trying to think of how to ask about the reindeer and Santa without making it seem obvious that she knew about them. This was the tricky part. A little white lie wouldn't hurt, would it? "Ray Ashworth, since you're here, may I ask you a question?"

Ray looked up, slightly surprised. "I was wondering if you knew anything about other pieces of the carousel that might be in storage somewhere? I think I remember hearing something about it from my grandma years ago."

"Ah. Yes, well, Hunter and I spoke about this the other day and I've had a chance to think about it. I remember something now. We have a couple of storage sheds on the property. I think maybe you might be able to find them in there. I wish I had a better answer for you."

"That's great, Ray. I would love to go check that out."

"Maybe you can go with her, Hunter. I can give you the keys," Ray offered, turning to face his son. She watched as Kat sighed and frowned.

Hunter nodded, ignoring Kat's glare. "Sure, we can go Saturday morning."

She nodded. "Sounds like a plan. I just want to thank everyone for coming out tonight and braving the cold. Once we review the sign-up sheets, we'll be able to see where help may be needed. Please, if you have a neighbor who couldn't make it tonight, let them know what we discussed and have them contact me directly if they'd like to volunteer. Have a good evening everyone," she said, as people began to rise from the bleachers.

When Holly arrived home, Abbey was lying down next to the Christmas tree. "Hey, girl," she said, walking into the living room and plopping down on the couch. Abbey followed carrying a stuffed Santa Claus in her mouth and jumped up next to her. She'd planned on waiting until Christmas to give Abbey the new toy, but it turned out she wasn't very good at keeping the surprise. The anticipation had overwhelmed her. Abbey bit down on her toy, as if saying how grateful she was.

Squeeeak! Squeeeak!

She smiled as she put the stack of sign-up sheets on the coffee table. "How could anyone resist your cute little face," she said as she stroked Abbey's cheeks while she continued to maul the corduroy Santa.

From a quick perusal of the sheets at the end of the meeting, it looked like there would be more than enough volunteers for getting the park up and running. But when she'd glanced at the carousel restoration sheet, there were only a handful of people who'd signed up, and she'd been the first one to do so. She leaned forward, curious now to see who she'd be working with on the project, wondering if she'd recognize any of the names under her own. She hoped at least a few of them would be good at painting and repairing. A good carpenter and an electrician would sure come in handy.

She thumbed through the pile, looking for the carousel sign-up sheet.

"Ah-ha," she said, slowly wheedling it out from the pile.

Hunter Ashworth was the very next name after hers, followed by Kat McDougal, in the same handwriting. *Interesting.* So, I guess I'll be spending more time with Hunter, and Kat, she thought. Holly didn't know if Hunter had any talent with woodworking, but it would be in keeping with his family's lineage of craftsmanship if he did. She suspected Kat, on the other hand, with her perfectly manicured nails and dainty hands, had probably never even so much as held a piece of sandpaper. *Now, now, Holly, don't judge a book by its cover,* an inner voice cautioned.

She would at least give her the benefit of the doubt, although after her behavior tonight, she wasn't so sure she deserved it. She'd practically run up to Hunter as soon as the meeting ended and dragged him by the arm to extract him before any chance of additional discussions. By the way they'd raced out of there, she was actually surprised he'd had time to sign his name at all.

After reviewing the other names on the sheet, none of which she recognized, she sat back and put her feet up before pulling her phone out of her pocket. She knew someone else who could help, quite a crafty lady indeed.

"Hi, Mom, it's not too late, is it?"

"Not at all Holly. How are you? I feel like I haven't seen you in ages."

"I'm great. I have some good news."

"Really? What? Are you and Greg getting married?"

"Mom! Really?"

"Sorry, dear. You sound very excited, that's all."

"Well. How would you like to come up next weekend to help us restore the carousel at the park for our Merrysville Christmas Village?"

"What? The park's going to reopen? How in the world did that come about?"

"It's kind of a long story. Turns out, inside that egg Abbey found in the garden was a miniature Christmas Carousel ornament. I had a dream about fixing up the carousel, so I talked to Hunter Ashworth about it and he finally agreed." It was sort of true, although she still wasn't quite sure how to categorize what had been happening to her in the middle of the night. Calling it a 'dream' sounded almost a degradation of her surreal experience.

"Whoa. I'm afraid you'll have to back up sweetheart. It sounds like I must've missed a few things."

"I can explain it all later. We've got a few other things to tend to this weekend, but I'd love for you to come up next weekend. Hopefully the weather will hold out for us."

"I'll mark my calendar. I can't wait to hear all about it."

"Oh, and I almost forgot. Ruby said she'd love to sell some of your wreaths in her store. And you might as well bring some to sell at the Christmas Village too."

"That's a great idea. I'll be sure to bring some with me."

"Great. I'll let her know. Love you, Mom. See you soon."

Whew! She'd managed to get off of the phone without talking about Greg, other than her mom's glib comment about getting married. She settled back into her couch cushion. Speaking of Greg, she might as well get it over with. She dialed his number.

"Hi Holly, it's good to hear from you. How are you?"

"Great. I just wanted to say, I think that it would be better if you wait until next weekend to pick up the cabinet. I'm a little busy this weekend—I have a project I'm working on."

"Oh. Sure, I guess that's fine. Is there anything I can do to help?"

"No, not right now, but I'll let you know. Thanks, though."

"Okay."

He sounded a little let down. "But definitely, I'll see you next weekend," she added, hoping to mitigate his disappointment.

"See you next weekend, Holly."

She hung up, glad that the call had gone so smoothly, and glanced toward the darkened corner of the room. She'd forgotten to plug in her Christmas tree. She walked over to the tree and bent down to plug in the power cord. As she stood up, she reeled backwards when she saw it. There it was, back in its original spot, the Merrysville Christmas Carousel ornament.

Just then, Abbey jumped down from the couch and walked over to the tree. "Do you know something I don't know, Abbey?"

Abbey picked up her head to look at her and lowered herself to the floor with a little whine.

"Guess I'm on my own then, huh?" she said, staring at the ornament. "I'm pretty sure Hunter didn't break in and put it here—which leaves only one explanation—there is no explanation." She frowned as she listened to herself. Technically, the explanation was perfectly reasonable, if she lived in the supernatural. It must be another miracle from above. But why? she wondered, realizing the question for now would largely remain unanswered. The only thing she did know at this point was, for whatever reason, she'd been chosen, and her job wasn't finished yet.

Chapter Twelve

Searching for Santa

It was Saturday morning, and the day was looking up. Hunter texted her at seven to let her know he'd been able to obtain the keys to the storage shed and he'd like to meet as early as possible. She couldn't explain it, but she was feeling a little giddy, like a schoolgirl about to go to recess. By the time she'd made it out the door, the sun was shining brightly. It was supposed to reach an unseasonable sixty degrees today, with some possible record-breaking highs later in the week, and she was ecstatic that, so far, the weather had decided to cooperate with their little venture.

The effervescence in her spirit fizzed away as soon as she pulled up. Hunter was there, standing next to the antiquated Merrysville Amusement Park sign, with Kat by his side, squeezing his arm like a boa constrictor. And unlike during their previous encounter, she appeared to be in a great mood.

"Good morning, guys," she said, walking up to the couple.

"Hi Holly," Kat replied, with high-pitched over-enthusiasm as she bounced on her stiletto boot heels.

"Hi Holly," Hunter added, tossing her his hand. "I took

the liberty of rounding up some transportation since we'll be traveling around the fairgrounds." He pointed toward a four-person golf cart with a striped canopy parked a dozen yards away. "And I couldn't talk Kat out of those ridiculous boots. It's not like she doesn't have twenty other pairs she could've worn."

"Oh, don't be silly, *Silly*," she said, poking him in the side with her index finger. "You know these were the best match to my outfit. A girl's gotta do what a girl's gotta do, right Holly? Coordinating the right outfit is *so* important. In fact, Hunter promised to take me shopping at the boutique after this," she said, chipper as a songbird as she looked toward *Patterns* across the way. "I'm going to need some new outfits for when we move to Baltimore."

"Oh, wow, that's great. I think Ruby got in some new suits that you might like," Holly said, turning toward Hunter, who was giving her a facial expression that was as close as it could've gotten to actually speaking the words *don't encourage her*. "And thanks for borrowing that," she said, looking toward the cart. Unlike Kat, she'd come prepared to work, wearing her Levi's and some lace-up Timberlands. She didn't mind the walking at all, but the cart was a nice gesture.

"Sure. You know, I'm kind of looking forward to this. The last time I rode around on one of these I was in high school. In the summertime, a bunch of my friends and I would take turns riding on them after the park closed." He laughed to himself. "I remember Dan and I goofing off and trying to race each other once. But these things never went as fast as we'd wanted them to."

"And it's a good thing they don't, Hunter," Kat said, scoffing. "Or someone might have ended up in the emergency room."

He nodded. "You're probably right, Kat. Shall we?" He led the ladies toward the cart.

"Let's keep it under fifty, Speed Racer," Holly kidded

as she jumped into the back seat.

Hunter waved her off. "From what I recall, I think there's an access road to the storage shed over by the carousel," he shouted over the sound of the little gas engine as he looked over his shoulder at Holly. "I think it's on the other side of the picnic area." Hunter didn't know it, but he was heading exactly where Joe said they should be able to find them.

She proceeded to flash a healthy grin and a thumbs up. *So far, so good.*

They putted along on the gravel path, now overgrown with patches of knee-high brown weeds and green moss until they came to the access road. Holly could hardly bare to look to her left, where the majestic carousel stood less than glorious, a gargantuan cry from the shining beacon it had been only days before. She forced herself to turn toward the makeshift plywood partition, her eyes scanning the graffiti-ridden boards. A small heart on the bottom caught her attention and clawed at her heart. Someone had recently painted a red heart with writing inside: Joe + Wilma, TLA. *True Love Always.* She smiled fondly. She bet she knew who that someone was.

The cart suddenly jerked to a stop, and she grabbed onto the arms of her bench seat. "Whoa!"

Hunter said, "Uh-oh."

"That's never a good thing to hear," Kat replied. "What's wrong? Did we run out of gas?"

He shrugged. "I don't think so. I checked the level—unless there's some sort of leak or something clogging the tank. Could be anything—it's a pretty old cart."

"Maybe it's the battery," Holly said.

"It could be. I had to jump it to get it started." He rose from his seat. "Sorry, guys, looks like we're walking from here."

"Great," Kat said, "my heels will be ruined."

"Why don't you take them off?" Hunter asked.

"And what? Walk in my cashmere and wool Ralph Lauren socks? I don't think so." She began to sulk. "See, I told you this was a dumb idea. Every little bit of it."

"Calm down, Kat. It was just a suggestion. Don't worry. I'll buy you a new pair of boots, and socks, too, if you'd like," he replied, patting her on the back.

Kat smiled, her temporary tantrum grinding to a halt. "Oh, Hunter! Thank you," she said, throwing her arms around him.

His face flushed slightly as he glanced at Holly over Kat's shoulder. "No problem."

In the meantime, Holly had grabbed her phone from her pocket and busied herself with deleting old emails while they discussed Kat's terrible footwear dilemma, trying not to listen. She looked up. "Are you ready, guys?" she asked, hoping to disperse the awkwardness, as she put her phone back in her pocket. Whatever overdramatic Kat's appealing qualities might be, other than the undisputable fact that she was gorgeous, it was lost on her. *Feeling a little jealous are we, Holly? Well, yes, as a matter of fact, I am.* If you can't be honest with yourself, who can you be honest with?

After walking for a few minutes, Hunter turned to Kat who'd been making loud sighing noises every couple of yards. "Okay, so, we're not that far. It's just up ahead. See it, Kat?" Hunter said, pointing beyond the picnic pavilion to the old shed. Holly could just make out the corrugated roof.

"Yes, I see it," Kat replied. "It seems pretty far to me. I don't know if I want to walk all the way there. I'm feeling a little tired. I didn't get much sleep last night. I think I need some coffee." She stretched her arms in the air and forced a yawn, as if trying to prove her point.

Hunter spoke in a low voice. "Kat, you said you wanted to come. Why don't you just try?" he pleaded.

"Okay, fine," she replied, looking down at her boots

that were now splattered with streaks of orange-brown mud.

A few minutes later, they arrived at the shed. There was a large aluminum roll-up type door covering the front of the structure. As they walked closer, they could see that the padlock on it was nothing but rust on rust.

"Let's go around to the side. There's an entrance door there," Hunter said.

"I hope you have the key," Kat said, turning the corner, as Hunter dug into the pocket of his denim jacket and pulled out a ring of keys. He began to thumb through them, searching for the storage shed key.

"Luckily, they're all labeled. Ah-ha!" He grabbed a key and held it up. "This should be it." He pushed the key into the lock.

Holly was thrilled that they'd finally made some progress. "Great!"

Hunter turned the knob and pushed the door open. Then he reached around the corner to flip on the overhead light. Miraculously it turned on. "Wow! I brought a couple of flashlights, but I left them in the cart. Good thing we don't need them. After you, ladies," he said, bowing his head.

"Oh no. I'm not going in there with all those little creepy bugs and spiders. There're probably snakes and rats in there too," Kat said, drops of disgust spewing from her clenched teeth.

"Now who's being silly, *Silly*?" Hunter said, putting his hand on his hip. "I'm sure it will be fine."

She leaned on the side of the building and began to examine her fingernails. "Even so, I'll just wait outside, just in case."

He shrugged. "Okay, have it your way. We'll be right back."

Holly looked down as she entered, making sure not to trip on the raised metal threshold. The shed was almost empty, except for some old signs and pieces of roller coaster track, and other things she couldn't recognize. There was a set of wooden stairs to her right and she grabbed the wooden two-by-four banister. "Wow, I don't see much down here. It's pretty much cleared out."

Hunter walked over and climbed the first step, putting his arm out to block her ascent. "Wait. Let me go check the upstairs. I don't want you to fall. Who knows how safe these stairs are?"

"Okay, fine. I'll wait here." He started to climb the rickety steps one by one. When he got to the top, she heard creaking floorboards, then nothing. She waited a minute before calling out into the silence. "Hunter, are you okay?"

"Yep. Just like I thought—empty," he said, turning to walk back down the steps, "except for some old costumes and things that some of the employees used to wear for the theater productions. Let's go."

Her hopes were dashed. "I don't get it. They have to be somewhere, don't they?"

"No luck?" Kat asked with a little grin forming on the corner of her mouth when she saw their faces. "Oh well, no big deal. I thought the whole thing was a bit silly anyway." She raised her eyebrows. "I guess that means we can go shopping now."

"Is there another storage shed?" Holly asked, ignoring Kat's inane comment.

Kat's annoyance was visible in her body heave. "Really?"

"I can call my dad. Maybe he can give us some direction." Hunter turned to Kat and pulled out his wallet. "Why don't you head on over to the boutique? It's not that far, probably a half mile. Here's my credit card. Just put everything on this," he said, handing her his Citi card.

She glanced toward Holly as she snatched the card from his hand. "Can I talk to you for a second, Hunter? In private?"

"Sure," he said, taking her arm and leading her over

toward a mass of overgrown hedges.

Holly was not trying to eavesdrop, but Kat wasn't being too shy about her words. She was quite sure she'd heard "be careful" come from her lips, followed by "don't worry about her" coming from Hunter's. She felt the blood rushing to her head as she tried to focus her attention on her task. She wondered, Could Kat be jealous of me? If she was, Holly knew she couldn't afford to let some petulant child's jealous streak affect her—she had more important things to worry about.

"Great," Kat said, bouncing on her mucky heels, causing them to sink into the soft dirt even further. "Thanks, babe," she replied, kissing him on the cheek before turning to run off. "Bye, Holly," she called a second later, as an afterthought.

"She suddenly seems energized," Holly said, pretending she hadn't heard a word. "Guess shopping is a cure-all."

Hunter laughed. "It seems to be." He watched her walk off, stumbling in her heels through the gravel. "Let me call my dad and see if there's another spot we could look."

"Doesn't hurt to try," she said as Hunter dialed his dad.

"Hey Dad, any chance the carousel rides are somewhere else?"

Holly mouthed the words "thank you" to Hunter as she listened to one side of the conversation.

"Yes, okay. Yes. I think I know where that is. Okay, yes. I have the keys. Yes, we'll be careful. Thanks, Dad," he said, ending the call and looking at Holly.

"Well, are you okay with a little more walking?" he asked, putting his hand on his hip.

Holly's eyes lit up. "Sure. Where to?"

"Dad said there's another shed on the opposite side of the park. It's probably only a quarter mile or so if we use the path. I have to warn you though, it might be a little more dilapidated than the last one. Our company has marked it for bulldozing."

"That's no problem. I can handle it, except, I'm not very fond of snakes."

Hunter smiled. "I promise to protect you."

"I'll hold you to it," she replied as they set off.

Holly thought of ways to bring up the next topic as they walked together down the path through nature's overgrowth. "Hunter, can I ask you a question?"

"I think you just did."

"Okay. Well, seriously. What did you do with the ornament?"

Hunter stopped smiling. "I, um, threw it in the trash," he said quickly under his breath.

"You what?" she asked, looking at him wide-eyed.

"Sorry, Holly. I can give it back if it means that much to you," he replied, stopping to look her in the eyes.

She was silent, unsure what to tell him. From a quick assessment of the situation, odds were, he'd think she was a looney tune if she mentioned that the ornament had somehow found its way back to her Christmas tree. And now didn't feel like the time to make him wonder about her sanity. "No, that's okay. What's done is done. Let's go see what we can find."

A few minutes later, they arrived on the backside of the park. Beyond an old white picket fence that had long since fallen victim to the thick jungle of trees and vines and fallen over under the deadweight of massive jagged broken limbs, was a second storage shed, similar to the first one.

"Well, they've got to be in there," he said.

"You lead the way."

"You got it." Hunter turned to look for the easiest way to crawl over the rickety broken pickets and tree limbs. "I think I see a path. Let me take your hand, Holly. There really might be some snakes in here."

"I hope you're joking," she replied, her heart rate quickening as she gripped his hand and held onto it for dear life.

"I wish I was," he said, turning back to make eye contact as he helped her over the last of a section of broken fence. There wasn't even a glimmer of a smile on his face.

"Wait, I think my boot's stuck," she said, a few seconds later as they skirted over the broken fence, unable to loosen her ankle from a space between two limbs. She started to yank at her boot, and felt it give an inch. "I think I almost got it." She gave another pull, this time, as hard as she could. As it came free, she torpedoed into Hunter, causing him to fall back into the brush. She fell forward, hitting the ground with a jolt as she landed right next to him, eye to eye.

"Are you okay?" he whispered, looking into her eyes.

"Yes," she managed to say, sounding like one of Abbey's worn-out squeaky toys.

A smile formed on his lips. "At least we didn't find any snakes."

Just the mention of the word 'snake' had her catapulting off the ground quicker than she'd believed humanly possible. "That's one way to look at it." As she brushed the dirt and pine needles from her jacket and jeans, she looked at Hunter, who seemed more than comfortable to just remain lying on the ground. Just the brief moment of locking eyes with him had rattled her to the core. Not only was she out here in the wild battling Mother Nature, but at the same time, battling her own human nature. She was conquering the forest quite well, but when it came to her feeling for Hunter, she had to admit, she was starting to cave in like a sandcastle during high tide. She cleared her throat. If she stood there another second, she'd wash away. "I'm ready when you are."

"Darn, and I was just getting comfortable." Hunter jumped up and quickly brushed himself off. "You are a woman on a mission, I have to give you credit for that," he said, assessing the shed in front of them. "Let me get the key."

"Okay," Holly said, heading for the side door just as they had at the other shed.

Just as easily, as they'd hoped, the door unlocked, and Hunter pushed it open with his outstretched fingers. When he reached to flip the switch, though, nothing happened. "Great. No lights. Well, the sun's shining, so at least we have some natural light."

"Yeah, whatever can filter through the dirty windows," Holly replied. "There's a lot of stuff in here, Hunter," she added, looking at structures draped with large drop cloths in the center of the room. She walked over to pull the first drop cloth.

"Careful, Holly, it might be a little dusty," he said, just as the cloth dropped to the floor, raising a cloud of dust that covered his hair and face.

She fanned the air with her hands, coughing. "I'm so sorry," she said, unable to hold in a grin when the dust finally cleared and she looked at him, covered from head to toe in a fine layer of particulate.

He began to sift his fingers through his hair. "You think that's funny?" he replied, giving her a stern look that lasted only a second, before his lips parted to reveal a bright smile that was accentuated by his gray-powdered cheeks.

"Yeah, I guess I do." She turned to look at what had been uncovered. "Well, what do we have here? It looks like an old dunking booth. Wow. I wish we had time to refinish this. On second thought, I guess no one but a polar bear would volunteer to get dunked this time of year." She glanced at Hunter who was busy wiping the dust from his face with his shirt sleeve.

"I think I'll go look at that end," he said, pointing toward some tarped objects in the corner of the shed, "in case my allergies get triggered. I wouldn't want to start— *achoo!*"

Too late. "Bless you!" she said.

"Thanks. I'll be over there," Hunter replied, pointing to

the corner. "Maybe we can just look under the cloths without removing them?"

"As you wish," Holly replied as she walked toward the next covered object.

After spending about ten minutes lifting drop cloths and looking at treasures from times past, she heard Hunter yell.

"Hey. I think I found something!"

"Really?" She walked toward the back where Hunter had his head partially buried under a pile of material. He stood when she approached.

"Have a look," he said, pulling back the cover.

Holly gasped. Underneath was a large Santa Claus sitting in a sleigh, with a bench acting as the back seat, holding reins in his hands. Hunter pulled the tarp back of several smaller objects nearby, which turned out to be Rudolph and the other reindeer, all skewered with the same candy cane striped poles as the animals on the original carousel. "It looks like they're in great shape," she said, running her hand along the smooth contours of the artwork, admiring the colorful paint that had held up astonishingly well after all of these years in the suboptimal conditions of the drafty shed.

"This is amazing," Hunter said. "Just think. My company was set to bulldoze this shed. We would've destroyed all of this."

She tilted her head toward him. "So, are you saying you're glad you were able to save them?"

Hunter shrugged. "Yes. I guess. Thanks to you, Holly. Just think, once we restore it, I could probably sell the carousel for quite a bit of money to a park somewhere— after the Christmas Village is over."

"Yeah," she replied, frowning. "I guess you could."

There goes my idea. He's just thinking about profits again.

"Well, it's getting late," Hunter said, glancing at his watch. "I better go find Kat and see what kind of damage she's done. I'll call my dad and let him know. We can probably get some guys out here to move this to the first storage shed. I was thinking, since it's cleared out, we could use the shed to work on the carousel pieces."

"That sounds like a great idea," Holly replied as they walked back, forcing herself to stay positive even though discouragement was trying to wiggle its way into her heart after the unforeseen turn in their conversation. Up until a few minutes ago, she thought she had a really good chance at changing Hunter's mind, especially after the look of delight on his face after finding the long-lost carousel creatures. But now, after his comments, she was having some misgivings. She wasn't going to let it ruin her mood, though. She'd think of something to make him see the light, no matter how dim the circumstances. "I'm looking forward to getting started, Hunter. It should be a blast."

"Me too, Holly. I'm thinking maybe we can start as early as Monday, during lunch, if you're game?"

"Great. Just let me know."

Chapter Thirteen

Tropical Christmas

After saying goodbye to Holly, Hunter walked over to the boutique to find Kat. He couldn't explain it, but he'd felt elated when he'd found the missing parts of the carousel; they were like ancient relics. An inner voice was telling him that he owed it to his grandfather to get the park up and running again, and Holly Edwards had been speaking exactly the same language. And overall, it had been a pleasant morning, a nice break from twelve-hour workdays, exploring the old park, except for Kat's constant complaining. He could only hope she'd be in a better mood now that she was in her natural habitat—one where clothing hung like fruit on trees ripe for the picking. He smiled to himself as he opened the front door.

"Hi Hunter," Ruby said, looking up from her register, before he even had a chance to put both feet on the entry floor. "I've been waiting for you."

"Hi babe," Kat said, beaming ear to ear. She was sitting on the stool at the cash register, waiting for Ruby to finish ringing up her last item. "Perfect timing. Ruby said you'll have to sign the receipt."

"No problem."

Ruby handed him a copy of the receipt and a pen. He almost went into cardiac arrest when he saw the total. "Ouch," he said, grabbing his chest, before taking the pen from Ruby's hand. "You did some damage alright."

"Well, I had to get a new pair of boots, too, so—"

"Say no more, Kat. I'm just glad you got what you wanted."

"Here you go, Kat," Ruby said, walking around the register to hand her several large bags. "They're pretty heavy. I'm glad you have Hunter here to help you. Maybe you should take another look, too, Hunter. We got in some new arrivals just this morning."

Kat practically leapt from her chair. "That's a great idea, Ruby!"

"I don't know, I'm kind of tired," he replied, looking at his watch.

She began to lead him toward the men's clothing rack in the back. "Come on, babe, it will only take a minute."

"Take your time guys. I'll watch your bags," Ruby offered, taking them out of Kat's hands and putting them safely behind the register.

"So, did you and Holly find anything?" Kat asked, once they were in the back.

"Yes, as a matter of fact we did. There was a second storage unit on the other side of the park. Everything was in there."

"Great!" she replied enthusiastically.

He looked up from the suit rack. "Kat? Are you okay? You seem really happy."

"What's wrong with that?" she asked, looking as if she was trying to hold onto the smile.

"Nothing. It's a good thing. It's just a little, I don't know . . . uncharacteristic."

"Well, sweetheart, now that you mention it, there is one little teensy-weensy little thing I wanted to talk to you about," she said, squinting her eyes and pressing her thumb and forefinger together.

He crossed his arms, bracing himself. He knew it. Something was up.

"I was thinking, with all of this crazy park business going on, maybe we could skip out of town for the holidays and just let someone else take charge of it. The weather here is wretched this time of year. And besides, it's already giving me a headache, this whole carousel restoration project. I just think it's a waste of time."

"Kat!" His words came out louder than expected. He glanced up at the front where it looked like Ruby was busy reading the newspaper. Hopefully she hadn't heard. He decreased his volume. "You know I can't leave. I have to stay. I'm trying to save face. How would I look to the town if I just bailed?"

Kat shrugged. "The same as you've always looked."

"That's what I'm trying to avoid." He thought about it for another second and shook his head. "No, I can't leave. Not right now. I've made a commitment."

"Well, then, since you're going to be busy working on the carousel, maybe I could go?"

"Go where?" He put his arm out to grab the rack as he leaned in toward her. She wasn't making any sense.

"Well, my parents decided they're going to go island jumping in Hawaii for Christmas, and they asked us to come along. And if *you* can't go, I was thinking maybe just *I* could go with them."

"You mean, not even be here to spend Christmas with me? I can't believe I'm hearing you correctly. Wait. You've been planning this all along, haven't you Kat?" he asked, as his eyes searched hers.

Kat turned away. "It's not a big deal, Hunter. Didn't we both agree when we started seeing each other that it was going to be just for fun? Quote, unquote, *nothing serious*?"

Hunter grimaced. She was right. He hadn't even wanted to call it *dating*. He supposed it wasn't that big of a deal; he had a lot of work to do and having her around could become a distraction. But he was usually the one trying to keep his distance. Being on the receiving end of a big box of indifference wasn't fun at all. *Two can play at this game.* "You know, Kat, I guess you're right. If that's what you want to do, then go ahead."

"Thank you, Hunter," she said, giving him another hug that somehow didn't seem sincere—as far as one-armed hugs go that only lasted a second. It was like hugging a stranger. Who knew? Maybe she felt the same.

"Wait. What about your job?" he asked, suddenly realizing the impact on his business.

"I've already talked to a couple of temp agencies. They can have someone as early as Monday morning—all you have to do is call."

"You've thought of everything, haven't you, Kat?"

"I sure have," she replied, giving him a smile as sweet as cherry pie. "I thought you'd be proud."

That's one word for it, he thought.

"So, any luck?" Ruby called out as she headed to the back of the store to check on the couple.

"Um," Hunter replied, looking down at the rack. He'd only had the chance to grab one suit before he'd gotten lost in conversation. "I think I like this one. It's my size. No need to have it altered."

"Great choice," she replied, smiling at Kat who was nodding very enthusiastically in agreement. "I'll go ring it up."

"Great, Ruby," he said, wondering if she'd heard their conversation. He had to give her credit. If she had, she sure could've fooled him.

Chapter Fourteen

Shedding a Little Light

It was midweek, and Holly was impressed with the progress her groups of volunteers had made. Just walking through the park, she could see that the grounds team had already made great improvements. New large trash cans had been dispersed, and volunteers were starting to fill them with litter and trash that had accumulated over the years. The entire carousel had been dismantled, with the key components being transported to the storage shed. And she'd been relieved to find out that Jack Haywood, the third name on her list of carousel restorers, was an electrician. After tearing away the plywood, he'd been able to get into the main controls of the carousel to look into the wiring issues. It turned out to be an easy fix. A few mice had found their way into the circuit board and chewed through some of the little wires, making themselves a nice little home in the process.

"There's no telling what other little vermin might have made this carousel their home here over the years, but not anymore. I'm making it critter proof," he told her.

"Well, I'm just glad you found the problem," she replied, before heading into the storage building to continue her sanding. She was currently working on the white unicorn; it only made sense, seeing that it was her favorite. The wings were in need of a new coat of paint, which the local hardware store owner, Rob Evans, had donated. Everyone was doing their part, even Hunter Ashworth.

"Hey Holly," Hunter said, looking up from the carpenter's table where he was using a palm sander to remove the old coats of lacquer on the Bertazzon sleigh. After closer inspection, a few of the Christmas components also needed a little reviving, just some minor repairs of little chips in the paint on Santa and Rudolph. They were next on the list.

Holly took a deep breath. For the past three days she'd been trying to keep her distance from Hunter, not letting herself get too close. After finding out that Kat had decided to abandon them, she was ecstatic; but her enthusiasm waned when she realized what that meant. She was obviously falling hard for Hunter, and that was not acceptable. The more her heart did somersaults when Hunter said her name, the worse her predicament. She decided to focus on her job at hand, no matter how difficult it was becoming. And Hunter wasn't making it any easier. He seemed happier each day. That was exactly the point, though, wasn't it? she thought. "Hey, how's it going?"

"Great. Come check this out," he said as she walked closer. "See, I've already finished sanding the sleigh. It's ready for a new coat of lacquer. Bob Cole is going to be using a spray gun from his automotive shop to shoot clear on them."

"That's great, Hunter," she said, looking at Hunter's station a little closer. "What's that?" she asked, pointing to a couple of paintbrushes covered in plastic wrap.

"Oh, just my brushes. I figured if I wrap them, I don't have to worry about the paint drying and having to throw them away."

"Good thinking, Hunter. That's what I always do with

my paintbrushes. I'm impressed with your frugality."

"I'm trying to do my part to save money."

She looked at her watch. "Well, I'm going to go make my rounds and check in with the ladies setting up the craft booths before I change clothes and get to my sanding."

"Mind if I go with you? I could use a little break." He wiped his hands on the thighs of his faded jeans.

"Uh, sure, I suppose," she said, leading him out the door.

They walked together past the dismantled carousel, watching the volunteers rake and pull weeds from the well-worn gravel paths that had been so desperately overgrown only last week.

She turned to him. "It's coming along, isn't it?"

"Yep. Thanks to you, Holly."

She turned her head toward the street just as a community van of children drove by. They looked at them and the park wide-eyed, their little faces lighting up the windows like jack-o-lanterns.

Hunter waved. "They look so excited."

"Yes! A lot of those children have parents that are both working, they don't have a lot of extra money laying around, so, for them, this is going to be a big treat. We're working with local charities to make sure all of them get to come to the park for free if their parents can't afford it. There's a lot of need out there. And not just for the kids. I've seen a few adults struggling, too, not able to afford gas, riding their bikes around town this winter."

"Really? I had no idea. I guess I'm more blessed than I realized," Hunter said in a low voice. "Hey, maybe we can do something more than just free admission for the kids."

"What do you mean?"

"Well, I'm kind of surprised that there are so many volunteers willing to help out the town. It's inspiring to see. Maybe we can have an Angel Tree event so kids whose parents can't afford to buy presents will have something to open for Christmas."

She thought about it for a moment. "How? The park's not going to be opened until Christmas. How would people sign up?"

"Right. I know! We could do it online. I'll see if my mom would like to work on getting it set up. She's pretty good with website design. We could talk to the local charities and then put an ad in the paper directing everyone to pick a name online. And then we could open the park for a few hours on Christmas Eve and invite everyone and pass out the gifts."

She was impressed. Even after this short amount of time, Hunter's heart had really seemed to be transforming, literally right in front of her eyes. "I think that would be amazing, Hunter. Really." Maybe light was finally filtering through all of the walls he'd built during the years, just a little, like through the layers of film on those storage shed windows.

"Awesome. I'll give my mom a call." He reached into his pocket just as his phone began to ring. "Hold on a minute, Holly." He answered, "Hello, Kat, how's Hawaii?" while putting up his finger to signal for her to wait.

She nodded and sat down at a nearby bench and watched him walk off toward a large oak tree, trying her best to ignore his conversation. Part of her was slightly curious, though, and she tilted her ear up just a little, catching a few bits and pieces:

"Kat, no, I can't increase the spending limit. Yes, I'm with her at the park. Kat, wait, like I said before, we're in different leagues. Okay. Yes, I miss you too. Bye."

Different leagues, huh? *I guess he thinks he's out of mine.* She tried to put his insulting words out of her mind as quickly as they'd entered. He walked back and sat down next to her on the bench. If Kat was in the same league as he was, she was glad *she* wasn't.

"So, how's Kat?" she asked, trying to sound interested.

"She's shopping, so, she's good. Says the weather's great too."

Holly nodded. She couldn't deal with her emotions right now, especially sitting next to Hunter, who'd once again made her feel unworthy to be in his presence. It might have been sunny skies in beautiful Hawaii, but here in her microcosm of turmoil, a wintry storm was just about to blow through. "Well, I suppose it's time to start sanding," she said, jumping up from the bench. "I still have thirty minutes."

"Do you want me to walk you back, Holly?"

"No, I'm sure you have to go back to work, but let me know what your mom thinks about the online Angel Tree project."

A look of confusion crossed his face and he shrugged. "Okay, are you sure?"

"Absolutely." She flashed a smile and turned away, tearing down the path toward the shed as quickly as she could, unwilling to let him see that he'd upset her.

He called out after her, "I'll text you."

Chapter Fifteen

Four Eyes
Dream on

"Mind if I have a seat, Holly?" Joe asked, walking up with Ralphie chasing his heels, before parking himself next to her on the bench by the carousel entrance. He was dressed to the nines in his black sharply creased dress pants, crisp white shirt under his carousel barker striped vest, and shiny golden shoes, reminiscent of particles of pyrite on the bottom of a creek bed glinting in the sun. "You certainly seemed to be in a rush to leave Hunter today."

Golden shoes? Why haven't I noticed those before? It was a humid summer evening, and the moon was less than a quarter full. Nonetheless, the shoes were sparkling, as if reflective of something beyond earthly boundaries. "Are those new?" she asked, wiping her forehead with the back of her hand.

"Nope. Same old shoes. Here, my dear," Joe said, handing her a soft white towel. "It's only going to get more intense. You'll need this."

"Thanks, Joe." She took the towel and laid it in her lap. "I wonder why I never noticed them," she said in a low voice, glancing at the shoes again. She'd never seen anything like them.

"There are a lot of things right in front of our faces that we sometimes never see."

"That sounds almost philosophical, Joe," she replied with the hint of a smile. "Are you trying to teach me something?"

Joe winked. "You know me, Holly. So, tell me, why the rush?"

"You seem to know things, Joe. I'm sure you must have heard what Hunter said to Kat about me. I don't want to be where I'm not wanted."

He sat back and crossed his arms. "Why don't you tell me what he said?"

She took a deep breath. "Fine. He said he was out of my league. It figures. Just when I was starting to think he was a good guy. And before you say anything, I know that shouldn't bother me. This is about getting the carousel rebuilt and helping Hunter with his priorities. It's not about me." She glanced at the ground, avoiding his stare. At that moment, Ralphie walked over and sat down next to her, panting.

"Are you sure that's what he said, Holly?"

She spun her head to look at him. "What?"

"I heard something different. I heard him say you two weren't in the same league."

"And? Isn't that what I said?" she asked, reaching out her hand to pet Ralphie.

"Not at all, depending how you look at it." He began to stroke his white bristly beard. "Why I'd imagine he was right on target. *Aren't* you in different leagues?" He looked her in the eyes. "When I think about it, I don't think I've never met two people who were *more* opposite—except maybe Wilma and me."

She slowly sat up, wiping her brow again with the towel. "I guess I just thought he didn't approve of me, like maybe I wasn't good enough for him—as if Kat is."

"You seem a little bitter, Holly. Do you ever wonder why you feel that way? Why you sell yourself short?"

The question rang out into the hushed night and she realized for the first time that evening that the carousel music wasn't playing. She didn't know what to say.

"You're wrong about something else too," he added.

She turned to face him, silently inviting him to expound with the raising of her brow.

"This isn't just about Hunter, Holly."

"Wait. I thought I was getting better—more independent every day. What does this have to do with me?"

"When you signed up for this, you said you wanted a challenge, and that's exactly what you're getting. Maybe it's time to challenge some of the ways you think about yourself—and others."

"If you're talking about Kat, I know. I'm trying *not* to judge her. But she's just so *spoiled*."

"Maybe you should try putting yourself in her shoes, Holly."

"Which pair?" she huffed.

"Ouch! Mercy, child, mercy. I distinctly remember someone else I know being an only child whose parents did everything for her, until very recently."

He'd hit the nail on the head with that one. She frowned, feeling the conviction ping her right in the heart. Yes, maybe she was recognizing a little bit of herself in Kat—the part of herself she didn't like.

He continued. "You don't know her past. If I told you she was a foster child who craved security and was adopted by her loving parents at age twelve, would it change your perspective?"

She swallowed the lump rising in her throat. Like someone adjusting the magnification on a microscope, the reasons behind Kat's actions came into focus. She could even feel a little empathy for her. "Yeah, I guess it would."

"Holly, dear, when I told you it was only going to get more intense, I wasn't speaking about the heat and humidity. Do you think you're ready for a stroll down memory lane?" he asked, standing up and holding out his hand.

She inched toward the edge of the bench and squeezed her eyes shut as she placed her palm against his. "I sure hope so."

She heard his fingers snap and opened her eyes, almost losing her footing. "Whoa!" At first, she couldn't comprehend what she was seeing other than spots. It was like she was standing at one end of a kaleidoscope and spinning the other, watching pieces of color dance and form patterns. "Can you stop the spinning, Joe?"

"Let's back up a little, Holly, so we can see more clearly."

When she stepped back, the spinning stopped. "That's better." In front of them was a bulletin board full of construction paper mosaic artwork. She gasped. They were in Mrs. Kula's second-grade art class. She glanced at the top of the bulletin board and felt her heart drop to the soles of her shoes. The date was February 14. A date she'd rather forget. But she made herself scan the room. There she was, sitting in the back row, wearing her new tortoiseshell-rimmed glasses. Her hair was in a ponytail and she was wearing a pink plaid button up shirt and a pink romper. Next to her was her friend Mandy, the only other girl in class who admitted her parents bought her clothes at the thrift store.

She looked at Joe. "This must be a mistake. Why did you bring me here?"

"Don't worry, Holly. It's okay," he said, squeezing her hand.

Memories of being made fun of for her clothing came rushing back into her mind. She looked at her younger self, happy as a lark, working away on her valentine without a care in the world in her favorite class. But all of that was about to change.

Mrs. Kula spoke and began to walk down the rows slowly, examining her students' handiwork, from glued pink and red heart clusters to white paper doilies cut into the shape of little hearts. "Okay, class. Finish up your valentines now and go ahead and hand them out. We only have a few more minutes before the bell rings. That's very nice, Holly," she said glancing at her intricately cut heart. "Whoever receives that one must be very special," she added before moving on.

"Thank you, Mrs. Kula," little Holly replied. She was right about that. The valentine was for the cutest boy in the class, Chad Nissley. Just as she put it in the yellow envelope that Mrs. Kula had provided, she looked up and saw none other than Chad himself standing over her desk.

"I have something for you, Holly," he said, handing her an envelope and smiling.

"Really? I have something for you too," she replied, handing him her valentine.

Before she could say another word, the bell rang, and he bolted for the door.

"Okay, class. Have a nice Valentine's Day. Please take a lollipop on your way out," Mrs. Kula shouted.

Little Holly was smiling ear to ear. She leaned back in her wooden chair and opened the envelope, pulling out a big red folded heart. On the front smaller white hearts were pasted on haphazardly. She was so happy she was squirming in the chair. When she opened it up, though, she froze, and her face began to crumble.

Dear Four Eyes,

Happy Valentine's Day. Maybe you wouldn't have to wear such thick glasses if you sat in the front row. Love Chad

She slumped down in her seat and glanced at the door and then to the floor where the valentine she'd given to Chad was laying, unopened and rejected.

The trip down memory lane came to an abrupt halt, and Holly found herself sitting back on her unicorn on the carousel, with Joe in the sleigh by her side.

Joe whistled through his teeth. "That was brutal."

She wiped her face with the towel. "Tell me about it. I don't know if I felt worse *then* or *now*. Why did you show me that, Joe?"

"I think maybe you gave this memory too much weight in your heart for too long. Maybe deep down, you've let it hold you back from going after what you want. I think it's time to let it go, Holly—to see it for what it is—a silly little boy who didn't know any better."

"I forgot all about Chad Nissley."

"Why'd you save it Holly?"

She whipped her head to look at him. She shouldn't be surprised that he knew, but she was. "I forgot about that too. I don't know." Her mind began to churn, wondering when she'd last seen the valentine. Nope, she couldn't remember.

"In my personal opinion, I think Chad was a bit jealous."

"Huh? Of me?"

Joe nodded. "You were a very talented little artist, dear. He, on the other hand, couldn't draw himself out of a paper bag."

She couldn't help but giggle. "Come to think of it, the valentine was pretty ugly. But his message sure hit home. I remember begging and pleading with my mom to get contacts after that. I never told her why, but maybe I should have. She said I was too young." She hung her head. "And I used to cry when she made me wear clothes from the thrift store to school. I guess I should've told her about being made fun of too. I just felt too ashamed."

"Why, Holly? No one could tell. You looked just as nice as everyone else in that class, didn't you? And you were just as worthy as anyone else to receive a proper valentine."

She looked up. "Hey, I just remembered something. After I ran into Hunter at the park that summer and he complimented my glasses, I stopped begging my mom for contacts. Suddenly I liked them. Like Hunter said, they made me look smart."

"Why don't you wear them now?"

She shrugged. "I don't know."

"Meeting Hunter back then seems to have been a good thing. And I think it's a good thing now. Look at you both. Two people who probably never would've given each other the time of day are forced to look beneath the surface and get to know each other, really know each other, and their true selves in the process. I couldn't've orchestrated it better myself."

"As usual, Joe, you're right. But I thought you *did* orchestrate it."

"You give me too much credit, Holly. I was as surprised as you when all of this started."

"Really?"

"All I know is that I prayed for Hunter and I was given a chance to make a difference. And now my time is almost up. I have until Christmas Day, or I should say, *we* have until Christmas Day to help Hunter."

"Do you think it's enough time?"

"It has to be Holly, it's all we've got."

"If you don't mind me asking, what happens to you then, Joe?"

"Don't worry about me, dear. I'm in better hands now," he said, his eyes sparkling as he scanned her worried face. "Are you ready?"

"For what?" she asked, looking into his eyes, before full comprehension could take hold. "Oh," she said, glancing toward the mechanical arm in front of them. "If it's all the same to you, Joe, I'm kind of worn out. I think I'll skip reaching for the brass ring tonight."

"I understand completely, Holly. The healing process can take a toll."

Chapter Sixteen

Bruised Bones and Broken Egos

Her phone rang, jolting her from sleep. She stirred, peeling her waffle-patterned cheek from the rough couch cushion. On the coffee table was her empty dinner plate. She must've drifted off after eating. Working over her lunch break was starting to take a toll of its own.

"Hi Holly. Did I wake you?"

"Oh, hi, Mom." She yawned and stretched her free hand over her head. "What time is it? I guess I dozed off early." She looked across the room at the clock and then the unlit Christmas tree. There was Abbey's form, sprawled out on the floor beneath it, snoring like a well-oiled chainsaw.

"It's a little after nine."

"Oh. Wow. Nothing like a three-hour power nap." She stood to turn on the living room light. "What's up?"

"Well. I was just calling to inform you that your father had a tiny little accident. He's okay, though."

Her mind started to race. "What happened?" In the background, she thought she heard a couple of low-sounding moans. "Is he okay?"

"Yes dear, I just repositioned him on the couch." She raised her voice, obviously trying to make her point. "He decided he was going to go out on the roof this time of night to set up our nativity. If you ask me, he was just doing it to compete with the neighbors."

She bit her lip. She could only imagine her mom's stern facial expressions as she scolded her poor father. It wasn't funny, well, maybe a little. "He fell off the roof? Are you sure he's okay?"

"Well, he's able to walk just fine—and he can wiggle his toes."

"Mom, maybe you should take him to see the doctor. He might have a compression fracture in his back. Remember when Uncle Will fell off of his roof?"

"Your father was only on the fourth rung of the ladder it turns out, and the rose bushes caught his fall. I gave him some ibuprofen and an ice pack. He'll be okay. He's just a little bit scratched up is all."

She sighed with relief. Her mom could be a little dramatic. That was something, luckily, that they didn't have in common.

"Anyway, dear. I wanted to let you know that I'm afraid I won't be able to make it to see you this weekend. I'm going to stay here and nurse your poor father back to health. But I would like to hear about what you're doing at the park."

"Well, I guess since I'm wide awake, I can tell you all about it."

"Wait, let me get your father another pillow. I'll be right back."

She heard the phone clunk onto a hard surface. A minute later she heard her father's grumpy protests in the background.

Finally, she heard her mom fumble with the phone and plunk down onto her seat with a sigh. "Okay, dear. I'm ready."

She proceeded to fill her in with the details of the ornament and her talks with Hunter Ashworth, all the way up to the town meeting and carousel restoration project, leaving out the tiny details of her dealings with Hunter's Grandpa Joe.

"Wow, dear. I'm impressed. You sure sound confident about everything. I'm surprised I never heard about the Christmas Carousel. So, what's Hunter Ashworth like when you really get to know him? Is he the unredeemable man we all think he is?"

"Well, I'm no expert Mom, I still don't know him very well. But I guess you could say he's got potential."

Her mom was silent for a moment. "Hmm, sure, I guess we all do."

"You know, Mom. I was just thinking that I'm kind of glad I didn't have new clothes growing up. I think it made me more creative."

"Where did that come from? I didn't think you even remembered that."

"Of course, I remember, Mom. Anyway, I think it's given me a greater appreciation for what I have. I think it's why I like to restore things too."

"I suppose you're right, dear. Our experiences are what make us what we are. And speaking of that, I hope this experience helps Hunter reach his *potential* as you call it. Maybe you can get him to fall in love with the park after all."

That's the plan. "That would certainly be a step in the right direction. Have a good night, Mom. Kiss Dad for me." She hung up the phone and sat back on the couch. *Falling in love* with the park. What an interesting way to put it.

"So, I was just speaking to Kim Darnell from the party

store. She's going to be taking care of arranging the rentals, and earlier today I spoke with the advertising department of the *Merrysville Banner*. They're going to start running the ad for the park tomorrow and so is WMAB radio." Ruby stood in the doorway of the break room, studying her. "Holly?"

"Huh?" She jumped at the sound of her own name, realizing she'd been sitting with her face resting on her fists, staring at the ceiling, completely oblivious to what Ruby was talking about.

"So, you didn't hear a word I said, did you?" Ruby asked, shaking her head. "What has gotten into you? Or maybe I should ask, *who* has gotten into you?"

She sat up in her chair and stretched her neck from side to side. "I don't know what you're talking about, Ruby."

"Hunter Ashworth. You suddenly seem to be very excited everyday right around lunchtime, ever since last week. And that's also around the time I started to notice that little glimmer of infatuation in your eyes. Tell me, can you really say with a straight face that *you don't know what I'm talking about*? Good heavens, Holly! How could you not?"

"Oh Ruby, don't be so dramatic. I'm just excited about working on the carousel and getting the park up and running." The truth was, she had been thinking about what Joe had said all morning long. Why had she been selling herself short for so long? Why didn't she think she was worthy of unconditional love? Should she go after what she wants, whatever that may be?

"So, you aren't the least bit excited to see Hunter?"

The sound of his name made her lips start to curl into a smile as much as she tried to fight it.

"See! I knew it. You can't fool your cousin!"

"Oh Ruby. Even if I did find Hunter . . . amazingly attractive . . . and even sweet, it seems like such a long shot. He's dating Kat." *And she's nothing like me*, she wanted to add, only reminding herself just before the words slipped out that maybe that wasn't quite true. She dropped her head into her hands on the counter, finally surrendering to her internal struggle. "What am I going to do, Ruby? It's crazy, isn't it?"

"I'm just glad you can admit it, Holly. You have to follow your heart. Maybe you need to listen to it a little closer. Besides, I don't think there's anything serious between the two of them."

She sat up straight in her chair. This she had to hear. "What do you mean? How do you know?"

"That's the thing about being the shop owner. Sometimes people talk about stuff and forget I'm here. I become the proverbial little fly on the wall." She gave her a wink.

She wanted to jump out of her own skin. "Ruby, what did you hear?"

"Well, I guess I can tell you, considering the circumstances. They weren't really being very private about it. But please, don't say anything to Hunter."

"You know I wouldn't do that Ruby."

Ruby took a deep breath and continued. "And that's why I'm going to tell you. When Kat was here the other day, she invited him on a trip with her parents and he said he couldn't go. Then she mentioned how their relationship wasn't serious after all. They were just *seeing each other*." Ruby put up her hands and emphasized the last phrase with air quotes.

She gasped. "Wow, Ruby. I thought things were serious between them, with her moving to Baltimore and everything."

"That's not all. She arranged for a temp to fill in for her at the office. I'm not quite sure she even expected him to go in the first place, with this park project going on."

"I wonder how he feels about her?"

"Why don't you ask him, Holly?"

"What? I couldn't do that," she replied, appalled by the very mention of the idea.

"Just a suggestion." Ruby looked at the clock. "It's about lunchtime, I think you have somewhere you have to be. See you this afternoon, Holly—and good luck." She gave her a big, knowing smile.

"I'm just going to go work on the carousel, Ruby," she replied as she grabbed her change of clothes and headed for the door, acting as if she'd not been subconsciously counting down the seconds until she could go.

Ruby laughed. "Whatever you say, Holly," she muttered under her breath just loud enough for her to hear as she closed the door behind her.

Hunter had just finished putting on his padded navy coveralls to get to work on Santa's small surface imperfections when his phone began to ring from some unknowable pocket—either in his dress pants or coveralls. He'd picked up a light tan pair for Holly to make it easier for her to work without having to change clothes. The last few times he'd been in the shed, he noticed that it was a little drafty, even with the space heaters, and it might be nice for them to have the extra insulation. But now that his phone was beyond reach, he was having second thoughts about what was turning out to be a more than cumbersome *convenience*.

He rushed to unbutton what he'd just buttoned and palmed around until his fingers found the flat little rectangle. No time to glance at it, he slapped the phone to his ear.

"Hi Hunter. Is this a good time?"

"Oh, hi Kat. Sure. What's up?"

"Are you okay? You sound a little perturbed."

"I'm fine, Kat. Just having some technical difficulties," he replied, before taking a deep breath and sitting down on the nearby metal stool by the workbench. He strained to keep the aggravation out of his voice. "So, how's Hawaii?"

"It's wonderful. I absolutely love it. I think I want to move here."

"I wish I could, but I've got a company to run. Maybe someday. My parents are moving there, after all."

"No Hunter, I'm serious. I really want to move here, like soon. Maybe I could open my own boutique?"

"What are you trying to say, Kat?"

"Well, I've been thinking—about you, my job, my life—and I've decided that it's in my best interest to quit working at the company."

"What? Quit working for me?"

"Yes. There are other things I want to do with my life besides be a secretary."

"What about us?" He held his breath. Deep down he thought he knew the answer. She hadn't been answering his texts for the past day and a half. He could take the hint.

"Well, it was fun. Maybe if you were willing to compromise and move with me, I'd consider making our relationship long-term."

"Compromise? How's that a compromise, Kat? It's not like I can just pick up and leave. How would you survive? You don't have a job, and you *really* like to spend money. Are you sure this isn't about me not increasing the spending limit on my credit card?" His voice unwittingly increased in volume, causing him to look around to make sure no one was listening.

Hunter could hear her tone soften. "Sorry, Hunter, it's not about you. Don't worry, I'll figure it out."

"Did you meet someone else?" he asked, half-hoping she had. At least that would be an explanation.

"Does it really matter, Hunter? I mean, really. Are you more concerned about losing a secretary or someone you're seeing?"

She had him there. She couldn't even bring herself to use the term girlfriend, at his own insistence. His first concern had been the company's welfare, not hers. He hated to admit it, but his feelings for Kat weren't quite where she wanted them to be. Part of him figured they might get there eventually, but now he'd never know. "Uh—"

"Relationships aren't supposed to be this difficult, Hunter. I shouldn't have to wonder how you feel about me or how I feel about you."

"I know. You're right, Kat. Neither of us should have to wonder," he said, finally relenting, as he rubbed his forehead with his thumb and index finger. "So, what are you going to do now?"

"See if I can find a job and start looking for a shop to rent. It can't be that hard. Of course, I'll have to fly back and pack up my apartment after Christmas."

"Sounds like you have it all figured out then. Well. I'll see you later, Kat. I wish you the best. Have a Merry Christmas."

"Bye, Hunter. Merry Christmas."

"Hey there, stranger, I like the new look," Holly said, waltzing across the room. "They seem really warm."

"I'm glad you like them, I got you a pair too." Hunter held up the tan coveralls.

"That was sweet of you. We can be twins." She threw her duffle bag on the floor by the wall. "I guess I won't need to change into these then."

"Just think about where you put your cell phone before you put them on. It could get lost."

She laughed and gave him a questioning look. "Okay. I won't even ask," she said, stepping her legs, one at a time, into the coveralls and then buttoning them up. "How do I look?"

"Prepared to work." He grabbed a new piece of sandpaper to slap onto his palm sander.

"Oh, I am, believe me. So, how's your day been so far?" She began to pry the lid off of a new can of iridescent light-blue paint with a flathead screwdriver. Her hand slipped, causing the top to fling off, and a smattering of paint to fly across the table and land on Hunter's cheek with a *splat*.

She froze, horrified, as she watched the paint drip slowly down his expressionless face. "Oh no, I'm sorry Hunter!" It took her mere seconds to locate a clean rag and reach across the table to wipe it away.

"Blue's a good color for you," she said, pressing her lips together, trying to contain her amusement. It was no use, she burst out laughing. "I'm sorry Hunter, I don't mean to laugh."

At first he looked at her with narrowed eyes, but finally his face gave way to a grin. "Why do I feel like you're trying to sabotage me, Holly?"

"I'm not, I promise," she said after wiping her eyes and sighing as the last trace of laughter left her lungs. "Here's a tissue."

He reached for it and wiped his cheek. "Did I get it all?"

"Yes. I think we can safely get to work now." She proceeded to reach for a paintbrush.

"And, since you asked, my day's getting better and better," he said, "now that you've come along. I can't wait to see what else is in store. Maybe I'll come down with a case of chicken pox or break my leg."

"Hunter! Don't say that. What else happened? Is everything okay?"

"Kat wants to move to Hawaii. She just called to break up with me."

"I'm sorry, Hunter." Her mind started to race with all sorts of questions, none that were appropriate to ask. But she knew how to be a good listener, so she sat. "Do you want to talk about it?"

He sighed and followed her lead, sitting down on the edge of the table. "I don't know. I guess I have some thinking to do. I don't know how I feel. Honestly, maybe my ego's bruised more than anything," he said, looking into her eyes before shaking his head. "I don't know why I'm telling you this."

"Because I care?" She could feel her emotions start to swirl so she took a deep breath and tried to calm herself. "It's okay, Hunter. No judgements here, believe me. I've had some recent clarity on that."

"I don't know what happened, really."

"Well, from what I could tell, you did everything right. I mean, you seemed to be generous and thoughtful, and a gentleman." She paused. *Maybe I'm saying too much.* "But what do I know?" she added, shrugging her shoulders.

"You think I'm a gentleman?"

Her throat suddenly became hoarse. How in the world did she get into this predicament? *Me and my big mouth.* If only Joe was here, he could snap his fingers and she'd disappear. "Well, sure. You can be when you want to," she replied. *Whew! Saved by ambiguity.*

Hunter nodded. "I see. Thanks, Holly. Well, I think I'm going to call it quits early today. I feel a headache coming on."

"I have a Tylenol in my bag."

"No, that's okay. I think I just need to take a nap," he said, as he started to unbutton his coveralls and step out of them.

"Thanks for the coveralls, Hunter. It was very thoughtful of you. I hope you feel better."

"I'm sure I will. I'll see you tomorrow, Holly," he said, turning to walk out the door.

Chapter Seventeen

My Treat

By Friday afternoon, Holly was up to her eyeballs with sanding and painting. She was ready to switch gears and focus on something that required a little less manual labor and a little more mental acuity. Hunter hadn't been able to make it to the shed at lunchtime due to a small crisis with the temp agency Kat had gone through to hire her replacement. But he'd texted later that afternoon that everything had been cleared up, and he wanted her to meet with his mom, who was currently in Hawaii, on a video call to discuss the Angel Tree project. Now, he was following up:

HI HOLLY. DO YOU WANT TO MEET AT THE BEAN DOWNTOWN? WE COULD GRAB A BITE AND TALK ABOUT THE PROJECT. I'LL BRING MY LAPTOP.

THAT WILL BE FINE, she texted back.

SIX?

SOUNDS GOOD!

Hunter was already set up with his computer at a table when she walked in. She eyed him immediately, sitting in the corner with his blue scarf and blue-and-red striped sweater, sipping on a cup of coffee. He looked up and blinked, as if hardly recognizing her for a minute. "Oh, she's here Mom, hold on one second," she heard him say as he stood to greet her.

"I like your glasses, Holly."

She smiled. "Thanks." She hadn't worn her glasses outside of the four walls of her home in years, but when she was getting ready earlier in the evening, she decided, on a whim, to wear them. Maybe just to see if Hunter still approves? she found herself wondering. It was a different ball game now, with Kat out of the picture.

"I hope you don't mind. I took the liberty of ordering us some soup and salads. I'm not sure what you like, so I got a variety." He motioned toward the table where two bowls of soup, one French onion, and one chicken noodle sat steaming, along with a couple of salads.

"Thank you, Hunter," she said as he helped her with her coat. She sat down next to him in the chair that he'd pulled out for her. "I'm not picky."

"Well, it's very nice to meet you Holly. I've heard good things," Stacey Ashworth said, her face smiling at her from Hunter's computer screen. She was a pretty woman with delicate features and brown hair swished back into a ponytail. Holly could see that she was on a balcony and the red sun was still glowing in the background where palm trees and sandy shores were visible for miles.

"Thank you, Mrs. Ashworth. I'm so glad you can help us out with this."

"Oh, believe me, this is one of the easiest decisions I've had to make. I just love the Angel Tree project. It's so rewarding. And I'm looking forward to returning for the Christmas Village next week. I'm so excited to see what all you've done."

"It's been an amazing transformation so far. I think you'll see that when you get here, Mrs. Ashworth."

"Thanks to you, dear. And please, call me Stacey. Don't mind me, just go on and eat, and I'll talk about the website."

"Thanks, Stacey." Holly grabbed a spoon and began to eat the chicken noodle soup in front of her.

"So, I was just telling Hunter that I sent him an email with the link to the new website. You can look at it now if you'd like."

"Okay," Hunter said, pulling it up.

"Wow, this looks great, Stacey!" Her eyes scanned the screen. On it was a beautiful Douglas fir decorated with large silver balls.

"Thank you. It will be live after I get approval from both of you. I was able to get a list of children from Ruby and put their requests in the system. Do you see the big Christmas tree?"

"Yes, that's the first thing we saw when we opened the page, Mom."

"Well, you can click on one of those silver ornaments and it will tell you what the child wants. Then you can choose to accept. Once it's chosen, it disappears from view. So, the goal is to have a tree with no ornaments by next week. Go ahead, click on one."

"Okay," he said, choosing one near the top. Once he clicked on it, it flipped over and revealed the name of a child, the age, and their wish list of several items.

"Excellent, Mom."

"Oh wow, that's awesome," Holly added.

"There are instructions at the bottom on where to bring the presents on Christmas Eve. Ruby said she has a few volunteers that will be there to make sure the packages go under the tree and are labeled correctly."

She and Hunter glanced at each other knowingly. It was happening, the tree was going to be a big success and all the children would get a present.

"I don't know what to say, Stacey. You've done a great job. I couldn't be more excited."

"You're so welcome. I'm just so glad that you were able to talk Hunter into opening the park again. He wouldn't listen to his father or me. You must be a special lady."

Holly looked at Hunter out of the corner of her eye; he was looking down at his bowl of soup. She couldn't quite tell, but it almost looked like he was blushing.

"And Hunter could use—"

"Mom. We don't want to keep you. I'm sure you've got stuff to do. Have a good night," he said before starting to shut down his computer.

"Hunter, wait. There's something else I need to talk to you about."

"Can we talk about it later, Mom?" he asked, almost pleaded, with steely eyes.

Holly figured he was trying to stop her from saying anything too embarrassing. What was it with moms? Some of them just loved to watch their adult children squirm sometimes. She rested her chin on the palm of her hand and covered her lips with her fingers. It was a little entertaining to watch, she had to admit.

Stacey exhaled deeply. "I suppose. This is probably the wrong time anyway. Have a good night. Bye Holly. It was a pleasure to meet you."

"And you, Stacey. Thanks again."

After ending the video call, Hunter turned towards her. "How was the soup?"

"This is my favorite. It's excellent, as usual. Your mom seems really nice. I like her."

"I can tell she likes you, too, maybe more than she likes me," Hunter said.

Holly let out a laugh. "Oh, come on, Hunter. She loves you."

"I know. She's always been a rock for me, even when I wasn't such a great son to her."

"You? Not a great son? Do tell."

"You know how it is, a little teenage rebellion. Nothing serious, just trying to come to terms with who I was as a person, what I wanted, that sort of thing. But she took it in stride. She always said *you'll figure it out*. That's probably her favorite thing to say."

"And you did, didn't you?"

He nodded. "Yes, I guess I did. Hey, how would you like to go for a walk? I'm feeling a little cooped up in here."

She pushed back from the table. "Some fresh air would be nice. I don't mind the cold. I've got my hot coffee. Thanks for dinner, Hunter."

He stood and gave her a little wink. "Just trying to be a gentleman, *when I want to*."

"So it seems," she replied, as he helped her into her coat.

Out in the night air, they began to stroll down the sidewalk, inevitably toward the Merrysville Amusement Park. She glanced at Hunter who seemed to be lost in a thought.

"I almost forgot to ask, how's everything going with the move to Baltimore? Have you started packing up your house yet? I'm sure you're busy."

"Well, I'm probably going to commute for a while. I scheduled the movers for after the holidays. It's a pretty chaotic time with my parents moving, the park, and work, so I'm just trying to pace myself. I realized there's no rush. And honestly, I'm glad I don't have to think about it. Maybe I shouldn't've let Kat talk me into the move in the first place. It feels strange to say this, but now that she's not in the picture, I feel a little less pressure."

"It's good to take a step back. Sometimes it helps us see more clearly," she said, realizing as she spoke, that they had been the exact words Joe had used when they popped into her second-grade art class.

"Words to live by. How did you become so wise, Holly?"

She shrugged. *If you only knew.* "Maybe it's the

glasses."

He looked down and kicked a small pebble from his path. "You know, I was kind of wondering about something."

"Yes?" she asked, glancing at his face.

"The guy you were with last spring, I can't remember his name . . ."

"Greg, I think you mean."

"Yes, him. Greg. I haven't seen him around. Are you and he—together?"

"Uh . . ." *That's a good question, Hunter.* She pictured one of those Love Meters at the arcade that ranged anywhere from *cold feet* and *cold lips* to *sizzling hot* and *on fire.* In Greg's case, she figured the needle might be somewhere in the *fizzling out* range.

Before she could answer, the familiar voices of little girls started yelling her name. "Holly! Holly!"

Across the street, she could see Ruby and Dan and the three girls walking down the steps from *Patterns Boutique.* Talk about timing, she thought, grateful for the interruption.

"Hey girls," she said, as they rushed to greet her. She bent down and threw her arms around them.

Ruby followed closely behind, watching for cars. "Hey Holly, hey, Hunter. We just stopped by the shop to pick up some papers I forgot. Now we're headed for some dinner at *The Bean.*"

"I didn't know you wore glasses, Holly," Danny said, pulling back to examine her rims. "Mommy said *I* have to have glasses."

"Really?" Holly asked, glancing at Ruby who mouthed, "She doesn't want them."

"Well, I think glasses are great. They make you look smart," she said, looking Danny in the eyes.

"I agree," Hunter added.

"Really?" Danny asked.

"See honey, I told you. You'll look great," Dan said.

"You should try the chicken noodle soup, Ruby, it was excellent," Holly said, changing the subject. Even though Ruby was maintaining a nice wide smile on her the face, Holly knew there were multiple unasked questions looming behind her inquisitive stare, like: *Why are you out here with Hunter? Are you on a date?*

Holly took the initiative. "So, Hunter and I had a conference call with Hunter's mom over the Angel Tree project." In other words, no, this is not a date, don't even think it, dear cousin. She stared at Ruby waiting to see what she'd say next.

"Oh, good. How's *that* going?" Ruby asked with a little sparkle in her eye.

She ignored Ruby's subtle innuendo. "Couldn't be better. I'll have to show you the website on Monday. It's fantastic."

"What's an Angel Tree, Mom?" Danny, who'd been listening to the conversation asked, while her sisters had started singing their own rendition of "Jingle Bells" that they'd made up earlier that day.

"Well, honey, that's where children who might not have someone to buy them presents can sign up to receive a present on Christmas. And thanks to Holly and Hunter, lots of children will have a very special Christmas. He's also the one who was nice enough to let us have a Christmas Village at the park this year, and we're all very thankful for that."

The twins stopped singing and looked at Hunter with wide eyes. "Thank you, Mr. Ashworth. We love the park," they replied in unison before going back to their ditty.

Danny tugged on her mom's coat sleeve. "Mom, could we buy a present for one of the children?"

"Well, sure honey. I think that's a great idea," she replied, patting her on the head.

"Each of you girls could give a gift," Dan added.

"Yay!" Danny said, bouncing on her feet.

"Well, I need to be getting back to check on Abbey. Why don't we walk with you?" Holly suggested. "Our cars are parked in front of *The Bean*."

"Okay, sounds good. Come on, girls," Ruby said to the twins.

"Abbey?" Hunter asked as they walked back toward their cars.

Holly smiled. "Yes, my golden retriever."

"Oh, yeah. The one who found the Christmas Carousel."

"You got it."

"I was thinking about getting a dog, but I'm so busy with work. I wouldn't want him to be lonely."

"Get two then."

Hunter smiled. "You have an answer for everything, don't you?"

She looked down. *No, not really. Not by a long shot,* she wanted to say.

As they arrived at *The Bean*, Danny walked over to Hunter and tugged on his coat. "Mr. Ashworth?"

"Yes, Danny?" he replied, squatting on the ground to come face-to-face with little Danny.

"Can I give you a hug?"

His face lit up with delight. "Sure you can."

"Us too, us too," the twins yelled and ran to hug him. Hunter looked up at Holly and she winked.

"Okay, girls. Let's go get dinner," Dan said. "I think Mr. Ashworth has to go now."

"Alright," they said, before letting go and running up the steps to the café. "Bye Holly," they called out as they pulled open the heavy door.

"Those girls are little angels. You're a lucky man, Dan," Hunter said, clearing his throat.

"Thanks Hunter. They're a blessing, that's for sure," he replied, grabbing Ruby's hand and walking up the steps.

Hunter called out to him. "You know, Dan. I was thinking. Maybe we could get together and hang out sometime. You still like to race golf carts?"

"I'll race anything with a motor."

"Okay. Sounds like a challenge. We'll talk soon."

After waving goodbye to the girls, Holly turned to Hunter, who was standing with his hands in his pockets and a strange look on his face. "Are you okay? You look a little dazed."

"I guess I didn't realize what an impact the park had on the children. I don't know why I never considered that. It seems like the park brings out the best in everyone."

She nodded in affirmation. "Yeah, I think you're finally starting to see it now, Hunter." They stood for a moment in silence looking at each other at the bottom of the steps. "Well, it's time for me to get going. It's a little cold out here." The last thing she wanted was to ruin the moment by continuing their earlier conversation about Greg. She'd have to prepare for that topic.

Hunter continued to look into her eyes, maybe one second longer than a friend might've, causing her heart to pitter-patter in her chest. He seemed to want to say something more. She held her breath, hoping he'd forgotten what he'd asked her earlier.

Finally, he broke the gaze. "I guess you're right. Anytime I can see my own breath in front of my eyes, it's time to go inside," he said before blowing a cloud of white vapor from his mouth.

She laughed. "I hear the weather's supposed to be nice this weekend. We'll have all day to work." By the time they'd reached their cars, her heart rate had returned to normal.

He opened his car door. "Sounds good. I can't wait."

"Me neither. Thank you for such a good night, Hunter."

"It was my pleasure, Holly. See you tomorrow."

After letting Abbey outside, Holly sat on her couch, still in her coat, motionless, as her mind played through every moment of her evening with Hunter. There was no telling how things would have gone had they not run into Ruby and Dan. All she knew was Hunter must've had at least a teeny, tiny bit of interest in her to be asking about her relationship with Greg, right? *Unless he was just trying to make conversation.* No, she wasn't going to think the worst this time. She'd explore the idea that he might like her, after all, why not? As she stood to unzip her coat, she glanced at the Christmas Carousel and remembered something.

She walked into her bedroom and slid open one of the mirrored closet doors, wincing when her eyes fell on the large number of boxes crammed onto the top shelf. She went to get her little step stool from the laundry room, making a ruckus as the metal clanked against the washing machine and wall as she tried to slide it out. When she returned to her bedroom, Abbey was sitting next to the closet waiting for her.

"Hey girl, don't mind me. I'm just about to look for something," she said to Abbey who tilted her ears forward and lowered to the floor. "Where to start? Eeny meeny miny moe," she said, pointing at the boxes until her finger landed on a large white box in the corner.

It was an old box, the top of it caving in after years of being on the bottom of a stack in her mom's closet. "That looks like a good one, Abbey." She reached into the corner to grab the box and set it down on her bed. Inside were old papers that Holly didn't recognize at first. She began to sort through them, realizing some of them were drawings from grade school. "Jackpot!" she said, looking toward Abbey, who raised her head and barked.

"I know, it's exciting, isn't it, girl?" She dug to the bottom of the box, pulling out an assortment of colored construction paper. The red color near the bottom of the pile caught her eye. She gasped as she slowly pulled at the corner of it, teasing it from the stack. There it was, the infamous valentine from Chad Nissley. She sat up straight and adjusted her glasses on her nose. Taking a deep breath, she opened up the card, half-expecting it to say something different, but it was exactly as she remembered—the same old stupid insult. But not the same vulnerable Four-eyes reading it.

"It's time to say goodbye, Chad. You've been in my head for way too long," she announced ceremoniously, holding the valentine out in front of her with one hand. Using two fingers, she slowly pulled from the top downward, ripping it in half; and then ripping it in half again; and again, until it was a shredded pile of confetti.

Chapter Eighteen

Wrenching

"Hey, who's this? This must be Abbey!" Hunter said, getting down on one knee to greet the shiny-coated golden retriever as she ran from behind Holly and rushed to greet him with a wagging tail. "She's definitely friendly," he said, scratching her around the neck. Abbey put her paws on his shoulders and proceeded to lick his face.

She laughed. "Okay, Abbey, that's enough. Sorry about that." She looked around the shed, admiring the carousel animals that were resting against a plywood partition, some of them still glistening wet with polyurethane.

"It's fine. She's just excited. Aren't you girl?" Hunter asked, scratching her head as he stood.

Abbey barked and situated herself down next to Hunter.

"So, anyway, I just talked to Bob Cole. He sprayed a couple of the animals on Thursday, so he thinks they're dry. We can start putting them back on the carousel," she said. "He said to start with the ones on the far left."

"Great! I'll grab the tools and we can ask a couple of guys to help us cart them outside."

Holly began to rub her palms together. "Only seven more days. I can't believe it! We've come so far."

Hunter buckled his tool belt. "I know. It's exciting."

She turned to leave the shed.

"Aren't you forgetting something, Holly?"

She turned back. "What?" she asked, turning to see the coveralls he was holding up in his hand.

"Oh, yes. I can't forget those," she said, taking them from his hand and glancing at the tools hanging from his tool belt. "I guess you know what to do with those things?"

He looked down. "The tools? Of course. I know you would never guess by looking at me now, but I worked as an apprentice with my father for a few years in high school. Dad wanted me to know all of the ins and outs of the furniture business firsthand. You might even go so far as to say I have a little talent in the woodworking department."

"I should've known. You seemed to know what you were doing with the sander. And you look mighty comfortable in your coveralls I might add." *And irresistible!*

He winked. "You seem pretty handy yourself, Holly."

"Yes. I refinish furniture. I like the redemptive process. I've been doing it for years," she replied as she stepped into her coveralls. "Okay, I'm ready."

They made their way from the shed and rounded up a couple of volunteers; Holly and Hunter found themselves working to attach the white unicorn assembly. It took them, plus the muscle strength of two hulky men, to carry it to its original position.

"Are you sure you want to do this, Holly? I think it'd be more fun for you to work on the Angel Tree project, you know, something that didn't require a tool belt," Hunter said as the two men walked off.

"Are you kidding? I love this part. Now we get to put it back together and see how beautiful it is!" She held the unicorn in position as Hunter stood on a ladder to tighten the bolts at the top of the pole. Next to the ladder sat Abbey. Ever since arriving, she hadn't left his side. For some reason, she seemed to be drawn to Hunter. Maybe it was his cologne, it had woodsy, earthy undertones—like petrichor. Smelling it again reminded her of the moment in the shop when she was pinning his suit and almost passed out. No, something told her it was more than just simple cologne that had attracted Abbey, and her, to Hunter Ashworth.

"I think Abbey really likes you, Hunter. I've never seen her act this way." Well, except for with the ornament, she thought.

He smiled and puffed out his chest. "What can I say?" He climbed back down the ladder and stepped back, looking at the unicorn. "Well, what do you think?"

"I think it's amazing," she replied, her eyes traveling from the unicorn's iridescent rainbow horn to its mane, and lastly to its wings. She'd just ridden it in her dreams, and it looked exactly the same. "It's just like I remember. I can't wait to put up the rest of them."

"Hey guys, I was hoping I'd find you here," Ruby said, walking up to them holding a clipboard. "It's looking good."

"Thanks Ruby," Holly said, ignoring Ruby's huge grin and more-than-obvious delight at seeing the two of them together. She put up her clipboard and gave Holly a little wink from behind it while Hunter was checking the bolts on the bottom of the unicorn's pole. It was everything she could do to not just shoo her away. She could feel the blood begin to flood her cheeks.

Ruby directed her gaze toward Hunter. "I have a favor to ask."

"Whatever you need, Ruby."

"I've just been at the craft booth. Looks like we're going to have quite a few items to sell, everything from freshly baked apple pies to dried lavender wreaths. I was hoping we could use the shed to store some of the nonperishables?"

"Sure. That shouldn't be a problem. There will be plenty of space, even more when the carousel animals are moved out."

"Great. I'll let everyone know." Ruby turned to walk away, but not before giving Holly a knowing look.

She looked down and put her palm to her forehead, hoping Hunter hadn't seen the exchange.

"Well, I guess we can go get another one. Are you up for it, Holly?" Hunter asked, stepping down from the carousel platform. Abbey followed right behind as he put out his arm to help her. "Here, let me help you."

"Thank you," she replied, taking his hand for a brief moment. It was enough time, though, to remind her that when it came to Hunter, she found herself only wanting more of him, his presence, his closeness, his conversation.

As they walked back to the shed, Greg popped up in her mind. She'd forgotten to call him to let him know she'd be busy working today and that tomorrow would be a better day for him to pick up the cabinet—a day when she wouldn't be so distracted. She started to pat her pockets.

"Did you lose something?"

"My phone. I think I left it in the car. Oh well, it can wait."

"Yeah, after almost losing mine the other day, I decided to leave it behind as well. It's kind of nice to have a break from it."

"I know what you mean," she said as they ambled back toward the shed.

A few moments of silence passed before Hunter turned to look at her. "You know, Holly, I'm really glad you persisted in this park project. I know it sounds kind of funny, coming from me, but I almost feel like it was meant to be, you finding the ornament—"

"I feel the same way, Hunter." Truthfully, she really did, but for her it wasn't just 'a feeling.' She knew it was meant to be, and his Grandpa Joe was her proof. But she

still had questions about the extent of what, or who, the phrase 'meant to be' applied to.

"I'm starting to think maybe you and I were meant to meet too," he said, glancing at her as they continued their stroll.

It was like he'd just read her mind. She could tell he was a little apprehensive, just like she was. She let out a slow, steady breath. "This is all very—unexpected." She was thinking of a way to broach the next subject—the one that had been weighing on her mind for a few days. She'd gone back and forth over whether or not she should mention the ornament, or anything else for that matter, like her new friendship with his Grandpa Joe. She figured she'd dangle her little toe in the water; mention the carousel and see how he reacted. It was only fair that he knew what was going on. "You know, I want to tell you something, Hunter, but I don't want you to think I'm out of my mind."

Hunter narrowed his eyes. "Yes?"

"Seriously, I know you have no idea what I'm about to say," she said, stopping to face him. "I, um, noticed the other day, the day after I saw you at your office, that the Christmas Carousel ornament was back on my tree." She held her breath and searched his face, trying to gauge his reaction.

"I don't know what to say," he replied after a long pause. "I could ask if you're sure, but it looks like you are. I mean, are you sure there wasn't more than one?"

"I don't think so. I took it off my tree and brought it to you, and now it's back."

Hunter scratched his head with his forefinger. "Yeah, I guess I'm at a loss here."

Holly began to open her mouth to bring up his Grandpa Joe, and then decided against it. She'd already ruined the moment. And who knew what he was thinking. Maybe it was better to just let the dust settle. They walked the rest of the way back to the shed in silence.

"Well, I guess you have it back now," he said shrugging, as they stood outside the shed as if things like this happened every day. "It's where it's supposed to be." He opened the door and walked in.

"Holly? Is that you?" a male's voice yelled from the distance, causing her to stop in her tracks. She recognized the voice alright. *Yikes!* She instantly regretted leaving her phone in the car.

Planting a smile on her face, she spun around in the doorway. "Greg, hello there."

"I thought that was you. I almost didn't recognize you with the—whatchamacallits," he said, pointing to her coveralls.

She couldn't've invoked a faker giggle if she tried. "Yes, not my usual kind of outfit. So, what brings you here?" She managed to glance over her shoulder at Hunter who appeared to be half-listening, and half-organizing his tools in the corner.

"Well, I didn't hear from you so I thought it would be okay to come and pick up the cabinet. And when I got here, you weren't at home. So, of course I called your mom. She always knows where to find you—and here we are," he said, walking past her into the shed.

"Great," she said, although deep down she was thinking just the opposite. This should be as fun as having a tooth drilled. She followed him reluctantly. "Um, I'm kind of busy right now, Greg."

"Holly, if you have to go, I can finish without you. It's fine," Hunter called out.

"Oh, hey, aren't you Hunter Ashworth? It's good to hear about the park. I'm Greg, Holly's boyfriend."

"Thanks. It's nice to meet you," Hunter said, walking over to shake his hand. He looked at her and she glanced down, suddenly fascinated with her bootlaces.

Yes, she could feel herself shrinking inside. "Are you sure, Hunter? I can come back later. He's just going to pick

up—"

"Absolutely. You don't have to come back. Just go have fun," he said, fanning his hand in the air. "I got this."

After pulling off her coveralls, she followed Greg out the door. "I almost forgot. Abbey!" she called, walking back inside. Abbey, who was lying by the table near Hunter, sat up. "Come on, girl."

Abbey wouldn't budge.

She clapped her hands onto her thighs. "Abbey, come!"

She still wouldn't budge.

Hunter smiled smugly and crossed his arms. "Looks like I won her over."

Holly sighed and walked over to her, "Come on, Abbey." She grabbed her collar and gently lead her out, glancing back at Hunter one last time. "See ya later, Hunter."

He looked up and gave her an unexpected smile that made her insides turn to jelly.

Abbey wasn't the only one he'd won over.

After loading the cabinet into the back of his truck, Greg walked back into her house. "The cabinet is beautiful, Holly—a piece of artwork in and of itself. I think Mrs. Bradley will be extremely happy." He walked into the living room and stopped in front of her, sitting on the couch. "You'd better watch out. I have a feeling more orders will be pouring in after this one." She looked up at him as if he'd magically appeared out of thin air. "I've missed visiting you, Holly. What would you like to do tonight? I've got all evening."

She gave him a weak smile and continued to pet Abbey.

He took a seat facing her. "Are you okay, Holly? You've been a little quiet since we got back."

"Oh, yeah, I'm fine. Just thinking about the park." *And Hunter.*

Greg rested his elbows on his knees and wove his fingers together. "You know, I was thinking, maybe we should talk about our future." He looked her in the eyes. "I know you said you wanted your space. And I've given it to you, haven't I?"

She gave him a small nod. "Yep, you've definitely given it to me."

"You make it sound like a bad thing, Holly. I was just doing what you asked."

Holly couldn't help but think he might have tried a little harder if his heart was really in it. "Sure. I know."

"Well. Have you had enough time to figure out what you want? I'm more than ready to start dating again."

By the tone of his voice, she would have thought he was talking about going to the grocery store for a loaf of bread. "Greg, why do you want to date me?"

"Because you're fun, and smart, and creative, and independent. I mean, I don't mind living an hour away at all. I actually think it works well for me—I mean, us."

Holly held her peace for a moment. "Thanks, Greg. Yes, I think I have had enough time to figure out what I want. But it's not *this*," she said, waving her hand back and forth between them. "Where's the passion? We should have been super excited to see each other today, and we didn't even hug."

"I can hug you now," Greg said, putting his arms out.

She shook her head. It was time to speak her mind. "No, that's not the point. I just don't think we're in love. I think we're better off as friends. I mean, it's kind of what we've always been."

"I hear you, Holly. And believe me, I've thought about it. And you know what I've figured out?" he asked, searching her eyes and smiling as if he'd made a rare discovery. "We're just not *that kind* of couple. We've gone above and beyond that passionate phase that always fades. Our relationship makes sense. It's based on reality, not fantasy."

He really believes that? "Sorry Greg, I don't agree. I think love should become more and more exciting as it grows."

"I think that's unrealistic, Holly."

"I know. That's my point," she replied, slumping down in her seat, "you don't believe in true love, and I do."

It was quiet for a minute until he straightened and turned towards her. "I guess we're really breaking up, then?"

"Yes, we're really breaking up, Greg. I'm sorry."

"Don't be sorry, Holly. It's better that I know, so I can move on. I do have to say, though, you've changed quite a bit since moving here. Overall, I think it's a good thing."

"Thanks Greg. I think so too. Maybe we can stay in touch. You know, just in case someone else has a cabinet they need to have painted?"

Greg stood up slowly from the couch. "Sure. I do have a question, though, Holly."

Her eyebrows tented. "Yes?"

"What do you think of Hunter Ashworth?"

That's a curveball, she thought, blinking twice. She could feel herself start to smile, as hard as she tried to conceal it. "Hunter Ashworth? What made you think of him?"

Light spread across Greg's face as if he'd just won at Bingo. "Yes, Hunter Ashworth. I'm getting a funny feeling that you might have a thing for him. And I saw how he looked at you."

Her jaw hinged open. Anything she'd say right now in protest would be completely inauthentic and they both knew it. It was better to just not say anything at all.

"Be careful. I know his type. And you, Holly, are *not* it. Remember, a leopard never changes his spots. I know everything looks good now, with the park, but just wait, it'll benefit Hunter Ashworth in the end—he'll make sure of it."

Holly cleared her throat and stood, resisting the urge to defend Hunter. Turned out, Greg could be passionate about something after all—his dislike of Hunter Ashworth. But it was far from fair. Greg just didn't know the real Hunter— plain and simple.

"I just don't want you to get hurt."

"I'll take that into consideration, Greg," she replied, trying as hard as she could to keep her cool as her emotions came to a slow roaring boil.

"I'm sorry, Holly. I guess I just feel like I have to protect you, that's all," he said, putting his hand on her shoulder. "It's for your own good."

"I get it Greg, really. I know you mean well, but I'm not a child. I'm more than capable of taking care of myself—I think I've proved that. But no hard feelings. You're more than welcome to come back to visit the Christmas Village. You should check out the Angel Tree website too. There're a lot of kids out there who need presents."

"Maybe I will," he said, nodding slowly.

"We're distributing gifts on Friday, Christmas Eve, at the park's opening. I'll text you the website address."

"Sounds good," he said, as she walked him to the front door.

He put out his arms. "Can I hug you now, friend?"

"Sure. Have a safe trip home."

Chapter Nineteen

Returned

Well, that was weird. And even more weird that I'm about to do what I'm about to do, Hunter thought. It was Monday morning, and he was sitting at his desk thinking about his conversation with Holly. He'd been trying to come clean with his feelings, so to speak, when she'd brought up the Christmas Carousel ornament. Up until that point in time, he thought she was a completely down-to-earth woman, but he had to admit, her comments had thrown him for a loop. And then when her boyfriend showed up, he decided the writing was on the wall: *Retreat! Retreat!*

Yet here he was ready to dive into his trash can to see if it was really true. Was the ornament really gone? When he walked into his office this morning, he'd been relieved to find that the trash can had not yet been emptied. *Here goes nothing.*

And thus, his rummaging began. Luckily it was mostly wadded up papers and a few protein bar wrappers. As his fingers scraped the bottom of the can, his heart rate began to speed up just slightly. No ornament. He ran his fingers around the base of the can one more time. Finally, he sat back and glared at the trash can, studying it, before picking it up and dumping it over on the floor in one swift motion. After sorting through the trash on his hand and knees, he sat back. *It can't be.*

The intercom buzzed. "Mr. Ashworth?" Then he heard shouting from his new secretary, Belinda. "Sorry, ma'am, you can't go back there!"

"Yes, I can," was the reply. There she was, Kat, appearing in his doorway, slightly taken aback as her focus shifted from his empty swivel chair to the floor where he was sitting on his heels, trash spread out before him like puzzle pieces.

Belinda was right behind her. "Sorry Mr. Ashworth. She wouldn't listen to me," she said over Kat's shoulder, giving him a strange look as he rose from his knees.

"It's fine, Belinda. Would you hold my calls, please?" he asked, staring into Kat's eyes as he took his chair.

"Yes sir," Belinda replied, and quickly turned to march back to her post.

"Hi, Hunter," Kat said, giving him a sweet gleaming white smile that accentuated her Hawaiian tropical tan. She was holding a pair of leather gloves in one hand and a shopping bag in the other. "I brought you a present."

He was not at all in the mood to smile back. "Kat? What are you doing here?"

She took a breath. "Mind if I have a seat?" She barged into the office without waiting for his reply and plopped down in a chair.

"Sure, help yourself," he muttered.

"Well, I thought about what you said on the phone. And I've decided to give you another chance."

He stared at Kat, unable to comprehend what she was saying. *Give me another chance?*

"I think we can work things out. Maybe I could stay here a little longer and work for you and when the time is right, we could move to Hawaii."

"I'm not quite sure what to say, Kat. This is certainly unexpected."

"Say you'll think about it, Hunter. And there's something else."

As if this isn't enough. "Yes?"

"When I was out on the beach in Hawaii, I was thinking how nice it would be for you to be there with me. I missed you. And I still do, more and more every day. So, I came back here just to see you and bring you a gift, well, sort of a gift. I had to use your credit card," she said with a tremble in her voice. "But it's the thought that counts, right?"

He was shocked. She actually sounded sincere. "Kat, I don't think—"

"Wait, Hunter. Don't say anything else. Just hear me out." She pulled a small box out of the bag that looked a lot like a jewelry box and placed it in her lap while clearing her throat. "Hunter Ashworth, I've had time to think. Our relationship might not have been perfect, but I think we can work on it. I know we can find love together. Will you marry me?" she asked, opening the lid to reveal a wedding band studded with a small blue diamond in its center. "It's titanium."

His mouth fell opened. Was this really happening? "Kat, I don't know what to say. I, um, wasn't really prepared to see you so soon, not to mention, have you propose. I mean, you did just propose right?" he asked, delicately choosing his words. His mind raced. Deep down part of him was a little skeptical. Was she just manipulating him? Was she flying on the seat of her emotions? Was she desperate? Maybe all three?

"Say yes, Hunter. I promise you won't regret it. Say you want me too," she pleaded, walking over to his side and wrapping her arms around him from behind, breathing lightly into his neck.

He pulled forward in his seat and cleared his throat. "Um, well, I think I just need time to process this. Will you let me think about it?"

Kat's eyes teared up and she nodded. "Yes. Take all the time you need." She set the box on the desk. "Will you at least wear the ring?" she asked, sniffing, as she pulled it out and held it up to the light. "It's so gorgeous."

"Kat, I can't . . ." he said, brushing his hand through his hair. "It's too much right now. I—"

"Just think about it," she replied, drawing back like a wounded animal as she struggled to place the ring back in the box. "I'm going to go now," she said, before turning to rush out the door, leaving the ring and the shopping bag behind.

"I'll call you tomorrow," he yelled out, before sitting back in his chair. He looked at the mess on the floor and then back to the desk where his eyes locked onto the shiny ring. At least he'd bought himself a nice one. He slipped it onto his finger just to check to see if it fit. He smiled and placed it back in the box. Surprisingly, she'd gotten the size right.

But what in the world was she thinking? He wasn't sure what to do. Besides the gut feeling growing inside that she only wanted him for his money, he did feel flattered. He picked up the phone to place a call, hoping for some words of wisdom.

"Hey, Hunter. I was just thinking about you," his dad said, answering on the first ring.

"How's Hawaii, Dad?"

"Great. I don't know why we didn't move here sooner. Well, on second thought, I do know why. It's because I refused to listen to my own dad, but he was right. I'm glad I finally did listen. Your mom and I couldn't be happier. Oh, I heard that there was a really nice article in the paper about Ashworth Furniture, and you Hunter. Sounds like your reputation's improving a little now that we're opening the Christmas Village. Maybe this would be a good time to think about settling down—become a family man. I think it can only help improve your reputation more.

"What do you mean, Dad?"

"Well, when you move to Baltimore, maybe you should think about your future—and a family. Aren't things between you and Kat heading in that direction?"

"Well, actually Dad, she broke things off."

"Oh, I'm sorry, Son. I just assumed you were an item. You seemed to get along really well."

"I guess as far as our business relationship went, it was pretty good. But I need some advice, Dad."

"Sure, Son. I'll try."

"So, Kat came back from Hawaii and just came to see me at my office."

"Oh, really? Did she want her job back?"

"She proposed."

"What? *She* proposed to *you*? I thought you said she broke things off?"

"She did, but it seems she's changed her mind."

"Well, what did you say?"

"I told her I'd think about it."

Ray exhaled into the phone. "Probably not what she wanted to hear. I'm not really sure what to tell you Hunter. You know certain people walk into our lives for a reason."

"Yes, I agree with that. But she did walk out. Maybe she'll just change her mind again."

"Or maybe she's the one. People do make mistakes. Listen Son, I don't know her very well, but if she makes you happy, then you have your answer."

"Yes?"

"Well, sure. I mean, you are in love with her, aren't you? You must be if you're even considering marriage."

He paused, stuck in his thoughts. "Um, I think so. I guess that's what I have to figure out."

"Take your time, then, Hunter. The answer will come. Oh, I almost forgot, since I have you on the phone. I've got some good news."

"What?"

"Well, you know how we've been looking for a buyer for the carousel and the other rides at the park?"

"Yes."

"I think I found one. He's really interested in the carousel. He said he'd like to come look at it as soon as possible."

"Great, Dad. I guess that's one less thing I have to worry about now."

"I feel like a weight's been lifted off my shoulders, Ruby. I don't know how else to describe it," Holly said as she grabbed a handful of blouses that had been left in the dressing room and walked over to replace them on the rack.

"Well, then, it's obvious you made the right decision. Besides, I never saw any sparks between the two of you like I do with Hunter."

"Oh stop, Ruby," she said, shaking her head. She looked at her. "You really think there're sparks?"

Ruby laughed. "Helloooo. Like a Fourth of July parade!"

"Well, I guess we'll have time to see what happens now. But he said he's moving to Baltimore after the holidays."

"So. Greg lives in Baltimore. It's not that far."

"I suppose you're right. But I don't want us to get ahead of ourselves." She was wondering what Hunter's feelings were about the whole Greg thing, and she made a promise to herself that she'd talk to him about Greg the next time she saw him.

"Good morning," a too familiar and unwelcomed voice

sang out. "Beautiful day, isn't it?"

Holly's jaw involuntarily hit the floor. What was she doing here? She turned to look at Ruby, who had the same stunned expression on her face but was quickly able to mask it.

"Kat, so nice to see you. I thought you were in Hawaii," Ruby said politely. "May I help you with your coat?" She walked over toward her. Underneath, Kat was wearing a long-sleeved silk floral button up dress. "I love your dress. It's perfect for Hawaii."

Kat twirled. "I know. I wanted to bring a bit of the tropics back with me. I do so love it there. I'm afraid I'll have to wait awhile before I can move there, though, now that Hunter and I are going to get married."

It was like a ton of invisible bricks fell from the sky and hit Holly square on the head. She couldn't hide her shock, or her horror. This was the doozy of all doozies!

"I could've sworn Hunter said you two broke up, Kat," Ruby replied, glancing at Holly in her emotionally incapacitated state.

Kat gave Ruby her widest possible grin; the kind that shows off the back molars. "I figured you'd be surprised. That was just a silly little lover's quarrel. We made up. And both of you are invited to the wedding. I was thinking of purchasing my wedding dress and bridesmaids' dresses here. Would you be so kind as to help me? It all has to be perfect."

Ruby looked at Holly again, as if seeing if she was okay with the idea. She gave her a slight nod.

"Sure, Kat. We'd love to help."

"Great. I brought along a few magazines."

Just breathe, Holly, she told herself. She hadn't even noticed the large floral satchel of bridal magazines that Kat had carried in. *Talk about being blindsided.* She tried to unbuckle the belt of despair that was securely wrapping itself around her heart.

Ruby took the bag from Kat. "So, Hunter asked you to marry him?"

"Well, not exactly. I actually asked him."

"Wow, that's pretty neat, Kat. So, tell us the details. Was he in shock or did he say yes right away?"

"Um, yes, he was definitely surprised. But he practically said yes!"

"Practically?" Ruby asked, prying for more information. Evidently, something about all of this didn't seem right to her either.

"Yes, practically," she replied, nodding her head emphatically. "I know he'll say yes. I always get what I want. It's just a formality."

Ruby clasped her hands together and looked at Holly. She was still off in another world, completely unprepared, emotionally or otherwise, to process what Kat was saying. Ruby turned back to Kat. "Okay then, I guess we have a lot to do. Why don't you show me what you're looking for?"

Kat smiled and pulled out a magazine from her stack. "It has to be perfect."

By late afternoon, Holly was starting to come around. She was thankful that Ruby had suddenly remembered that she needed a few things at the store and sent her on an errand to get them. Ruby had never run out of staples and rubber bands, or any other office supply, since she'd opened her doors several years ago. It was just Ruby's way of saving her from hearing the excruciating details of Kat's Hawaiian wedding planned for the following winter in Merrysville, but she'd already heard more than enough before she managed to escape. Kat went on like a giddy schoolgirl about the honeymoon getaway she was planning in Maui—the only island, Kat touted, that she and Hunter hadn't visited together, *yet.*

When Holly returned to the store, Kat was trying on silver heels from the *Glass Slipper Collection* and Ruby was taking notes. Luckily, Kat had finished gushing and was down to business.

"I think I like these too. What do you think, Ruby?" Kat asked, marching around the room in a circle as if on a mission.

Ruby paged back through her notes. "I think you already tried those on, Kat. You said the heels weren't stout enough. My notes say that you've had a pair of shoes from this collection before, and you broke a heel the first time you wore them."

"Oh. Yes. I remember that! That was the worst," Kat replied.

"Hey, Holly," Ruby said, directing her attention towards her.

"Do you want to see the bridesmaid dresses I've picked out, Holly? I'm going with a lovely silk hibiscus fabric," Kat said, wedging her mouth into a huge smile between her tan cheeks.

Holly had to resist the urge to want to thrust the tip of her shoe into it. She glanced at Ruby who seemed to be reading her mind. "Um—" Her phone rang. *Thank God for perfect timing!* "Just give me a minute. I've got to take this," she said, setting down the large white bag she was carrying and walking toward the break room. She looked at the foreign number. Whomever it was on the other end didn't matter; he or she was her hero.

"Hello?"

"Is this Miss Holly?" an older male voice asked in a distinct Southern drawl.

"Yes, this is Holly."

"This is Jack Haywood, the electrician. I was calling

about the carousel."

Her ears perked up. "What can I do for you?" her heart starting to pound. He wouldn't be calling unless there was a problem.

"Well. I've got some discouraging news. I didn't want to bother you, or worry you before, but I just, for the life of me, can't figure out why the organ won't work. I've tried everything. I know it's getting power."

"Oh no. What can we do?"

"That's why I'm calling. I wanted to make sure to get your approval before I make a few phone calls. I may have to call the manufacturer and have them recommend someone to come and take a look at it. I have no idea how much that will cost, though."

She sighed and leaned forward, putting her elbows on the table. "Well, I guess we don't have much of a choice. Just do what you can Jack. I really appreciate you helping us."

"Don't mention it Holly. This is as important to me as to everyone else. I loved this carousel. I used to take my daughter on it all the time. It brings back the best of memories."

"Thanks Jack. I know a lot of the town feels the same way. Let me know how it goes."

"Will do. Have a good night."

Holly's thoughts of smooth sailing from only this morning had been disrupted by a surprise gale wind, rocking her little boat. Yep, it is most certainly true. When it rains, it pours—*and I get tossed overboard.* Nobody would need to ask if she was okay if they looked at her face, the answer was written all over it. But luckily, she'd made it back to the comforts of her home and to her canine companionship without having to explain her mood to anyone. Abbey understood. As soon as she sat down on the couch, Abbey walked over and rested her furry little chin on her knee, as if saying: *It'll all work out.*

After dinner, she spent the better part of two hours trying to lose herself in an old classic she'd picked out from her bookshelf. Books she'd read back in high school always seemed to bring comfort, kind of like her visits with Joe at the carousel, she was beginning to realize. She stood to get ready for bed. Maybe she could call for Joe, she thought. He'd know what to do.

"Please Joe, come back and help me. Even if things with Hunter aren't meant to be, at least come and show us how to fix the organ," she said out loud as she lifted her comforter and slipped underneath. After a few hours of tossing and turning, trying to will herself back to the carousel, she gave up. Where was Joe?

A few hours later, around four in the morning, she bolted upright, awoken by a nightmare. She could only remember the last scene just as it faded from the grasp of her memory. In it, Kat was parading down the aisle toward Hunter in her six-inch heels, gliding over a sandy beach, while she was plodding along behind her wearing coveralls and galoshes, holding Kat's veil, her boots getting stuck in the sand just a little bit deeper with each step.

Chapter Twenty

Hunter Visits the Future

"Knock knock," Kat sang as she opened the front door. Hunter walked into the room and watched as she carried a white shopping bag stuffed with all sorts of Christmas decorations, from garland to glittery balls, in one hand, and her satchel of wedding and bridal magazines in the other. For the past couple of evenings since proposing, she'd been stopping by his home, carrying her satchel like it was attached at the hip. She told him she wanted to spend time with him; but he noticed so far that she'd spent the majority of her time adorning his decidedly simple Christmas tree and the rest of his home with garish, over-the-top decorations that he figured she must've found in the dusty dark corner of someone's attic.

He stood and stared at her in his flour-coated white apron, holding a rubber spatula. "Hi Kat."

She set down her bags and walked over to him, keeping her distance, and leaned forward to give him a peck on the cheek. "What are you doing in that apron?"

"I'm making a batch of chocolate chip cookies for the children tomorrow at the Angel Tree event."

"Oh. That's very nice of you, Hunter. I didn't realize

you were a part of that."

"Yep," he replied, directing his chin toward her bag. "Not to complain, but where did you find all of these decorations? And isn't it getting kind of late for that? I mean, Christmas Eve is tomorrow."

"One can never have enough Christmas decorations. I was thinking it could be a new tradition for us. We can keep them up until Valentine's Day. I admit, it's a little less elegant from my usual style, but I didn't exactly have a *large* budget," she said, glancing at Hunter as she tossed a strand of her long hair back over her shoulder. "So, I went to visit my Grandma. She told me to help myself, so I did."

"I can see that," he replied, looking at the string of holly leaves with brass trumpets, French horns, and mini drums trailing from her bag. He wondered if she had a partridge and a pear tree or any of the other Twelve Days of Christmas paraphernalia in there. As far as he could tell, she was definitely trying to mark her territory, gawdy as it may be.

"She reached around his waist and untied his apron. "Let's get rid of this silly thing," she said, tossing the apron to the floor behind her and flinging her arms around him. She nestled her nose into his neck. "You smell like cookie dough," she cooed, before pulling back her head. "Can I ask you something, babe?"

He nodded. Here she was again, acting all *cutesy-whootsy*. He had a feeling he knew what was coming.

"So, I was wondering when you were going to let me know your answer." She glanced at his finger. So far, he'd not put the ring on his finger. It was sitting in its box on the mantle. "It's hard to plan a wedding this way. At least let me use a credit card so I can start making a few purchases—for the wedding. And then, of course, there's the honeymoon in Maui. I can't wait to show you the resort I chose," she said, letting go of him to reach into her satchel.

"I'm sorry, Kat. I know you want an answer. I just feel like I need more time to think. We haven't really spent a lot of time together lately. I mean, just last week you were breaking up with me. I feel like we need to get to know each other a little better. And that takes time."

She looked up at him and smiled. "Well, that's a simple fix. I can just move in," she said, patting his chest. "We'll have all the time you need."

He stopped himself from rolling his eyes. "Kat. Hold on. I feel like we're rushing into things here. Please, just give me a little time. I promise, I'll have an answer for you soon."

She put on a pouty face and all but whined, "When, Hunter? I can't wait forever."

"Fine. I'll give you an answer tomorrow," he said flatly, secretly wondering if that was even a possibility. *Don't make promises you can't keep, Hunter.*

"Okay," she replied bouncing up on her heels to give him a peck on the lips. "I'll leave you alone now. Remember, Maui is calling," she said, as she picked up her satchel. "I'll just leave these over here." She picked up the bag of decorations and set it by the tree. In what appeared to be a last-ditch effort, she picked up a travel magazine and laid it on his coffee table as he crossed his arms and watched. She turned to give him one last dripping honey-glazed smile and finally walked out the door.

Whew! Talk about pressure. He frowned as he walked over to look out the window to make sure she was getting in her car to drive off. So much of their relationship had been about Kat making decisions for the both of them. Why hadn't that seemed to bother him before? Just as he was about to head back into the kitchen, his phone rang.

"Mom! Hi. How are you?"

"I'm great. I'm very excited about helping to hand out the Angel Tree gifts tomorrow. Is everything ready for the Grand Opening of the Christmas Village?"

"Yeah, as far as I know. I've been keeping up to speed with the progress." The last couple of days, though, he hadn't heard from Holly, which had him slightly worried. But he'd finally texted her this morning to which she'd replied somewhat cryptically that everything was 'more than fine.' And when he went to finish up the carousel the day before, she sent a couple of volunteers in her place. None of it made any sense. Until recently she'd acted like the project was her top priority, now it seemed like she couldn't be bothered. Maybe she was too busy hanging out with her boyfriend.

"Well, I don't want to keep you. I know you're very busy, but I wanted to let you know something. Your father told me about the proposal."

"I'm sorry, Mom, I should have said something. But I guess I figured Dad would tell you."

She hesitated for a moment. "That's okay, Son. That's not why I'm calling."

"Okay, then why are you calling?"

"Remember when I said I wanted to talk to you about something the other day?"

"Yes, when I was with Holly."

"Yes. Such a nice young woman. Anyway, I figured you and Kat had broken up since you were with Holly or I would have said something sooner."

"What do you mean, Mom? Holly and I are just friends."

"Well, I wanted to tell you that Kat stopped by to see me when she was in Hawaii. I hadn't even mentioned it to your father. I figured it wasn't that big of a deal. But it was sort of confusing."

"What was?"

"Well. She asked if she could borrow money from us to open a boutique in Hawaii. Since you two were dating, I figured you knew about it. I just told her that it didn't really make sense, seeing that you two were moving to

Baltimore."

"Yeah. That is strange. I wonder if she knew she was going to break up with me when she asked."

"Or maybe she decided to break up with you after I told her no. It makes me wonder why she's proposing. Maybe she figures you'll move to Hawaii once you get married, and she'll be able to start her business. Don't get me wrong, Hunter. She seems like a nice girl. I just don't know if she's the kind of woman who likes to be told no.

"*If* we get married, Mom. And yes, I think you're right. She's a go-getter—she could make a profession out of it."

"It's not to say she couldn't be serious about you Hunter. I mean, I'm sure she really has feelings for you, and you obviously have feelings for her."

"You're right, Mom." He was beginning to wonder what Kat was really up to. Was she really in love with him? "I hate to say it, but this relationship business used to be a lot simpler when my heart wasn't really in it." He thought about Holly for a split second. It was probably better that she was already taken; he certainly didn't need things to be any more complicated.

"I'm sorry, Hunter. I know you'll figure it out."

He smirked in spite of himself. "You're right again Mom. Eventually I will *figure it out.*"

"I love you honey. See you tomorrow," she said before hanging up.

He sat down on his couch and let out a long exhale. How did he really feel about Kat? And what about Holly? Did he really believe it was better for Holly to already be taken? It certainly made his decision easier. But what would he do if Holly didn't have a boyfriend? The answer was pretty clear. He knew how he felt when he was around her. She'd turned him into a better man in a matter of weeks, miraculously. There was certainly something special about her that brought out the best in him. But what about the whole Christmas Carousel ornament thing? Now that was inexplicable. She seemed as shocked by it as he had, but she'd also seemed to be holding back. Was there something she knew that she wasn't telling him? Oh well, it was a lost cause now.

Maybe I should just cut my losses and move on. *Maybe Kat and I are perfect for each other after all,* he thought glumly, glancing one last time at the ugliest Christmas tree he'd ever seen in the corner of his living room as he stood up and headed for bed.

Maybe that's what he deserved.

Welcome to the Dream

"Wow, this looks better than I could have even imagined. They did such a great job. It looks just like it did when . . . wait, what's this?" Hunter asked out loud, rubbing his eyes before turning his attention to the fun house, and then the funnel cake stand beyond it. Everything was in perfect condition and operational, from the Ferris wheel in the distance to the dunking booth, but where is everyone? Where are the children for the Angel Tree?

He was all alone, except for the sounding of upbeat organ music drifting in the distance. *Wait, what am I doing here?* He mindlessly roamed toward the familiar sound. *The carousel is already up and running? Wow, it's been so long.* He looked down at his apparel. He was wearing a pair of khaki shorts and a Hawaiian button up shirt. *Did Kat have something to do with this?* "Kat, Kat. Where are you? Is this some kind of prank?" he yelled as he continued to wander toward the carousel. He made it around the corner to the clearing, past the lampposts, as the streetlights overhead were just coming on, and found himself staring at the carousel with lights blazing and music roaring as it rotated, full of animals, yet deserted.

The last thing he'd remembered was putting on his plaid fleece pajama bottoms and throwing on a long-sleeve shirt before turning out his bedroom light; and now he was standing in the Merrysville Amusement Park at dusk where the temperature must have been somewhere closer to the seventies. He walked over to the carousel. It was spinning fairly fast, but he timed it just right and was able to step up while grabbing the stationary pole of the mighty queen zebra. Someone must have put her back on the carousel without him.

"You used to do that a lot as a kid. Do you remember that, Hunter?" Grandpa Joe asked, appearing on a small pony beside him as he took a seat on the zebra. "You'd try to jump on it while it was moving. It made your mom very nervous, that's for sure," he said, giving him a wide smile as tears formed in his eyes that made them sparkle like the stars. "I've missed you."

He jumped down from the zebra and walked over to Grandpa Joe. It couldn't be. "Grandpa? How? Where? What *is* this?"

"Well, some people like to think of this as a dream," he replied while extending his arms and giving him a big bear hug.

"Yes. It's got to be a dream. I mean, you . . ." Hunter pulled away. He couldn't bring himself to say the word.

"Died?" Grandpa Joe asked, clutching his arms.

He looked down and nodded solemnly, feeling tears sting his eyes. "I'm sorry I didn't get the chance to say goodbye."

"Well, look at us now. Turns out, it wasn't goodbye after all," Grandpa Joe said, pulling him in for another hug. The carousel began to slow down and came to a halt just as the organ music softened. In the distance, Hunter heard a sound.

"Rruff! Rruff!"

"A dog?" He strained his neck to look behind him. Just then, a black-and-white Border collie pounced onto the platform, wagging his tail forcefully as he ran up to Hunter and rested both of his front paws on his thighs. "Ralphie?" he asked, knowing in his heart that it was. Hunter laughed and bent down to give him a hug.

"Rruff!"

He rubbed Ralphie's soft fur. "It's good to see you, boy!"

Grandpa Joe smiled. "He's missed you, too, Son. Well, it appears the ride is over. Time to go."

"Go where, Grandpa?"

The two of them stepped off the platform, followed by Ralphie. "Let's take a stroll," Grandpa Joe replied, waving his arm toward a sign a few yards away. It was composed of wooden arrows marking the paths before them. One on the left was labeled simply, *Past Regrets*, and another, on the right, *Promising Future*.

"Which way, Grandpa?"

"It's up to you, Hunter."

"Okay." He shrugged as he glanced at the signs, paused for a moment, and then walked instinctively to his right.

"Good choice," Grandpa Joe whispered.

Hunter looked at his grandpa's top hat, then down to his bow tie and striped vest, and finally, his black dress pants and golden shoes. "Why are you wearing that getup, Grandpa?"

"I thought it suited the occasion, seeing that I'm the carousel barker. What do you think, Hunter?" he asked, turning slowly around in an effort to model his outfit.

"Yep, it's a perfect fit."

"It's hard to find that sometimes, don't you think? *A perfect fit?*" Grandpa asked, staring at him intently.

"Are we still talking about your outfit, Grandpa?

Somehow, I don't think we are."

Grandpa Joe took out his pocket watch. "Very perceptive of you. I knew you wouldn't want to beat around the bush. You know, time's almost up for me, Hunter, but not for you. More than anything, I'd like for you to find happiness, and the perfect fit."

"Nobody's perfect."

Grandpa's eyes twinkled. "Now, that's for sure."

"This is about Kat, isn't it?"

"Maybe," Joe said, putting his finger to his lip. "She's one of them."

"Oh, I get it. Holly. She's kind of like this dream—too good to be true. Besides, she's already taken. I've decided to marry Kat. She seems like the perfect fit for me."

"Are you sure about that, Hunter? Whoa, watch your step," Grandpa Joe said, grabbing his arm as his foot caught the edge of a large rock protruding from the middle of the gravel walkway, causing him to fall forward and almost faceplant in the dirt.

He steadied himself. "What's that doing there?"

"There are always going to be obstacles on the way to our destination, Hunter. It's how you maneuver them that determines if you make it to where you're supposed to go."

"So, it's all planned out, is it?"

"Partly so. But part of it is up to us. I like to say the *best* parts are up to us—the decisions that define our lives and bring us joy, or sadness, if you so choose. I realize now that it's our choice. Unfortunately, I didn't choose joy for a long time. I didn't even realize that I could. I was so caught up in *distractions*, like work and making money. Those were the big ones for me."

"Is that why you asked me if I was happy, Grandpa?" he asked, turning toward him.

Grandpa Joe nodded emphatically. "Yes. I just wanted to make sure you were aware that you *could* be happy. That day, I saw the look on your face that I'd seen on my own a thousand times before I decided to change my focus from helping myself to helping others. Don't do what I did, Hunter. I waited too long. Make a decision now, while you still have time on your side."

He looked down. His grandpa was making him think. That day, when his grandpa had asked if he was happy, was the very day he'd crossed the *t's* and dotted the *i's* on the factory, and Kat had booked a trip for them to celebrate. Part of him knew his grandpa was speaking the truth. He hadn't even really had fun on the trip; he'd been bored stiff rambling from shop to shop with Kat. But now, he was just starting to change his focus, mainly due to Holly. He was helping the town with the park and the Angel Tree project. And it was indescribable how it made him feel.

"Looks like we're here," Grandpa Joe said, pointing to a sign overhead: *Promising Future.*

"I don't remember seeing this at the Merrysville Amusement Park."

"This dream's tailor-made just for you—just like one of your suits," Joe added, giving him a little wink.

"You are on a roll today, Grandpa," Hunter replied, envisioning Holly as she sat on the floor pinning the cuffs of his pants with little straight pins tucked between her lips. "And just where are we exactly?" There was nothing in front of them but an empty field. "This is kind of, I don't know . . . anticlimactic."

"You'll see. Are you ready?" Grandpa asked.

Hunter looked ahead expectantly and nodded, on cue, as Grandpa snapped his fingers.

The scene changed right before his eyes.

What was a square of dirt and grass below his feet seconds earlier had transformed into a sidewalk. Hunter turned and looked to his left and then to his right. He was standing in front of the steps of *Patterns Boutique* next to Joe and looking out toward what used to be the Merrysville Amusement Park. Erected in its place now was a huge complex of brown stucco buildings with metal roofs. Hunter recognized the small industrial complex right away from the drawings he'd gone over with the architect a couple of months back. He turned around and did a double take as he looked at the sign above the door. It didn't say *Patterns Boutique* anymore; it was a storefront for Ashworth Furniture Company.

"What happened to Ruby's shop?" he asked, frowning, as he looked at Grandpa Joe.

"Progress, I guess. She decided to move to Baltimore. So did a lot of the other townspeople. I guess they figured you were right. What was the point of trying to keep tradition alive? It seemed like too much of an uphill battle."

They started walking down the street. Shop after shop was vacant with *For Lease* signs in the storefront windows. "What's this about?" They came to *The Bean*. Hunter sighed with relief. "At least *The Bean* is still open."

"Not for long, though. The owner's wife talked him into moving. Business has been slow since so many people are moving out of town. Most of the people that live here now work at your factory in some capacity. But a lot of them commute from the suburbs surrounding Baltimore. They don't even know the history of the park."

"Seen enough?" Grandpa asked.

The pangs of remorse were beginning to stir. "More than," he replied gravely.

"Hold onto me," Grandpa said, as he snapped his fingers. Without another word they were transported.

He steadied himself against his grandpa's arm. "Whoa, where are we?" He looked around and realized he was in someone's living room. The room was filled with designer furniture and gorgeous rugs. His eyes were pulled toward the twelve-foot ceilings and elegant crystal chandelier above his head. In the corner was a floor-to-ceiling flocked Christmas tree decorated with silver-and-white ornaments and white velvet bows.

"You'll see." He pointed toward the double glass doors that led to the study. Someone was sitting behind the desk. "Come with me," he said, leading him toward the room.

"Honey, have you seen my passport?" Kat asked, stepping quickly down the hall and turning into the study. She was dressed in a red pantsuit and her hair was cut into a curly bob.

"Why do you need that?" the man at the desk asked. "I thought we were headed back to Hawaii for Christmas again this year."

Hunter was shocked to see that it was he himself sitting there, a tad older, with the beginnings of little gray hairs peppering his short sideburns and a couple of small creases forming around his mouth.

"Yes, of course, but after that I have to fly to Italy for a fashion show."

"For how long? Weren't you just there?"

"Yes, but only for a week this time. Besides, don't you have to fly to San Francisco the day after Christmas? I told you it would make more sense to just move to Hawaii. It's hard to run a shop only being there a week or two out of the month."

"Kat, my company is here in Baltimore. I need to be here."

"But you're never here, Hunter. You're always traveling."

"Well, that's what happens when you expand your company and make it national. Isn't that what you wanted? Besides, if I'm not traveling, you are," the older Hunter replied, looking up from his laptop for the first time since they started their conversation. "Did you do something different with your hair?"

"Yes, a month ago," she replied, standing in the doorway with her hands on her hips, eyes averted toward the floor.

Older Hunter pushed back from the desk. "Sorry, Kat, I

guess I've just been busy. Between traveling across the United States and trying to keep up with your fashion show schedule . . ." He began to rub the bridge of his nose with his fingers. "It's a little stressful."

"Like I said before, Hunter, you can let someone else run the company and we can move to Hawaii."

"And what would I do there? Won't you still be running your shop? I need to work. It's in my blood. I owe it to my family."

"I thought you didn't really care about traditions, Hunter. Why can't you just let it go?" Kat asked. "We have all the money we'll ever need."

The older Hunter glanced at his wall. On it, in a small black frame, was an old newspaper article in the *Merrysville Banner*, "The Merrysville Grinch." It was all just a distant memory now. The *Merrysville Banner* had gone out of business years ago.

"I don't know why you wanted to keep that, and mount it in a frame, of all things."

"I don't know, either, Kat."

Deep down Hunter knew exactly why. It was a reminder of why he couldn't let himself care too much about anyone but himself. In the end, everyone was a critic. Hunter looked at his grandpa Joe. "Any children?" he whispered.

He shook his head. "Nope. Kat didn't want any. She said it wouldn't be fair to the child. You both travel too much."

A melancholic spirit rose up from within and he spoke solemnly, "I think I'm ready to go now."

"Say no more," Grandpa said, raising his arm to snap his fingers. Instantly, they were back in the park, facing the empty field again, before he could get out his last word.

Hunter turned to look at his grandpa. "So, I'll ask. Why you showed me that—hypothetical as it may be. It is a hypothetical, isn't it?"

"You tell me, Son. How did you feel when we were there? Did it resonate with you? Are you and Kat *the perfect fit*?"

"Oh, it resonated. But I can't imagine that really happening."

"It didn't happen all at once. One little step at a time, Hunter. A decision here, a decision there. Next thing you know—here we are."

"Anyway, as I was saying. If I had to guess, you're showing me this because you want me to make a different choice?"

"Son, like I said before, I just want you to be happy. If you're happy, I'm happy."

Hunter looked down at the ground, kicking a few blades of grass with the tip of his leather sandal. "But what if the thing that will make me most happy is unattainable?" he asked, crossing his arms across his chest.

"How do you know?"

"Holly's got a boyfriend," he replied, glancing up to catch his grandpa's stare.

"Ah, so the *thing* isn't really a *thing* at all. It's a *someone*. Like I said, how do you know? What's your inner voice telling you?"

Hunter thought for a minute, trying to tune into his heart's frequency—something he hadn't done in years. But it wasn't that difficult now since his heart had been laid bare, along with his soul, all thanks to his grandfather and the guided tour of his future. Was it *promising* like the sign proclaimed? Was that the kind of life he really wanted? An ache in his heart that had begun to stir when he first saw himself sitting behind the desk talking to Kat was beginning to grow. He recognized it immediately—the feeling of loneliness and loss. "I guess I haven't made much of an effort. Maybe I need to stay in Merrysville a little while longer and find out. And in the process, I could help the town."

Grandpa Joe was shaking his head emphatically. "Yes, yes, yes. Now you're getting it, Hunter. You and I were blessed with our business for a reason. We need to steward our resources well. You can find a balance between work, and relationships. And best of all, you can be happy."

"Maybe Holly and I . . ." he stopped short as something caught his eye. He turned around. Right behind them now was the carousel.

"How did that get there?" he asked, shocked by the site of the magnificent carousel starting to turn slowly on its axis. The organ music began to play softly.

"Carousels have a habit of getting around, Hunter," Joe replied, laughing heartily, "and around and around," he added, watching the carousel pick up speed before he faded into the night quicker than a blink.

"Wait!" Hunter yelled as his grandpa vanished, leaving him standing there all alone.

He sat up in bed, his grandfather's laugh echoing in his head. "What?" he said out loud as he looked to the clock on his side table. It was still dark, 5:00 glowed back at him. It was quiet, except for the remnants of echoes, and a simple question rising from inside his mind. *Are you happy?*

"I think so," Hunter said as he pulled back the covers and headed into the kitchen. "Not really happy about being up at five a.m. though." His voice echoed in the hallway. He thought about his grandpa. It had been so real, like he'd really talked to him. Until now, he hadn't realized how lonely he'd been without Grandpa Joe to call—not that he'd called him much in the last few months.

"That's probably why I dreamed about him." He switched his coffee maker on to the brew cycle and reached for a mug in the cabinet. After a few minutes he poured himself a cup and walked into the living room. There it was—the ugly Christmas tree. He found himself wishing that eyesore was only a dream. He walked over to it to plug in the lights anyway. Today was Christmas Eve. He was excited for the Angel Tree. He glanced at the ornaments as he walked by, accidentally knocking one off of its position on the tip of the branch.

He still hadn't fully awakened from his sleep. As he bent over to pick up the ornament, his eyes flung open and goosebumps exploded all over his body.

"What in the world?" he asked, gasping in awe.

He turned the ornament over in his hand. "It can't be," he said out loud with the wonder of a little boy.

Carousels have a habit of getting around, he heard echoing from inside of his head.

In a partial daze, with his cup of coffee in one hand and carousel ornament in the other, he realized he had a choice to make. He put his mug on the coffee table and walked to the mantle to grab the jewelry box and sat back down.

Hunter held the ornament in one hand and the ring in the other. Even if it was only a dream, it had given him quite a bit of clarity. Now he just needed some courage to commit. He looked back and forth, from one to the other slowly, deliberately, thinking of the woman and of the future each represented, as he tried to figure it all out.

Chapter Twenty-One

It's a Pleasure Doing Business with You

It was only a few hours until the Angel Tree event. Hunter had been itching since this morning to talk to Holly, but he knew he had one other important issue to address first—Kat. He'd spent the better part of the day baking cookies and thinking. Somehow the therapeutic motion of stirring chocolate chips into vanilla-scented buttery dough helped. Maybe there really is something to aromatherapy, he wondered, sniffing the air as he remembered the little bottles of lavender oil and lavender wreaths that he'd helped Ruby store in the shed. He took another deep breath, as he placed the last of the cookies into a snowman-themed plastic storage container. There was no other word to describe it: Heavenly.

But the atmosphere was about to change. He walked around the kitchen, trying to dispel his nervous energy, hoping Kat would see things his way for once. The last thing he wanted was to have Kat hate him. If all went as planned, though, she'd accept it, and who knows, she might eventually come to see him as a good friend. And then there was Holly. He'd decided he had nothing to lose by admitting his feelings. He already made his choice, but she still had to make hers.

Right on schedule, the front door opened. "Hunter?" Kat called from the front entry, "I'm here."

"Hi Kat, I'm in the kitchen. Come on in."

"Hey."

Hunter was looking down, pouring some steaming hot liquid into mugs. "I made us some hot chocolate. I was thinking we could take it to the park." Hunter looked up at her, noticing her attire. She was standing in the doorway in a tight black wool dress with black fur collar, her head tilted seductively with her shiny red lips pursed into a little heart shape. "Oh, you don't quite look like you're ready to go to the park to give away Angel Tree presents to the children."

"Nope, I'm not," she said, smiling and shaking her head. "I think we have more important business to discuss. You said you would have an answer, Hunter," she said, walking toward him and carefully taking the mugs of hot chocolate from his hands and placing them back on the counter. "So, what's your answer, babe?" she asked, grabbing him firmly around the waist and pulling him close. "I figured we could go out to celebrate."

Hunter blinked, overwhelmed by her musky fragrance, and drew back. "It's funny you say business, Kat."

"Why?" she asked, confusion striking her face.

Hunter grabbed her hand and lead her toward the living room. "Come with me Kat. I want to talk to you about something."

"Okay." She was tentative as she took a seat next to him on the couch. "What's going on Hunter?"

He took both of her hands in his and looked her in the eyes, unwaveringly. "Kat. I can't marry you."

She withdrew her hands like they'd just grazed a hot stovetop. "What do you mean, you can't? Why not?"

"I'm sorry, Kat. I don't think we're in love. I know I'm not in love with you. And I don't think you're in love with me."

"Hunter. I already told you. I can fall in love—eventually. I know we both can," she said, her voice on the edge of cracking.

"Kat. I want you to be happy. My mom told me you asked her to borrow money for a shop in Hawaii. It's obvious you want to be in Hawaii. Why would you want to marry me and live in Baltimore?"

Kat looked down.

Hunter sighed. "Are you in love with me or my money, Kat?"

"What kind of question is that?" she asked, annoyance creeping into her voice.

"An honest one. Would you still want to marry me if I was poor?"

"But you're not poor, Hunter. What a silly question. Money is a part of who you are."

He pulled back and leaned against the cushions. After a full minute of bone-crushing silence he said, "I'm not moving to Hawaii, Kat. I don't think either one of us is who the other person wants us to be." He glanced in her direction. She was sitting with her arms and legs crossed, tapping her foot impatiently in the air.

"I don't know what to say, Hunter. You know I always get what I want. This can't be the end." She sat fuming, her swinging foot vibrating the couch. "Wait, what did you mean earlier when you said something about business?"

Hunter looked her in the eye, trying to gauge if she'd calmed down enough to listen to his offer. "Well," he replied, "I wasn't sure if, or how, I was going to bring this up, but maybe I can still help you out—if you want."

Her body shifted forward, and she uncrossed her leg. "What do you mean?"

"I've been thinking about this all day, Kat. I have an idea. I spoke with my father. He's got a banker friend in Hawaii. He's a young guy. Dad said he could set up a meeting with him and maybe help you with a small business loan to help you open your shop. My dad and I could put in a good word for you." Hunter looked into her eyes, trying to read her expression. "What do you say?"

Slowly, a huge grin emerged on her face. "Well. I guess if I can't have you, at least I can have my shop. And who knows what else . . . is he single?"

"Oh Kat." Hunter was surprised, and more than relieved that she was taking everything so well.

"I'm only kidding—maybe."

"Funny."

"Yes. I guess I could look into it."

"Great. I'll let him know."

"Thanks Hunter. So, what about you? Are you going to ask her out?"

He looked at her sideways. "Huh? Who? What are you talking about?"

"Come on, Hunter. You know exactly what, and who, I'm talking about. I guess a part of me knew all along too."

He smiled shyly. "Is it really that obvious?"

She crinkled her nose. "Unfortunately. And I have a small confession to make."

"Really? What?"

"I may have told her that we were getting married."

He jumped from his seat. "Kat!" he yelled, "tell me you're joking. Why?"

"I may have wanted to flaunt it a little."

Hunter crossed his arms and took a deep breath before settling back down on the couch. "And how exactly did you do that?"

"I went into the shop the other day and asked Ruby and Holly to help me pick out my wedding dress—and bridesmaid dresses," she added, mumbling her words.

"Oh, Kat," he replied, cupping his forehead with his hand. It was all starting to make sense, why Holly had been avoiding him.

"I'm sorry, Hunter. I guess I was jealous."

"Never mind. I don't care," he said, shaking his head. He looked up at the clock. "It's water under the bridge. Now, I just have to see if I can reverse some of the damage."

Kat stood. "I'm sorry, Hunter."

"Don't be. I think we both learned a lot from this. I wouldn't change a thing."

"Good luck with Holly. She's a lucky girl. And from what I can tell, you're a lucky guy, as much as I hate to admit it. I think I'm going to see if I can catch a flight back to Hawaii. Give me a call next week."

"Sure thing, Kat. Merry Christmas," he replied, leading her to the door.

Chapter Twenty-Two

Angels Bearing Gifts

Did he give up on me? she wondered, staring at the Christmas tree in her living room, minus one little, yet oh-so-significant ornament. The Christmas Carousel, it was gone. "Joe?" she whispered. "Where did you go, Joe?" she asked, not at all amused by the rhyme she'd inadvertently uttered. "Where's my carousel?" She looked at Abbey who was lying on the floor, whimpering quietly.

"Well, Abbey. Looks like our time is up. All we can do now is enjoy the park one last time," she said, crouching down to pat Abbey's head. "Don't worry girl. It'll be okay." Abbey touched her hand with her moist cool snout and rested it on her knee, giving Holly a look that made her insides melt like butter in a microwave oven. "Yes, you can come with me. Just stay with me, though. No running off to see Hunter," she said, standing up to go change her clothes.

On her way back to the living room she stopped to grab a roll of wrapping paper from the hall closet and walked over to turn on her favorite Christmas CD. She'd chosen sisters, ages six and eight, from the Angel Tree. They'd requested coloring books and watercolor paint sets. Girls after her own heart. She began to curl the ribbons she'd wrapped around their presents with the edge of her scissors. "There. Perfect," she said out loud, holding up her present with her outstretched hands to admire her wrapping job, "even if I do say so myself."

She was trying to stay cheerful, humming along to the instrumental version of "Frosty the Snowman" that had just started to play. Earlier she'd made herself a tall glass of eggnog with an extra-large dollop of whipped cream and a dash of cinnamon, as if the delicious, high-fat, *and worth it*, concoction would boost her spirits and keep her mind highly charged on all things merry and bright. But all morning thoughts kept returning to Hunter and the carousel. She felt like a failure. Joe must have read the writing on the wall. It was too late now. *But I tried my best, didn't I?*

Later that day, she thought about the carousel again as she opened the car door for Abbey, who she dressed in a dark-green doggie sweater. She'd decided to wear a pair of thermals under her jeans since they were predicting temperatures to drop to the twenties later in the evening. For whatever the reason, she still hadn't heard from Jack Haywood. He was cutting it close. She tossed her phone into the passenger seat, figuring they would have no choice; they'd just have to operate the carousel without music. How sad!

She drove toward downtown and glanced at the clock on her dash. It was still an hour before the start of the event. She'd have plenty of time to make sure everything was ready to go. Thankfully, Stacey Ashworth had flown into town earlier in the day and had been able to meet up with Ruby. But wasn't there something she could do about the carousel?

Just as she parked her car, her cell phone rang.

She pulled off one of her leather gloves. "Yes?" she said abruptly into the phone.

"Oh, hi, Holly? This is Jack. Are you okay?"

"I'm sorry, Jack. I'm feeling a little panicked about the carousel, I guess. I just need to take a deep breath."

"Don't worry, Holly. You can relax. I have some good news."

"Really?" she asked, exhaling slowly. "I'm so glad you said that."

"I'm glad I *can* say that. The organ is in working order!"

"Great! How did you fix it?"

"I was afraid you'd ask that. I wish I could take the credit."

"What do you mean?"

"Well, I think it's nothing short of a miracle, really. I'd just gotten off the phone with the manufacturer—it took me two whole days to get ahold of them—but anyway, the person I spoke with said their technicians were off for the holidays. But just as I was hanging up, another call came in from some unknown number. Some guy by the name of Joe told me all I had to do was get down behind the organ and find a little switch behind a panel at the base and flip it up. So, I did. And it worked!"

"Wow, Jack. Thank you so much."

"Don't thank me. Thank some guy named Joe."

Some guy named Joe. She smiled to herself. He was way more than 'some guy named Joe.' *You didn't desert me after all, Joe. Me, or the town.* "Well, thanks for flipping the switch, then. Hopefully I'll see you tonight. Merry Christmas, Jack!"

"Merry Christmas, Holly."

She started to hum again, almost skipping as she made her way toward the Angel Tree, with Abbey nipping at her heels. Volunteers had set up a large area with a podium and a microphone earlier in the day to do the gift exchange. She carried her shopping bag of presents and set them down by the tree.

"Well, look who's here," Ruby said, coming from

behind the podium, followed by Stacey Ashworth. "Just in time. I was just talking to Stacey about helping us with my boutique website. I was telling her how amazing the Angel Tree website looked."

"Yes, it's amazing," Holly replied.

"Oh, thank you, ladies," Stacey said. "It was nothing, really. And Ruby, I'd be more than happy to help you with that business website you mentioned. Now that I'm retired, I've got some free time."

"Wow, that's great. I hadn't even thought about it, but it makes perfect sense."

Stacey nodded. "That's what I thought. Well. We've got a few last-minute details to tend to. I see that the people are starting to pour in."

"Go take a seat, Holly. I'll welcome everyone," Ruby offered, glancing behind her to the front row. "I saved some seats."

Holly looked behind her shoulder. Smiling faces were walking towards them carrying bags while several groups of boys and girls were being ushered into the children's seating area. She took a seat on the end of the front row so Abbey could sit on the ground next to her and glanced at her watch. She wasn't sure when Hunter and his new fiancée would show up. Part of her wished they wouldn't bother. The park's days were numbered, and Hunter and Kat couldn't care less.

"Hi, honey," her mom said, sitting down next to her. "Look who I brought." She turned to face Greg who was dressed in a bright red puffy jacket and carrying a gigantic bag of presents with both arms that looked like it could burst open at any second. "Since your father's preparing for the Christmas Eve service, I thought I'd come up with Greg. I think we'll be able to make it back just in time."

"This is a surprise," she said, looking at Greg who'd peeked his head from around the bag. "I see you've done a little shopping."

"Ho, ho, ho," Greg said.

"Greg told me you guys are just friends now, so I figured you wouldn't mind us coming up together," Mom said.

"How are you Holly?" Greg set down his bag in an empty seat before taking a seat on the other side of her mom. "I took your advice and decided to buy a few gifts. It's the first time I've done something like this. I kind of like it."

Holly smiled. "I guess we have more than one Santa here tonight," she replied, leaning forward to give him a little wink. "Things are looking up. For a minute there I thought we'd have a carousel with no music. But I just got the word that it's been fixed."

"That sounds like perfect timing," Mom said.

"Excuse me for a minute. I'm going to go drop these off," Greg said, picking up the bag. "Be right back."

A few minutes later, after the seats started to fill in, Holly heard the unmistakable commanding voice of Ray Ashworth. He'd taken a seat right behind her. He was talking to another man dressed in a suit and wearing a long black dress coat whom she'd never seen before.

Her mom whispered into her ear. "Isn't that Ray Ashworth?"

Holly nodded discreetly; her ears instinctively drawn to his words.

"Well, Bill, I'm sure he'll be here soon. I know he's excited about meeting with you. I'd say the carousel is in almost perfect condition. It's quite a treasure, an antique, really."

"I imagine it's one of a kind. That's what I'm banking on," Bill replied. "I'd love to have it at one of my parks."

Holly sank down in her seat. It's priceless. How could you put a price on something as exquisite as the Christmas Carousel?

"Oh, look, there he is now," Ray said, pointing to

Hunter, who'd just walked into view carrying two large bags. He stopped to give one of them to a volunteer. "Looks like he's taking a seat in the back," he added just as Ruby stepped up to the microphone. "We can meet up with him after this," he whispered to Bill. "Then I can introduce you to my wife, Stacey. You'll see her on stage in a minute."

Holly had to stop herself from looking at Hunter. She didn't feel like seeing Kat anyway. She figured it would only dampen her spirits. So that was it, he was really going to sell it. Even after everything that had happened, she realized she'd still been holding onto the tiniest thread of hope that he would change his mind. But now, here was Ray Ashworth sitting with the man who'd be buying the carousel, right behind her.

"Good evening, everyone. Welcome to the Merrysville Christmas Village and our First Annual Angel Tree Event."

People began to clap and whistle. "I'd like to take this opportunity to thank the people that came up with this idea in the first place. You all probably know her, Holly Edwards," she announced over the cheers of the crowd. "And of course, Hunter Ashworth."

The applause continued. "Would you both like to come up and say a few words?" she asked, looking directly at Holly who was mouthing 'No' and running her finger across her neck in a decapitation-by-index-finger maneuver. Ruby only laughed. "Don't be shy Holly. And Hunter Ashworth, where are you?" she asked, shielding her eyes with her hand as she looked out into the sea of people. "Oh yes, there you are," she said, her eyes finding him in the back row.

Holly shook her head, as if upset with herself for not predicting this sneaky maneuver by her cousin. She'd told Ruby earlier that she preferred to stay out of the limelight and just work behind the scenes. Mostly, she realized, because she wanted to avoid Hunter. Evidently, Ruby had a different plan. "Mom, watch Abbey for me," she whispered as she stood and reluctantly started her short plod to the podium. When she got up on the small platform, though, she noticed Hunter had been sitting by himself. She didn't see Kat, and that didn't surprise her one bit.

Ruby looked at the crowd and continued to speak into the microphone. "Thank you, Holly for working so tirelessly to have this park opened one last time before . . . well, before we have to say goodbye to it."

People started to murmur in the crowd.

"But there is someone we can say hello to. Would everyone please welcome, straight from the North Pole, Santa Claus!" Ruby turned around and started clapping as one of the volunteers dressed as Santa walked up to the stage and took a seat by the tree. "He took time out of his busy schedule tonight to help us pass out the gifts!"

"Ho, ho, ho," he said, and waved his hand in the air. "Merry Christmas, everyone!"

Hunter approached the podium and stepped up on the platform next to Holly while everyone was clapping for Santa. She refused to look in his direction before walking to the microphone. "Thank you, Ruby. And hello Santa. I must say it's really an honor to be standing here. I'm so thankful for all of the volunteers who made this possible. Could you all just give yourselves a hand, please? There are so many wonderful people who helped us bring this about. I just want everyone to enjoy themselves. And I'd like to thank the Ashworth family for everything they've done as well," she said. She looked toward Stacey Ashworth. "And thanks to Hunter and his mom, Stacey, we are going to be handing out a lot of presents to the children tonight! Are you ready, kids?" she yelled into the microphone.

The children in the first several rows jumped up from their seats. "Yes!" they screamed, most of them jumping up and down in front of their chairs. She turned to Hunter. "I think it's only appropriate that Mr. Ashworth here reads off the names. He'll be Santa's Helper tonight. Once your name is called, you can come up to get your presents!" She was smiling ear to ear when she looked at Hunter, who smiled back just as she looked away. As long as she didn't make eye contact with him, she figured she could make it through the evening just fine.

As Hunter took the microphone, she walked back to her seat, noticing Ray and his friend Bill were no longer there.

"Honey, I'm so proud of you," Mom said. "And I'm sorry that the park's going to be torn down."

"I know. I just can't believe it. I thought that there was a chance that Hunter would change his mind." She glanced at Hunter who was busy reading names from the list and frowned.

Greg stood and walked over to her. "It's okay, Holly. Maybe he'll let you guys keep a small garden plot," he said, putting his hands on her shoulders. "You did great."

She stood. "Thanks Greg," she replied, giving him a hug. "I really appreciate you coming tonight." She looked up to the stage again just at the moment Hunter was announcing the next child's name.

"Isabel Straighter," he called into the microphone, locking eyes with her, watching as she hugged Greg. "Would you please come up?"

She looked away.

Fifteen minutes later, Ruby walked back to the podium. "Okay, everyone. The gifts have all been given out. I just want to announce that the park is now open for business! And I know most of you want to ride the carousel. Please let the children go first," she said into the microphone.

"Ah, come on, Ruby. We're all children tonight," someone yelled.

She heard a splattering of laughs coming from the crowd. "Nice try, Rocco," she replied, putting her hands on her hips.

"Well, Mom. You want to go take a ride?" Holly asked.

"I wouldn't miss it for the world, dear," she replied as they started for the carousel, with Abbey trailing behind.

"Hey Holly, wait up!" Ruby said, walking up from behind them a few minutes later. "Hi Aunt Judith, hi Greg. Thanks for coming."

"Merry Christmas, Ruby. Where's the rest of your family?" Mom asked, giving her a hug.

"Knowing the girls, they're probably already riding the carousel with Dan."

"They better ride it while they can," Holly replied, begrudgingly, as she crossed her arms across her chest. "I just heard Ray Ashworth talking to an interested party about buying it."

"Oh no, Holly. I'm so sorry. I wish Hunter would change his mind."

"Sounds like a done deal to me," Greg added.

Holly exhaled. Greg had been right, about everything, after all.

As they walked toward the carousel, they could see the line weaving itself through the trees and along the gravel path.

"Oh my, maybe I should reconsider. We might be here for hours," her mom said. "I can't miss your father's Christmas Eve service. What do you think, Greg?"

"It's okay, Mom. You can come up and bring Dad tomorrow. Just bring all the food and we'll eat at my place. The park will be open tomorrow night and all week."

"I think that's a good idea," Greg replied. "I'll come, too, if you don't mind. My parents are traveling abroad for the holiday, but my mom left me her famous chocolate pecan pie recipe."

"Sounds good," Holly said, half-heartedly, "the more the merrier."

"Give us a call and we'll come by to visit. Maybe we can all come back to the park together? I'm sure the girls will love it," Ruby said, looking toward the front of the line. "Oh! I think I see them in the line up there. I'll see you all tomorrow," she added before running off.

Holly looked at Greg. "Mom, would you mind if I talk to Greg for a minute, in private?"

"Not at all, dear. I'll wait over by that bench, Greg." She turned toward Holly and gave her a hug. "Merry Christmas, dear."

"Merry Christmas, Mom."

"What do you want to talk to me about?" Greg asked after her mom walked away.

She reached out her arms and gave him a hug. "Just wanted to say I'm sorry for how things turned out and I'm thankful that we can still be friends."

"Thanks Holly. Me too," he replied, hugging her tightly. "And, guess what?"

"What?" she asked, pulling back her head.

"I've lined up at least six new orders for you. No one seems to be able to get enough of your artwork. Maybe you should consider opening your own store up here."

Her eyes widened. "Wow, that's great," she said, rising onto the balls of her feet to give him a peck on the cheek. "It doesn't hurt that you talk up my work like I'm Claude Monet."

"Seriously Holly, you should think about it."

"I will, Greg. Let's talk about it after the holidays. Merry Christmas."

"Merry Christmas, Holly," he said, looking over his shoulder. "I wish I had some mistletoe right about now."

"Oh, stop," she laughed, lightly punching him in the arm.

"How about one more hug, then?"

"Sure. See you later, Greg," she said, giving him one last squeeze.

How will I get her alone? Hunter had been wondering ever since he'd seen her sitting with Greg in the front row, and then watching them hug. He was surprised by his own persistence. It was usually the women chasing him, but not with Holly. She had a boyfriend. What was he doing? He considered the happenings over the last few days. He was surprised with himself for what he'd almost said on the podium earlier. At the last second, though, he'd decided to keep his lips tightly shut. He didn't need to make any rash decisions. Everything he said and did had to be carefully planned. But after seeing the kids and the looks of wonder on their faces when they received their presents, he started to feel a shift; he was beginning to have a change of heart. Even if Holly wouldn't be by his side, he was starting to feel like he owed it to the town.

As he walked down the path, past the crowds of people, some stopping to shake his hand or just say 'thank you' as they passed by, he was becoming even more resolute in his decision. He could feel it in his bones—and it made him float on air.

"Thank you, Mr. Ashworth," a little girl with glasses said, giving him a smile that lit his heart as she walked by holding an older girl's hand.

"You are welcome, sweetie," he replied, flashing a smile in return. As he turned the corner, though, his smile faded. There she was, standing with Greg. She looked happy. She was laughing at something he just said. Maybe I should just forget about it. This is a bad idea, he thought.

"Hunter! There you are, Son. We've been looking for you," his dad said, walking up with a man by his side. "This is Bill Spears. The man I've been telling you about.

He came to see the carousel. I was just giving him a quick tour. But it's a little busy right now. Maybe we can go and talk?"

"It's a pleasure to meet you," he said, turning away from the sight of Holly to greet the man with a gloved hand. "Thank you for making the trip—on Christmas Eve."

"Oh yes, no problem. I brought my entire family. I think my children and my wife are on the carousel as we speak."

"Great. I hope they enjoy it," Hunter replied, trying to stop himself from looking back to see what Holly was doing. He just needed to forget about her.

"Let's go chat, Son. Bill's come a long way," Ray said, putting his arm around Hunter.

"Okay," he replied. "I know just the place."

Hunter couldn't resist one last glance back toward Holly. For a second, he thought she'd seen him too. What else would have made her smile decidedly turn to a frown so quickly?

Chapter Twenty-Three

The Perfect Fit

The park was closed now. Holly had waited in line for over two hours to ride the carousel. She'd noticed about an hour into it that Hunter and Ray, along with Bill, had made their way around the carousel, obviously so Hunter could show it off to Bill. And Bill looked ecstatic as the three of them walked off together. *Guess I better ride it while I can.* She hadn't really cared about the wait. After all, where else would she go? Her mom and Greg were gone. She wasn't exactly thrilled with being alone. It was a conundrum. She didn't want to be alone, but she absolutely didn't feel like talking to anyone. It was why she was so glad to have Abbey.

Where is Abbey? she wondered. A jolt of panic surged through her as she stood from the Bertazzon sleigh. "Abbey?" she called.

Abbey sat up from behind the unicorn and looked at her as if she'd just been napping.

"I'm sorry, girl, I thought you ran off." Relief washed over her and she fell back against the upholstered bench. It had been a long night and she was proud of the people who'd made the park's opening successful. And riding on the carousel? It had been just like it was with Joe. Unfortunately, she still hadn't been granted the opportunity to reach for the brass ring. Perhaps she'd get one last chance before it was shut down permanently.

It was quiet. The blunt chill in the night air had grown more intense, unbuffered, now that the crowds had dissipated. Only a few volunteers were wandering around the park now, picking up candy wrappers and cups scattered on the ground.

"Miss Holly?" Jack said, walking over toward the carousel with a child fast asleep in his arms. She was bundled in a wool blanket. "Are you okay?"

"I'm fine, Jack. Thank you again. We couldn't have done it without you."

Jack smiled and spoke in a quiet voice. "My little granddaughter here, Irene, I think she had more fun than she believed humanly possible. You should have seen her face. Thank you, Holly. What you did here won't be forgotten—even if the park is gone."

"Thanks Jack."

"Do you want me to walk you to your car?" he asked.

"Oh, no. You go ahead. I'm going to just sit here and take it all in for a while."

"Merry Christmas, Holly," he whispered before turning to walk away.

"Merry Christmas," her lips quivering from the cold. She reached for her ChapStick. "Oh, Joe. I'm sorry we couldn't save the park," she said quietly, hoping that he'd make one last appearance. "And I can only hope I've made some kind of impression on Hunter." She glanced at her phone. It was close to eleven. It was probably too late now. She crossed her arms and leaned back into the seat. Maybe Joe would still show. She nestled her chin into her wool scarf and shut her eyes. *I guess I'll just wait a little longer, just in case.*

"Hunter Ashworth? What are you still doing here?" Ruby asked as she entered the shed carrying a small box of unsold crafts.

He'd just finished up his meeting with Bill Spears, before his wife and children had to come and drag him away. Hunter felt good about Mr. Spears. He was a family man. And more and more, he was finding himself wanting the same thing. He sat at the workbench, putting a rubber band around a small stack of papers. He had to admit, the deal they'd struck had been a win-win, just the way his father had taught him, and it felt great. If only things with Holly had worked out so well. "I think the better question is, what are *you* doing here, Ruby? Where's your family?"

"You know how children are. They wanted to go ride the kiddie train around the park—over and over and over again," she said, her eyes orbiting around in their sockets. "One look at their little faces and pleading eyes, and they had Dan wrapped around their little fingers. But I really can't imagine anywhere else we'd rather be tonight. We love this town."

"Did they ride the carousel?"

"Of course. Only about ten times, give or take. They said it was their favorite. But then again, they said that after every ride."

He smiled. "Well, it is Christmas Eve. It's a night for celebration, right? I'm sure they've had lots of sugar too."

"Yes. It's an absolutely lethal combination for tired parents," Ruby replied before yawning loudly. "Anyway, I told them I'd meet them back at the house—I just wanted to put up a few more things." She began to organize the boxes in the corner and paused. "So, Hunter?"

"Yes, Ruby?"

"If you don't mind me asking . . . where's your fiancée? I haven't seen her around all night."

"I don't have a fiancée Ruby. I never did."

She spun around on her heels so fast she almost lost her balance. "What?"

"Kat and I broke up. She told me about what she said at the shop. She feels bad about it now. I think we do much better in a business type of relationship."

"Wow. I had no idea. You'd think from talking to her that you were both chomping at the bit to get married. I filled up an entire notepad with her ideas of a dream wedding in Maui."

He let out a chuckle. "I don't doubt it. But I've got a business to run. She wanted me to drop everything and move with her to Hawaii. And I'm not so sure if I wouldn't've if we'd gotten married. But this town's kind of growing on me."

"Really? Then why are you selling the carousel?"

He rested his elbows on the counter and narrowed his eyes. "Who told you that?"

"Holly did. She heard it directly from your father. He was sitting behind her earlier tonight—with the man who came to buy it. It's too bad, you know. I thought the two of you were starting to like each other too. She's really disappointed. I guess we all are—I mean, about the park."

"You think she likes me?"

She could hardly contain herself. "Ha!" escaped from her lips before she could stop it. "If she's the Queen of Understatement, then you're the King."

"What about her boyfriend?"

"What boyfriend? You mean, Greg?"

"Yes. Greg. He was with her tonight. And pretty much all the time lately."

She raised and lowered her eyebrows in a little dance. "Sounds like someone's been paying attention. But maybe appearances are a bit deceptive. You've got it wrong, Hunter. She broke up with him. They're just friends now, believe me. That's all they've been for some time." Ruby watched his face closely as the first inkling of light dawned in his mind. "He left with her mom earlier tonight to go back home—to Baltimore."

He slowly pushed back his stool and stood. "Oh. So, where's Holly then?"

"I'm not sure. But maybe you could call her."

Excitement was mounting as he pulled his phone from his pocket. "On second thought, maybe it's too late to call," he said, letting his arm drop to his side.

"It's never too late, Hunter. Now go find Holly," she said, giving him a hug before pushing him out the door and into the night. "And Merry Christmas!"

Holly heard a sound. "What?" she said in a startled tone, waking from a hard sleep. She looked around and tilted her head from side to side, stretching her neck muscles. "I must have fallen asleep. Brrr. It's freezing out here," she whispered to herself. She reached into her coat pocket to grab her phone. It was a few minutes 'til midnight, and her phone battery was draining quickly. She rubbed her eyes. It looked like she missed a call. Hunter Ashworth? Why would Hunter be calling her now? Whatever it was he wanted, it wasn't important. He didn't even leave a message.

"Abbey, we better get going. I'm too cold to wait any longer. Obviously, Joe's not coming." She stood up from her seat, expecting to see Abbey lying by the unicorn's hooves, but there was only an empty spot. "Abbey?" She began to look around the carousel. "Oh no. Not now. Abbey, please!" she yelled into the cold night air as she stepped off the carousel platform.

"Please pick up, Holly," Hunter said into the phone receiver, "please." He couldn't leave a message. What would he say? No, if he didn't leave a message, he could try again, maybe after Christmas. He hung up the phone after the eighth ring. Eventually they'd reconnect. But part of him couldn't wait any longer. Maybe he should just drive over to her house?

He walked down the street in front of the park toward his car when he heard a sound. First it was muffled, but then he heard it a second time. There was no mistaking it, it was a dog barking, and it was coming closer. Sure enough, in the distance, he saw the outline of a four-legged creature running toward him. Under the light of the streetlamp he realized it was a golden retriever—in a green sweater. It was Holly's dog, Abbey.

"What are you doing out here, girl?" Abbey ran over to him and almost bowled him over with the momentum of her body weight as she sprang up onto his chest with her paws, panting heavily.

"Rruff, rruff."

"Whoa," Hunter said, rubbing the sides of her body. Abbey jumped down and began to bark, running into the distance and then returning to where Hunter stood.

"Do you want me to follow you?" he asked, as Abbey barked and began to run off again. "Okay, wait up, Abbey!" He increased his stride behind her until he caught up.

They were headed in the direction of the carousel. In the distance, Hunter could hear a woman's voice calling out. As they continued to walk down the gravel path, he realized it was Holly, calling for Abbey. Just as he made it around the bend, he saw Holly rushing from the carousel platform.

He walked toward her just as she turned around.

"Abbey! Thank God! Hunter? What are you doing here?" she asked, as she bent down to hug Abbey.

"I guess I could ask you the same question."

"I fell asleep. She must've decided to run off while I was taking a nap."

"Why in the world are you out here by yourself at this time of night, Holly? I mean, it's Christmas Eve." He glanced at his phone. "Well, it's actually Christmas Day now."

"I guess you could say I was just saying goodbye to an old friend."

Hunter looked around. "Who?"

"The carousel, Hunter. It's like an old friend."

"I see. What if I told you that you didn't have to say goodbye?"

"What do you mean? I saw the buyer tonight. By the looks of things, he was very happy. You must have given him a good deal."

"I gave him a great deal."

Holly frowned. "I knew it."

He smiled and took her hands in his. "Holly, I'm not selling the carousel. I'm partnering with Bill Spears. He's an amusement park planner. We're going into a joint venture. Ashworth Furniture Company is now going to be making replicas of our Christmas Carousel for Bill to put in amusement parks across America."

She beamed. "What? Really?"

"Yes. Really."

"But what about the factory?"

"I've decided to build the factory on the other side of town. We'll be making the Merrysville Amusement Park bigger and better than ever. We'll need all the space we can get."

"Oh wow! That's great, Hunter. I'm so glad you decided to take our advice and listen to the townspeople. But who's going to run things when you move to Baltimore?"

"What would you say if I told you I've decided to stay, Holly?"

"I'd say that would be great for the community. But what about Kat? Where is she, by the way? I bet she's not too thrilled with the idea. From what I can tell, she's pretty set on moving to the tropics."

He looked up. "I don't know. But I would guess she's probably in the sky as we speak, flying back to Hawaii."

She gave him a puzzled look. "I don't get it."

Hunter reached for her hands. "We're not getting married, Holly. I realized Kat and I aren't right for each other."

She took in a gulp of cold air swirling around them. "I need to tell you something about Greg. We—"

"I know. Ruby filled me in. She said you guys are just friends." Hunter looked her in the eyes. "And I have a confession to make. I was a little concerned about you when you said the carousel ornament was back on your tree."

"Well, it's gone now, Hunter. Maybe I just imagined it was there."

"And maybe I imagined seeing it on my tree today."

"Really? It's on your tree now? Wow. I wonder why."

"I'm not sure, but I had a very interesting dream last night."

"Oh yeah? I've had a few of those myself recently. In fact, maybe I'm *dreaming* now," she said gazing into his eyes.

"Maybe we both are. Is it just me or is it getting warmer out here?"

She laughed. "Things started to heat up when you got here." Out of the corner of her eye she watched Abbey walk over toward the entrance gate of the carousel and sit.

He moved a step closer. "I have something to tell you Holly, all joking aside."

"What?" she asked, tilting her head.

"You'll have to come just a little closer." He drew her in and cupped her hands in his, locking eyes with her. "I'm in love with you Holly Edwards. You make me a better person. I should have known it from the way my heart almost leapt out of my chest when I first saw you."

"That day at the shop? Really?"

He shook his head. "No, that day at the park, when you dropped your Hello Kitty wallet."

A single tear streamed from her eye down her cheek and she gasped. "You remember," she whispered as new tears formed in the corners of her eyes. "I'm in love with you, too, Hunter."

He leaned in, his lips grazing hers through her salty tears before pressing into them. He felt a wave of adrenaline coarse through his body as he kissed her with passion he hadn't felt with another woman, feeling her tears graze his cheek as she held his face lightly with her hands and he wrapped his arms around her tightly, enveloping her. "We're the perfect fit," he whispered into her ear before his lips found hers again.

Suddenly the carousel lights flashed on, illuminating them where they stood, by the entrance gate.

"What . . .?" she started to ask, as the carousel began to turn slowly, and organ music filled the air.

He smiled and took her hand. "It's definitely warmer out here. Looks like we're in this dream together." With that, they walked toward the carousel and jumped up onto it.

"The unicorn's my favorite," she said, looking at Hunter.

"Mine too. We'll share."

Holly jumped up on the unicorn and he stood next to her, holding the pole. "Hey, look!" she yelled, pointing toward the gate where Abbey was still lying. He could see Grandpa Joe standing with Ralphie at his feet and Abbey right by his side.

"Do you think he's been here this entire time?" She waved at Joe, who tipped his top hat in their direction. He had a wide smile on his face as they watched him snap his fingers.

The carousel increased in speed.

"Grab for the brass ring Hunter and Holly!" Grandpa Joe yelled over the music. "This is your moment!"

Hunter could see it, Holly too. "I've never been able to reach it before," he said, looking at Holly. "Are you ready?" he asked, looking into her sparkling eyes.

She was more than ready.

He said, "On the count of three. One . . . two . . ." They both leaned in for the shiny metal ring as they approached the mechanical arm. Holly stretched her arm as far as she could while he boosted her up, and she held her breath and jolted forward just as she came to the mechanical arm.

"Three!"

In the blink of an eye, she was sitting back down on the unicorn, her fingers wrapped tightly around the cool smooth metal ring.

"You got it!" he said, wrapping his large hand around hers as the carousel slowed and the music quieted.

She laughed out loud. "*We* got it!"

They stayed on the carousel, with the ring in their hands, and looked again toward Grandpa Joe. Without saying a word, he winked, and then turned to walk away. The two dogs sniffed noses before Ralphie ran off after Joe and Abbey walked over and hopped up onto the carousel to sit by Hunter's feet.

All of a sudden, they felt something tingle in their hands and they looked at each other wide-eyed, words unable to describe what had just happened. Slowly opening their fingers, they saw what had taken the place of the brass ring, laying in Holly's palm: a wedding ring. They both gasped as they looked at it, before a huge smile formed on his face.

"You know, Grandpa told me they couldn't find my grandma's wedding ring when she died. I have a funny feeling this might be it. What do you say, Holly? Would you like to try it on?"

She threw him a quizzical look. "What are you saying, Hunter?"

He slowly crouched down on one knee. "I've been waiting for you my entire life, Holly Edwards. Will you marry me?"

It seemed crazy, but somehow the whole thing made sense in a way that couldn't be explained. "Yes, Hunter Ashworth. I will marry you," she cried. Fresh tears flowed down her cheeks as he stood and slipped the ring onto her finger.

"Well, what do you know? It's the *perfect fit*," he said, as she threw her arms around him and kissed him again.

"The perfect fit," Grandpa Joe called out somewhere in the distance.

THE END

Jill Van Horn is a family physician trained in Fort Worth, Texas, who has decided to pursue her passion to become a full-time writer of romance and cozy mystery novels. She lives in Whitsett, North Carolina, with her husband, two dogs and lots of cats in a fixer-up Victorian. She's a proud member of the North Carolina Writers' Network. The Christmas Carousel is her fourth published novel, and her current projects include a southwestern cozy mystery series, as well as a couple of summertime romances.

When she's not writing, she spends her time gardening, experimenting with recipes, working out at the YMCA, reading, and refurbishing her house and furniture.

www.jillvanhorn.com